SAM

Around the conference room, immortal men and women assembled at the hieroglyphic stone table in the underground bunker of Home Base One, their projected holograms beaming from similar ultra-compounds around the globe.

My boss, Mr. Ethan Anderson—the tall, tan, forty-five-year-old founder of Defying Death Industries (DDI)—sat at the center of the Egyptian Room, sharp blue eyes emanating competitiveness as he explained the new legal ruling, DDI's double infinity logo rippling across his chest. "It means we're going to have to source donors elsewhere, inventory will price us out otherwise. There's plenty of bodies in Africa. I sent a strike team the second the news broke."

"But, boss," the man across the table began, "wouldn't patients need to fly there?"

Ethan shook his tough guy head. "That's an option. But a few competitors have set up holding bays stateside. That's our cheapest option, a lock-up. It's better than enlisting more American donors, minimum age and payouts being what they are."

A few nods. Killing that many Americans would cost a fortune.

"Besides, stock's up twenty percent this quarter alone. Market loves us. Who cares if life donors aren't local? We've added more quality years and saved more lives than anyone, except maybe SLI. And it's not like we'll face any ballbusters, half the senators and congressmen are lifelong customers. Even the president herself."

"Screw the stock, Ethan. It's protests we're worried about."

"Protests come and go."

"Not like this. If more Americans starve because they're not getting death donor spots, that could go viral. The word catastrophic comes to mind."

"It's not our fault they're unemployable. And let's be real. Who actually cares where the dead schmuck on the slab next them is from when come to after a rejuve? People just want to live longer and feel great. The cheaper, the better."

He was right. The people had spoken.

"That may be," the woman said, 'but you need to keep local donors happy."

Why? Hadn't she seen lines wrapping the building day and night, donors begging for a few thousand. Ethan seemed to agree, and laughed. "Supply's through the roof. And once we expand, it'll drive prices further down. Donors have zero leverage."

"You'd better be right."

He smiled. "Have I ever been wrong?"

The meeting wrapped after each of DDI's heads reiterated their action items, and the company's cheesy mantra: "Live long, prosper, and profit."

Once they'd left, Ethan rose, pacing. "Fifty-five-million unnecessary deaths a year," he said to himself.

I was a statue at my post, my back to the Anubis door, despite everything being locked down. This was the subbasement of Ethan's favorite home, equipped with state of the art sensors, an army of weaponized drones, a dozen attack dogs, and a three-meter concrete fence surrounding the five-acre property. Money had its perks.

Without warning—like most things Ethan did—he spun and left. I followed at a distance. Like an apex predator, he liked his space. I could relate.

We took the reinforced lift to Subbasement One, and Ethan

beelined for the kitchen. His triple-espresso-infused smoothie was on the obsidian countertop. He downed the disgusting, optimized weekly, brown slop in three gulps before Maria, the mouthy Argentinian who did Ethan's red meats—and probably *a lot* more—emerged from the far pantry. Daron would say she was a looker if he was with the guys. But I'd kick his ass, and he knew it.

My shift ended four hours later. After a brief report to Mr. Anderson and his head of security, Vlad, I was more than ready to leave. Three lifts later, I arrived topside two, sun blazing my eyes. That had taken getting used to.

The security chip in my palm opened automatic double doors as I strode through the first parking garage checkpoint. A combination of gait analysis and biometric sensors, along with Quinton's okay, let me pass to the waiting Tesla at the staff self-driving section.

The scratched up, dinky two-seater opened, and I hopped in, laid back, and closed my eyes. Long day. Time for a slog home in Atlanta rush hour.

My seat buzzed as we reached my street, and I tapped my temple to activate my high-end display, a perk of the job. A dashboard appeared in my ARlense contact retinas, an entire operating system and all the world's information. It was 5:45 p.m.

Shit, Daron was going to kill me.

The car dropped me in the gravel driveway of our two-story suburban rinse-and-repeat home. No used needles on the sidewalk or missing persons signs, that was a plus. But the darkening stain on the water-damaged front porch looked worse. Avoiding the creaky step, I grabbed the newspaper the city insisted on wasting valuable tax dollars to produce, and stepped into 105 Abbott St SW.

Another violent riot in San Francisco's slums, Amazon's profits hit an all-time high, and a ridiculous report on same-race death donors increasing efficacy, something to do with genetic similarities. As if dicing the brains and organs of a Caucasian would be any different than an African, or an Asian... Ethan would be furious. There was still a dent by the weight rack from a similar story two years ago.

Not that it mattered. I had twenty more years on the job before I'd earn our death insurance. At least that'd buy me more time with my little girl, Malea, if I made it that long... But guard duty for Ethan was low key and paid enough to keep the hospital loan sharks at bay.

"Oh, you're home." It was Daron, brown hair swept back, face a dimpled smile. "Forgot it's Wednesday."

Plopping a wet one on him, I dropped my messenger bag on the whitewashed linoleum of our cozy-at-best sized home, the best we'd ever be able to afford despite my lofty salary. Even in death, Daron's mom strangled our life. Why'd I agree to those last-ditch treatments? We'll be paying off the debt from now to eternity.

"We still on for tonight?" I asked.

He shrugged. "You sure you want to go?"

Was he kidding? We hadn't had a "real" date in ages, not since Ruby Tuesdays, which almost shouldn't count. "It's our anniversary, babe. Thirteen years, today." To think, I almost didn't go to that Army ceremony. I hadn't thought about Saudi in years, repressing every-thing, that's what the psych said after my one and *only* appointment.

"You're right," he said. "I'm pissed, that's all."

Uh-oh. He'd always had swings, and his mom had been on SSRIs forever... Taking his wiry shoulders, I guided him to the beat-up blue couch in our little living room. It'd been a wedding gift. "What's up, baby? Everything okay at school?"

He shrugged. "I mean, these kids..." A sigh. "The prospects aren't great."

What could I say? He was right. "DDI's always hiring," I said in what I hoped was an encouraging voice. "Broke twenty thousand refreshes last year. Company's swimming in cash." If only Daron and Malea could get moved up the list...

"I know, it's just—" The door creaked open. "Hey, Malea, that you?"

"Yes, *Mom*." Here come the sassy teenage years, and she was eleven... It felt like yesterday. I touched my iron-forged stomach. "Can I sleepover at Karen's?" She walked into the kitchen, opened the fridge, and groaned. Payday wasn't until Friday.

"No, baby, it's Wednesday," I said. "You can't spend the night."

Malea stepped through the opening and rolled her eyes. "Dad, can you help me with my math homework? We're doing Southern slave trade economics. I'm having trouble."

I rose. That was my cue. This new-agey teaching was beyond me. Walking into our IKEA Basic plastic and plywood kitchen, I grabbed a cup and turned on the tap. At least the filter worked, making the sludge drinkable. *Remember to check Sunday.* Didn't need Malea getting sick again.

An hour to kill. Opening my ARlenses, I outlined a rectangle on the flimsy table and a virtual keyboard materialized. In a new browser, the NYTimes appeared. NYC protests over donor compensation, Africans undercutting the market...

At half-past six, Daron appeared in a pullover and slacks, messy flop combed into something presentable. Finally... standing room seats filled fast and we couldn't afford guaranteed ones. He'd be so disappointed if we missed the movie.

ETHAN

It had been another one of *those* days. The stock—on a tear for years—had taken a nosedive. The pseudoscience bullshit was killing our image on Wall Street.

Envisioning Sun Lee's smug face and fake, deferential smile as he beat me by two fucking points on our first Applied Genomics exam, I slammed the heavy bag one last time. The move to Tunis was the right one, it was close enough to Europe for fly-in treatments. Plus we could use seventeen-year-olds there, not the absurd eighteen limit here. Cells should have better performance and longevity. We needed a cheaper price to stay competitive.

Stripping, I walked naked through the fitness center to the heated sauna at the back. I cranked it to 180°F and meditated fifteen minutes—no longer. Learned *that* lesson years ago. A ninety-second cryo shower, and jeans and a tailored blazer made me ready for date night.

Back to the elevator, Boris at my six, an invisible ghost watching my back with those hard Russian eyes. We rode in silence.

A lean blonde stood at the far side of the living room by the fireplace in a scandalous blue dress. Which one was this? Tira? Or was tonight Yasmine? Didn't matter. The fireplace brought it all back, all those nights, Bobby, Mom, and I cuddled to stay warm. So much had changed. I couldn't be alone again, not tonight.

Ms. America was examining my prized possession, the Pieter Claesz masterpiece—bleached skull beside a dying wax candle in misty fog. She recoiled at my constant reminder of the horrors of death, and my mission to conquer it.

"Why, hello there." I strode forward. "I'm Ethan, welcome to my home." We made idle chit chat until Boris reappeared, leading us past the grass tennis center to the southernmost landing pad.

Gonzalez sat in the VTOL's cockpit, checking knobs and switches. He was the best money could buy—ex-Colombian special forces after a career running cartel shipments. The big Colombian gave me a grin.

We lifted off—vertical take-off and landing—and raced over Atlanta's burgeoning skyline toward DDI Arena and the Knicks. We landed at the elites' entrance and additional security led us to my tank-tested owner's box.

The party was underway, bottles out, hors d'oeuvres covering mahogany buffet tables, tuxedoed waiters with polished deference. You only live once… haha.

Senator Evans caught my eye and signaled me over. She was dressed in a becoming pantsuit, matching Prada real-leather purse and blood diamond earrings making a statement. She was on several over-sight committees. Her next DDI Christmas card should have a matching necklace.

"You look lovely, Zara." I offered a hand.

She rolled her eyes and gave me a hug. "Always so formal, Ethan. A handshake won't do, not after you reversed those wrinkles," she added in a whisper. "Five treatments he's done for me." She smiled at Isabella. "Even before I was elected."

Worth every penny. "I'm just glad you got re-elected. Saw a few bills you're working on. Couldn't have written them better myself."

"Speaking of, I need to talk to Senator Hayes. He's supposed to do something about those news stories we talked about."

"Don't let me keep you. Besides, I've got a beautiful woman to take care of." I put my arm around Isabella's recently rejuved waist.

The game tipped at seven-thirty and the night passed in a blur of cannabis, micro-dosing, and excitement as the Hawks beat the Knickerbockers 101-to-97 in a nailbiter to squeak into the playoffs. Buying the team was a good idea.

SAM

The next morning was brutal despite only a bottle. I rolled out of bed to a hangover and hurried to pee. Thursday; my turn to make breakfast. Stumbling to the kitchen, I slapped my face and filled old faithful. The sputtering Nespresso machine hissed to life. A moment later, coffee. That was more like it.

The fridge was a sorry affair, but it was almost Friday. Bacon and eggs would have to cut it. I guess I'd eat at work.

A door creaked open as I flipped the eggs. Soft footsteps scampered my way. "Hey, Malea? Hurry, before Dad's up.

Wooly socks skidded to a sleepy hug from behind. "How was last night? Did you two have fun?"

I told her about the movie, some chick flick—Daron's idea, thought I'd like it. Men were hopeless. A poor Indian girl and e-commerce billionaire that run off to VR. Really?

She rolled her eyes. "Lame." Mommy's little girl.

I flipped the bacon, stomach rumbling. "You know your dad. Always the idealist."

"An idealist, that right?" Daron laughed as he walked into the kitchen. "You used to be an idealist yourself, before the war."

"Who wants eggs?" My hand quivered as I changed subjects.

I'd never told either much about Saudi Arabia. Good men and great friends, traded for a few barrels. Henry had been nineteen...

As they left for school, Malea asked, "Can we volley later, Mom? Coach said I should practice setting and digs for the game."

"Sure, baby. After your homework."

"You'll have time tonight?" she pressed. "You won't be late again?"

Again... Guilt wracked me as she gazed up. I promised to do my best.

Only one crazy jumped on the car on the way to work today. Nothing to stop my documentary about. It was a good one, the military coups in Italy and India after the UN's legalization of life extension (LE). Even governmental-religious alliances couldn't stem the tides of LE... Before I knew it, Ethan's towering white complex came into sight. Rogers would be reviewing my security clearance.

At the halfway point, the doors opened and I exited. The car backed out, rejoining the city-sponsored pool as Rogers greeted me with a wink. The hairy hulk of a man with a scar below his eye smiled, flashing two chipped teeth and gums that never got the memo on smoking.

"How was last night?" he asked with a Boston twanged smirk.

"Watch it, big boy." I hurried to check in with Vlad, who was in the command center; a dark room of desks, two pots of coffee, and testosterone enough to impregnate a Grizzly. The pale Russian with the inverted hammer and sickle on his chiseled forearm sat in his haptic chair, hard eyes monitoring fifteen virtual screens in his augmented view. "Ethan's been waiting. Haven't you seen the news?" he asked. "Yosemite Room."

Two minutes later, I was outside the oak-paneled door. A soft knock, and I entered. Ethan was half-seated at the head of the table, ready to pounce, three life-sized holograms projected in the seats nearest him. "Is this a joke?" Ethan snapped. "Tell me this is a joke."

. . .

The dark-haired woman next to him pursed her lips. "We're not sure. It's only the NY Enquirer, but there have always been rumblings from the church and conservatives."

"But raising donor age is rumor at best?" he asked.

Better be, I needed this job. Without it, how long until I was in line, healthy cells the last things I could sell to feed Malea and Daron —all so some pretty-in-pink could smooth her damn wrinkles. My skin crawled.

The woman nodded. 'According to the journalists we talked to.'

"Good," Ethan said. "I want that report in my inbox tomorrow evening." That was that.

After the meeting ended, Ethan strode to the door. "Oh, Jones, you're here. We're going to the office today, something came up. Can you arrange transport and security?"

I sprinted off. Six minutes and three rushed calls later, we were in the air. Ethan double-tapped his ear, activating internal headphones. 'What's the situation in London?'

He listened for a second. I loved London. HB3 was my favorite of Ethan's compounds, the bustling city, British accents, and occasional United games a great change of pace.

'You're saying it could be the Chinese?' Ethan asked, eyes narrowing at the mention of Sun Lee and Shanghai Life Industries (SLI). 'Trying to short our stock? Shit. How liquid is the market?' A pause. 'That dirty bastard. Do you have any sources inside?' Ethan curled his lip. 'Find out what you can.' He swiped to kill the call and made three others like it as we zipped towards DDI's downtown head-quarters, landing on the seventy-story megalith ten minutes later. The egos of some men...

Fancy company execs waited as we touched down. "Mr. Anderson, it's good to see you." The suits made their best ass-kissing faces, and led Ethan to a waiting elevator, through blue carpeted halls and past dozens of newspaper clippings and civic awards he and the company had won over the years in the fight to cure aging. Even a picture of

Ethan with a bespectacled Dhruv Patel, the Georgia Tech genius who pioneered the Nobel Prize-winning breakthrough: recombinant target-specific tissue engineering (*RTSTE*). Something to do with injecting processed, metabolically healthy donor stem cells to reset mitochondrial mutations and clean out cell waste. Or something like that... Ethan had explained it at least a dozen times, given me a copy of his book too... still sounded like a word jumble.

The boardroom door opened to an army of arguing, red-faced C-suites and their underlings. Ethan stepped in, and silence fell as he jumped into a signature hellfire motivational. No one said a word as Mr. Charisma outlined his vision for the company, ridding the world of death and suffering, and the results they were on pace to hit. No wonder he earned the big bucks and I was stuck at the door.

Toward the end, a hand in the back went up. The guy—whose age was impossible to guess, eyes suggesting eighty as his broad back and smooth skin pointed younger—said, "Ethan, where do we stand with New York Life? Are they pushing for price parity?"

Ethan nodded a half smile. "Want us to go down to $125,000 per. In exchange, they're willing to make DDI their exclusive partner. That's at least ten billion a year."

"If these stories about twenty-two-year-old donors are bogus," the man remarked. What was his name again? His dystopian eyebrows and creeper eyes always distracted me.

"They are," Ethan said without hesitation. "The last three scumbag analysts I talked to thought this was a ploy by Lee's folks. Any other questions or things to discuss?"

No one said anything. "Let's wrap this up." The others repeated the corny company mantra and one-by-one, sidled out of the sixty-sixth-floor conference room—Ethan's unrelenting mockery of superstitious fate. Men...

Once they'd left, only Li Na remained, DDI's sharp-elbowed CFO, nicknamed 'the Eraser' for her ability to make the numbers work.

"Seen the figures from Barcelona?" she asked. God, Barcelona. It'd been forever... Was a trip in the cards? I wouldn't mind that.

Ethan shook his head.

"You should," she continued. "A quarter of patients are demanding same-race donors and willing to pay more or go elsewhere. Have you looked at donor markets? They're pricing Croatians and Albanians three-to-four times higher than Ethiopians. If we lose clients to Beyond Human or Google Life, we could be in for a stock hit."

Wait, a stock hit? Those options were a third of my salary. And Daron's job was a joke. Shit. Was she serious?

Ethan rolled his eyes. "The science is clear, there's no correlation between—"

"It doesn't matter," Li cut in, voice rising. "It's public perception. Numbers don't lie."

Damn. We were struggling to get by as it was. Daron had always said to take the cash.

"Okay," Ethan said without skipping a beat. "I'll deal with it." The meeting ended and before the next one, Ethan looked up. "Sam, I'm going to need you to stay late tonight, okay?"

Shit.

I agreed and stepped into the hallway to let Daron know while Ethan hopped on a call with his 'fixers.' He wouldn't be happy.

Turning down the empty hallway, I enjoyed world class views of the tent-free blossoming park and lofty skyline below. Must be nice...

'Hey, babe, how's work?' I asked as soon as her face appeared in my overlay.

'I'm glad you called. I have to stay late tonight, parent-teacher thing. You need to be there when Malea gets home.'

Crap. Opening the door, I laid a paper protector on the seat. 'I can't. Something came up. Boss is freaking out, we're at *headquarters.*'

He winced. 'What happened? Everything okay?'

'Look, I'll tell you later. Malea should be fine for a couple hours, right?'

His eyes flashed disappointed daggers. 'Samantha, you promised...'

'We need this, babe. We can't afford to lose this gig.' Especially after what your mom saddled us with... My stomach tightened. Mom of the Year, here I come...

I'd make it up to Malea tomorrow.

'Okay, Sam, but promise you'll call her. I won't be out until seven.'

I promised and clicked off, finishing my business and hurried back. Ethan never stayed late...

MIKE

H ere we go again. Let's get this over with… "Come in."

The door opened and into my anything-but-ornate office strode Megan Larson, the third time in as many weeks. Confident as always, long legs propelled the Crossfit-forged brunette past a wide-mouthed Owens at the door and towards my cluttered desk, her poisonous brown eyes sizing me up. Tall, casual black Armani, and high cheekbones with just the right amount of makeup, no doubt from her various stylists or high profile clientele.

"How have you been, Senator? Have you considered our offer?" There was something about her, attacking and inviting all at once, a pitbull I wasn't sure I should pet.

"You're back?" Already…

She smiled, still standing. "We both know how important this deal is. You're coming up for re-election next year and I hear the mayor is considering your seat."

And you want me to sell my soul and take DDI money to beat that corrupt rat of a woman and be your marionette, that it?

It was a game to these dirtbag lobbyists. I wasn't perfect, not by *any* means, ask my ex-wife—if you had twenty minutes to kill. But thank god I never became a lobbyist.

"Look, Ms. Larson, take a seat." I gestured to the straight-backed mahogany chair facing my simple wooden desk. "What do you want?"

Her penciled brows twitched without so much as a wrinkle. "We're looking to bring jobs back to *your* home state, right in Atlanta. But Boston and Toronto are offering generous tax breaks. And DDI has its shareholders to consider."

I didn't respond, letting silence work for me.

"The polls don't look good," she said at last. "Our people have run the numbers, I'm sure yours have as well." She was right, Rodriguez was up ten points since we'd failed to raise minimum wage. Georgians were struggling and the economy was always make or break.

"What do you want?" I asked.

"You need funding and a few headline photo ops. We can make that happen." She outlined terms and what they could offer before leaving. Did she think I was *that* crooked? Next meeting. Shit, the Christian Life Group. They'd lost that battle years ago.

* * *

The executive-fleet Tesla pulled into my highrise's reinforced, guard-patrolled, underground bunker. It had been a long day. Everyone wanted something. Tax the rich, tax the poor. Why aren't we spending more on the military, healthcare, education reform...?

What had happened to that naive kid from Syracuse looking to change the system? When had I become so cynical? At least we weren't in session. Senate cats were a whole nother matter, asses tight enough to uncork Merlot as they slayed you for dessert.

"Sir, are you okay?" It was Reggie Owens, the tall black bodyguard who'd been at my side since my election, holding the door. Had I been daydreaming?

I chuckled. "Fine, Reg. One of those days... And, how many times do I have to tell you? Call me Mike."

He smiled as we headed for the lift. "At least one more, sir."

Everyone in the building was vetted and under constant

surveillance—pools, gyms, and 10,000 square-foot gardens protected by AI and facial recognition. The elevator opened to my favorite song — "Live Like You Were Dying"—and whisked us to forty-five.

We got off and followed plush carpeting into my empty apartment. Dang, it'd been ages since I'd seen Ann, my one neighbor. I'd been wanting to ask her out for a while.

I kicked off loafers on the brown *Welcome Home* mat Ava had picked out but never taken, sighing. None of this was *my* stuff, not really. Between secretaries, assistants, and Ava, everything about this put-together apartment had a touch too much class. At least I'd decorated the pad in DC and house in Syracuse myself so they weren't as lonely.

Starving, I headed for the kitchen, glad for heated tile. "You hungry?" I yelled.

Reggie grunted approval. What did we have today? Tupperware lined the stainless steel fridge, eight options. Larry, you're a godsend. He must have stocked up. I stuck the cultured bison with wild grains into my multipurpose oven, sneaking a few chocolate covered almonds while waiting, waistline be damned.

Waiting, I replayed the day in my head to ignore the antique kitchen table which haunted me with memories of making love to my ex-wife.

It'd be a fight with Rodriguez this November. She'd done a phenomenal job turning around downtown: crime, poverty, unemployment. Was this the year to call it quits?

My chip buzzed. Call coming in. I tapped my temple and an overlay appeared, activating my internal headphones. It was Jamie.

'Hey, Dad. How's it going?' She looked so much like her mother, the same fiery brown eyes, uncontrolled yet gorgeous hair and turned up nose up to no good.

'Hey, Jame! How was school? I missed you. Can't wait for this weekend.' I had it all planned out.

'Yeah, Dad, about that...' she said. Not again... It had been three weeks since we'd had a weekend at my place. 'Mom thought her and I could go to Rome. It's the last summer before my apprenticeship and all, and I've always wanted...'

Ever since that cheesy heist movie, she'd talked about going. Relegated again... I swallowed hard. 'Rome will be great, Jame.' I'd always called her Jame. Ava hated it. 'When?'

'That's the best part, Dad. We'll be there a month for summer. Authentic as it gets.'

I nodded, doing my best to mask the crushing blow, but even we politicians have tells.

Jamie's eyes clouded. 'You're disappointed, aren't you?' she asked.

'No, honey. It's great. You'll learn a ton, and we'll hang out when you're back, before your Google Life internship.' I forced a smile. A whole month without her...

'Dad, you're the best. Mom knew you'd say yes.'

Course she did, the selfish bitch.

Jamie had to go not long after. Ava had decided to eat out to celebrate, no thought for anyone else but herself and the little girl who was everything to her. Nothing had changed...

Dammit Ava.

Another lonely night...

* * *

A few meetings the following morning, senators and congressmen fighting for bipartisan support on this and that. Half were on DDI's dole, or Google's. There was so much money in corporate finance. Dad had railed against it growing up, root of all evil. He was right.

I'd seen a lot in the years since beating Joe Porter. He'd been the NRA-sponsored favorite, and me, the unknown upstart. He was conservative, and me, liberal, an upstate New York implant who'd witnessed enough inner-city violence to ban weapons outright. Talk about unpopular, especially in Georgia.

But knocking up a coked up underage girl, and Christian norms did the rest. The upstanding voters sent me packing to DC, in over my head. I'd come a long way.

On the ride, I called my ex-wife. Big mistake. 'Ava, Rome? Really?'

'Come on, Mike. Jamie's wanted to go since freshman year.'

And *we* could have gone any point since. 'You could have asked.' Not that you ever did...

She rolled a practiced eye. 'You were too busy for your family ten years ago. Why's today different? At least it's not a birthday you're missing this time...'

Ouch. Low blow. I clenched my teeth. 'When do you leave? I want to see her.'

'Sunday,' she replied without acknowledging my request.

Shit, two days. Not cool. 'I'll pick her up tonight, around seven.'

'I don't know—'

'Dammit, Ava!' I snapped, therapist's advice be damned. 'I want to see my daughter. I'll be there at seven.' I hung up and sighed.

Just another day as a divorced dad. Even politicians had shit for rights...

ETHAN

"Three more reps, sir!" Boris shouted.

I arched my back into the hard bench, inching the bar off my heaving chest. "Four, five…" The barbell froze midway, 315 pounds bearing down as Boris towered over me.

"Want help?"

"No!" Don't quit. Google wouldn't, SLI either. And this would be a new personal best. What doesn't kill you… The bar descended. Push, dammit. You should have been able to save Bobby. "Don't!" I snarled. "I got it."

The bar thudded on my chest and Boris ripped it onto waiting hooks. My eyes snapped open. "I said, I had it."

"I know, sir. But you were going to d—"

"Don't say die!" My arms shivered. "*Never* say die!" I hated that word.

Boris knew not to argue. After an ice bath and ultraviolet sauna, I showered and suited up: Nikes and a blue Lacoste t-shirt—perks of being CEO.

Footsteps. "How was your night?" I asked.

"Fine, sir." Jones took up position in the kitchen's Roman arches, furtive, sunken eyes never settling. Her back, normally West Point ramrod straight, slouched in the doorframe.

"Sure everything is okay?" I asked. Didn't look like it.

She sighed. "Mom stuff. Home late last night. Nothing to worry about, sir."

Some jobs required more sacrifice and I paid more than enough considering how many unemployed soldiers and bodyguards there were. She'd get over it.

Sipping exotic crude, Jones and I discussed the day's schedule before walking the soundproof bunker hallway to the main lift, walls lined with the best security money could buy. A boy scout was always prepared...

Jeez, boy scouts... It had been ages since Mom stepped up as pack leader, organizing camping trips, code academies... everything. She didn't give a damn how the other dads looked at her. "Her Ethan deserved a real childhood, good-fer-nothing father be damned."

Legal and HR waited as the coral-lined Tahiti Room doors opened. The call came at seven am sharp, Ethiopian and Croatian offices materializing above the driftwood table.

"What's the status of our permits and facilities, Deidre?" I asked, despite knowing the answer.

'Slower than expected. Croatian's are putting up red tape like it's Christmas. Could be 3E fighting for their turf, or perhaps Asia.'

"We need those fucking bodies!" I snapped to get everyone's attention. Sometimes it took a well-timed eff-bomb to get down to business. "Do *whatever* it takes. I want a donor pipeline by Q1 next year and a full-blown facility in Zagreb by Q3. Can you do that?"

She promised. Same thing with Ethiopia, albeit faster and a better price. The Ethiopian government was holding on by a thread, desperate for jobs and tax revenue.

SAM

Back-to-back travel was rare. Boris gave the all-clear sign and we hopped from the company VTOL to the second-story ivy-covered landing pad of Mayor Rodriguez's four-acre estate. Ethan had warned me of another late night. At least Daron hadn't read me his bloody riot act. Lunch with his department head to talk funding proposals. Never enough to go around.

Two thick-necked Brits sporting scowls and MP5s led us past pristine greenery to a disguised lift with palatial views of the walled manor compound. Servant quarters sat on either side of the main with fountains, searchlights and four concealed snipers none but my war-wrecked eyes would have noted as my hand went to my holster.

Rodriguez stood in the double-doored main entrance. "Ah, Ethan, you've made it."

She was short but trim, had wavy shoulder-length brown hair, fiery Colombian eyes, and a confidence matched by brown designer slacks. Full of herself.

As we entered the cavernous home with rich ebony chairs, a sweeping staircase, Persian rugs and polished lamps, a broken-nosed killer of a man confiscated my Glock and Boris' Makarov, an army of armed guards lounging in leather recliners behind him.

Skipping the "worthless small talk," Ethan got down to business. "Ms. Larson told me. Look, Ms. Mayor, we put Atlanta on the map. We commercialized Dr. Patel's research and made Georgia Tech and the city fabulously wealthy in the process."

A message from Daron flashed. I'd read it later. Naked without my pistol, I sized up the guards for weaknesses or potential weapons while they eyeballed me. Statue, stool. Both would work. Wouldn't be the first time Ethan's acquaintances tried some-thing... At least they'd underestimate me. The big ones always did.

"Ethan, there's an election coming up," Rodriguez said. She didn't say more, catty intentions lurking in murky yet obvious shadows to avoid scrutiny.

"When was your last treatment?" Ethan asked. "You're how old numerically? Biologically?"

She squirmed, eyes narrowing. "Two years. I'm fifty-five," she said at last. "But thirty-seven biologically."

"So, you've done what, three, maybe four treatments?" A tense pause. "Your businesses were successful before being elected. Not *that* successful though."

Her fake eyes narrowed. It was no secret she'd profited from her position. Tech companies had flocked to Atlanta the past three decades.

"So," Ethan said after a lengthy staredown, "what's it going to take?"

The mayor smiled. "Now we're talking." And they did, about all manner of under-the-table deals.

We left as the mayor's people brought out tea and crumpets. Ethan had no patience for niceties. Me either. The guards returned our weapons as we left.

On the VTOL, I read Daron's message. He'd be home late again too. I called Malea. 'Go to Ali's house. His parents will be home. I'll have Dad call.'

She'd like that. Malea and Ali had been inseparable since Ali's family fled the reincarnation revolts in Northern India five years earlier. Ali's father, Pranav, worked at DDI in R&D, and we got together every few weekends to grill or for exotic Indian cuisine.

"Dammit," Ethan murmured to himself. "We need to stop by the lab. Gonzalez, take us downtown."

"Yes, sir!" Upfront, Gonzalez pulled a 180 for the bustling city. He was pointless, the VTOL flew fine on its own, but after that Luftwaffe standoff over German VAT... "Always have a backup plan," was Ethan's favorite motto.

ETHAN

Why'd the State insist on unannounced visits? Was Schmidt playing hardball? Or Rodriguez? Omar could deal with this. Did I have to do everything myself?

And who the fuck forgot to dust?

My nose twitched as the elevator rocketed to the third-floor showroom. Up ahead, Omar's voice. "As you see, the place is state-of-the-art, only the best for our patients."

We caught the tour group at the sales lounges, dozens of prospects at ornate tables in action-shot-lined rooms, discussing their futures, goals, and expectations. People loved us. And unlike our less-scrupulous competitors, we had salesmen and clientele of every race and nationality—I'd made sure. Boosted conversions eight percent.

We strode through psychologist-designed rooms filled with binaural buying beats, taking it in.

"When can my daughter get on the waitlist?"

"Do you have bulk packages?"

"Is my fourth treatment covered?"

Our salesmen handled the flood well, faces calm, smiles wide—but not too wide—commissioned greed never entering their eyes. The regulators must have felt it too, and waved us on. Good.

We slipped into the overcrowded donor waiting room, line snaking out the door.

"You stole my spot." A tall scraggly man grabbed the disheveled lady in front of him and threw her to the floor. "Wait your damn turn."

"I need the money now. My son—"

"Shut it, lady!" another snapped. "We all need the cash."

The guard at the door stepped forward and yanked the pathetic woman to her feet, dragging her out. Under a minute, no blood. Not bad.

Passing automatic doors, we reached one-way glass, offices barren by comparison. Cheap IKEA furniture, whitewashed walls and piles of prospective donor cards. A twenty-something salesman with short blond hair was showing the curly redhead a holographic chart.

"Donor packages are running twenty-nine thousand for Anglo-Saxons." He pointed to the graph's peak. "It's a great offer." He ruffled a six-inch stack, at least two-thirds of which were fake to increase urgency, before saying, "Sorry, I can't guarantee the price beyond today."

She dabbed hopeless eyes. "I need the money. My kids…"

"I know *exactly* how you feel." He jumped into our analyst scripted spiel. "Fifteen years ago, my mom made the same choice…"

The woman broke down, sobbing. "I'll do it."

I wanted to pump my fist. I loved a good close. And five grand below market price. Kid was good, but he'd never touch my fifteen-in-a-day record.

The suits left to find Lin Na and review company numbers.

Later, I'd blow the dusty trio away at the Lif—my new project. I had a reputation to uphold, five Michelin stars and Atlanta's #1 Restaurant Ranking five years running…

Why settle for second?

MIKE

S tarbucks.

    For all the hassle my colleagues went to find fancy restaurants for lowkey meetings, the Seattle-based coffee chain was my favorite. Their coffee was some of the best, the atmosphere, perfect: wooden tables, lab-grown leather seating, artsy coffee maps on the walls... Plus actual human baristas. Hadn't seen that lately.

She was late again. Typical, not that I could talk.

Her latest project, designer babies from some biotech firm. The problem; they were illegal since the First Accords which every nation —except North Korea and Thailand—signed in 2041.

Megan Larson appeared with a heaping cup and serpentine slither. "Senator Schmidt." I rose and offered a hand. "Imagine if we could eliminate disease, eliminate deformity, cure autism... Do you have children, Senator?"

Of course she knew about Jamie. Probably what brand I wiped with as well. "Ms. Larson, what you're proposing is illegal."

"I'm not proposing anything, sir." She changed her tack to defer-ence, as if I was *that* easy. "Atlanta's a leading tech hub, but we could lose prominence if another *less-principled* country, say China or Korea, lead on this."

"Ms. Larson, the answer is still no. I'm not religious, but some things man shouldn't mess with."

"What if it could save your wife?"

What? I stiffened. "It's ex-wife. What do you mean?"

"You don't know?" Her lips twitched. "Never consulted a genetic counselor?"

A conspiratorial twinkle in her eyes froze me. "What are you talking about?"

"Based on her most recent results," she said, "she has stage three bronchial cancer. Proper screening and embryo enhancement could have prevented that."

What? Was this a joke?

At last, she said, "We'd like you to consider—"

Was she serious, a sales pitch? Crushing my half-empty cup, I smashed it into the recycler as I headed for the door. Wallace hurried after me.

Cancer. Stage three cancer… Jesus.

Why didn't Ava tell me? We'd been married for years...

Ambling through Midtown, memories flashed. That Tijuana beach, passionate love after spicy carnitas… Our wedding, her beautiful belly and snow-white gown, Jamie two months later. So much, both good and bad.

I called her. Wallace gave me a respectful distance. 'Ava, when were you going to tell me? Cancer?'

A sharp breath. 'Mike, how did you—'

'Long story.' It hit me, Rome. 'That's why you're taking Jamie to Rome. Why didn't you tell me?' It hadn't been *that* bad between us, had it?

'I wanted to go before, before…' She swallowed hard.

I couldn't bear seeing her like this. 'Where are you? I'll come over,' I said. 'We can talk about this. Find a way… Wait, does Jamie know?'

A sniffle. 'Don't blame her, Mike. I asked her not to tell you. Doctors said it doesn't look good. Six months…'

Holy shit! Six months? 'Let me come over. Let me help.'

'No, Michael. I'm sorry, I, I can't. Not now.' She clicked off.

Wow, six months... Six months? This wasn't happening.

I hadn't been this shellshocked since Regina missed her period in high school. Worst three days of my life, until now. I couldn't stand Ava. But deep down, I loved her too. And she was the mother of my child. Jeez, Jamie... How was she handling this? She needed me.

I called Jamie, and she answered on the third ring. 'Hey, Jame. I heard about Mom.'

'I wanted to tell you. I—'

'It's okay, I know. Where are you? How are you holding up?'

Tears came from both sides of the call.

She gave me the address—oh, duh, school—and I ordered a priority skylift before the call ended. She needed me, and it was only money. This time I wouldn't throw up.

A Waymo VTOL dropped from the sky, blue butterfly doors opening as Wallace and I strode over. It scanned my smartchip as, wincing, I slid into the empty ship. At least with Ava's prodding, VTOL rides had gotten easier, but my stomach still writhed like a raunchy porno as we lifted off.

The Old Fourth Ward slums looked worse than last time: ramshackle tents and huts, hundreds of homeless, several cars burning. Impromptu police lines along Boulevard and Ralph McGill held back the worst of it. Talk about a shitty existence. How many were ex-'immortals' victim to life without challenge? No wonder pharma made an SSRI fortune...

Twenty minutes later, Decatur Private High. The weather was beautiful, warm and cloudy, none of the usual Atlanta humidity. We passed a group of kids and a frazzled teacher with a portable microscope heading for the massive brick building, flag flying high.

Two armed guards in bulletproof graphenite vests and riot helmets greeted us from behind heavy glass. A full body scan to gain entrance? What happened to being a kid?

I beelined for the principal's office, a much less imposing place since I'd escaped decades earlier, yet my hand quivered at the door. Too many memories.

A simple AI speaker system greeted us in the empty waiting room. I explained everything.

'*I see,*' the algorithm said after a pause to appear more human, notifying her teacher.

Plush chairs lined the far corner, awards covering the walls. Fifteen plaques, nine straight *Top School in Georgia* placards and a handful of cliché motivation posters.

What should I say? What could I say? Cancer, six months....

The door opened. "Jame."

She rushed over, throwing her arms around me, face red and makeup smeared. "Dad." We stood in the center of the room, holding each other for what felt like eternity. I'd missed her.

"Want to talk about it?" I asked as we left the building. Wallace hustled ahead to secure the area, and at the grassy knoll overlooking the campus, we sat wordlessly. Jamie and I always had that bond, not needing to say anything. And we didn't, for at least five minutes. It took her that long.

"Wh—what'll happen?" she asked, lip quivering. She was close to tears.

"I don't know. But everything will be okay." It had to. "We have each other." I hated myself for lying.

She snuggled into my chest like she had since she could walk, twisting her shoulder into the best kind of cuddle. I fought back tears. My little girl...

We sat there until a shaggy, half-clothed brown man limped towards the entrance.

Shouting ensued. "A meal, a slice of bread!" the man begged. "Anything. I paid taxes for years."

The guards' voices were muffled as the man hammered the windows. The door opened.

BANG.

The man collapsed, and the door closed again.

Jamie sighed. "Why didn't he go to a clinic? He could have at least helped someone."

A cold, heartless world...

* * *

"Ready to order, sir?" The gaudy waiter gestured at the expansive menu with a manicured wave.

The Lourde and Lif was Ethan Anderson's place, one of Atlanta's most exclusive restaurants. I couldn't pronounce half the entrees. White linen tables topped with flickering pewter candles, dull chandeliers and Parliamentary red velvet seats. Talk about excess. I didn't come often. Senator Warren did though, Speaker of the House. She must really want something, all the way to Atlanta... Or was she visiting the eccentric billionaire? Imagine *those* two in the sack...

Duck. Yeah, I'd have the roast duck.

Senator Warren sipped 2005 Pétrus with the practiced swirl as she eyed me. "Make up your mind, Mike?"

A nod. Mike, eh? Were we on first-name basis? "Duck à l'orange. And you?"

"Braised lamb shoulder with a Caprese salad. The chef, Luigi, he's to die for." Quite the expression these days.

It was busy for a Thursday, royally-clad elites in all manner of deep conversation, from furtive glances to fundraising, adultery, and worse.

She leaned closer. "I'm putting together a coalition to rezone cities. There's too much violence and inequality, it's not sustainable, even with donor stipends. The cities need to be safe for major contributors to society."

Talk about not saying much.

"We'd designate 'verified-only' areas," she said. "Anyone with sufficient employment and income scores would have access, while riffraff would be screened at checkpoints."

Was she serious? "That's what you'll run on, segregating cities?" The Jim Crow president... She was old enough. "Is that even legal?"

"Technically, no," she said. "But that's why we are having this meeting, isn't it? I've had three attempts on my life in two years." Wonder why. "It's like people don't remember who's fighting for them day in and day out," she continued. I stifled a laugh. She was so full of shit.

"You know what this will look like?" I asked. "It could trigger rebellion."

"What choice do we have? You saw the camps. It's worse in New York, and don't mention California."

But that doesn't mean we can't do anything. "What about the actual problem? Have you changed your mind on UBI—universal basic income?"

She chuckled. "You're funny, Mike. This is America. People would rather starve than be socialist."

Dammit anyways, she was right. Freaking Cold War capitalism.

Ethan Anderson and group of rich execs entered as Senator Warren tried to steal the check. I tapped the tabletop scanner. No way I was going to owe her anything. "We'll split it," I insisted when the waiter voice-bot asked how we'd like to pay.

Ethan's party sat at the exclusive center booth as the head chef, Luigi, waddled over with his finest hors d'oeuvres, of which he'd sampled one too many.

As we left, an athlete of a broad with a bent nose and a pale shock leapt from the table and hurried into the hallway, tapping her ear to answer a call. "What happened, Daron? Where's Malea?"

SAM

My heart hammered. The VTOL couldn't get here soon enough. After prying information from Daron and giving Ethan a hurried explanation, I sprinted from the restaurant to the Lif's spacious patio. It'd been years since I'd booked a flight and our budget would take a hit. Screw it.

Where was Malea? I tried calling twice. No answer.

I'd lived through wars, but couldn't think straight. My baby, my little girl...

Hurdling our steps, I ripped open the door and the window shattered. "Daron!"

He appeared a second later, red-faced and teary. "I, I was late. She's not at the Aggarwal's."

I threw up my hands. "Slow down. What happened?"

He told me. Forty minutes ago, he'd gotten a call from Sonia, Ali's mother. When was Malea coming over? "Six forty, Daron. Six forty! She should have been there hours ago."

I unholstered my trusty gun, clenching it for reassurance. "You haven't heard from her?"

He shook his head.

"I'm going to look for her."

"I'm coming with you," he protested. But we both knew the tough guy face was an act.

"No, go to Sonia's. Find out what happened. I'll run there, check side streets, anywhere she could have gone. Call Kelly and Mika's parents too, see if they heard anything. We'll find her. We have to." I gave him a hug and raced to the main road.

Malea, where are you?

The Aggarwals lived three blocks away. What could have happened? I called five more times. Did she go to the park?

The playground at the end of the street was deserted. The swings she'd grown up in, the bumpy slide we'd ridden half-a-million times... Not a soul in sight. I dashed on, slamming neighbors' doors and yelling, "Malea! Malea. Malea!"

People came to the windows and stared without interest, just another panicked mom. Fuck 'em. I ran, calling school, her teachers, anyone... No one had a clue. She'd been at school, handed in her genomics.

A buzz, a notification. It was an email from Google. A geo-targeted ad, courtesy of Amazon Adventures. Screw theme parks... I was two seconds from deleting it when it hit me. Amazon tracked my location, duh. Yes!

Opening our family account, I pulled Malea's data. This would work, it had to. It was all there: maps, charts, everything—by day, time and year. I chose the last twenty-four hours.

Our lower west side neighborhood appeared, red dots marking each location she'd connected to. I fast-forwarded. She walked home, passed the abandoned Baptist and Methodist churches and the soccer field. Everything looked normal. It was only five blocks. What happened?

She got home and entered our house. Was someone there? Ten minutes in the kitchen, the bathroom. After, she headed for Ali's.

At the end of the street, she paused. What was going on? If only there was video. She turned onto Sims and entered an alleyway. No, Malea. *What* was she doing?

Nothing happened. Her dot hovered, I swiped forward. Nothing. It disappeared after twenty minutes. I scrolled further, nada. She must have passed out. My legs pumped, heart hammering. I'd found her. It was going to be alright.

A message to Daron. *I found her.*

It rang as I hit Sims. 'Sam, Jesus! Tell me you have her.' Daron's voice broke.

Into the dark alleyway. Mommy's here, Malea... 'Everything's going to be—'

No, how was that possible? The alley was empty.

A drip of crimson, a horrific iron smell. My skin shuddered, heart stopped.

It was blood. Where was Malea?

* * *

I was slumped by a dumpster when the cops came. Daron appeared, yelling and shouldering past uniformed officers. None of the cops said anything.

"Where is she?" His eyes caught mine and he threw his arms around me. "Sam, you said you found her. You told me..."

My mouth wouldn't work. I couldn't say anything. My hands were shaking.

The officer in charge, a tall brown-haired man with a faint beard and hard eyes walked up and stuck out his hand. "Detective Harrelson. Tell me what happened."

I did, with Daron's help. Twice, sobs wracked me but I broke the fear.

The officer's eyes never left mine, but there was little sympathy. When I finished, he said, "It's not the first—"

Another officer appeared and whispered in his ear. Harrelson gestured deeper into the alley and I followed, dragging Daron forward in stunned silence.

The cops bent and pointed to something, a fine powder. "Was your daughter into drugs or anything?" the detective asked.

What? "No, of course not." What weren't they telling me?

Harrelson moved and a flickering streetlight illuminated a clump of brown hair. It couldn't be... It looked like Malea's. I was going to be sick.

The detective produced gloves, grabbed the tuft and slid it into an evidence bag. "We can run basic tests here but we'll have to get this to headquarters to analyze further. Should take a couple hours."

This wasn't happening. Where was she? I should have been there. Guilt torched icy veins, vision blurring.

My god... was that the last time I ever saw my daughter?

ETHAN

I remembered my first trip to London—Europe, for that matter—like it was yesterday. I was fifteen at the time and had pestered Mom for weeks. Even as a kid, I'd been a salesman and known the buttons to push. My dogged tenacity had won out. It didn't hurt she'd felt guilty about Bobby and London had been 'my way' of coping, according to the three shrinks who'd tried to tame me. They'd been so full of themselves.

Shaking my head, I returned to the *Lourde and Lif*, listening as Atlanta's A-list discussed the latest happenings and talked shop. Each was impressive in their own right: Penny Wood, the billionaire media mogul; Rachel Ryans—today's da Vinci and Michelangelo rolled into one; and Damien Pierre—creator of work.com, where half the labor force that were gig workers earned their keep with long, benefit-less hours for thousands of faceless corporations in need of low-cost labor.

Despite their prowess, none came close to touching DDI's scale.

"Ethan, what do you think about the rumors?" asked the mousy-nosed artist. Her intense eyes were narrowed, hair wild, in contrast to the orange scarf around her pale neck.

She must be talking about designer babies. "It'll never happen, not in our lifetimes at least," I said with a fake frankness, revealing nothing of our skunkworks projects. "And since you're all DDI members, that will be a long time indeed."

Talk turned to dessert, a personal favorite of mine.

When holograms materialized, announcing the night's lineup, there were gasps. The sugar-and-sweetener-free (SS-F) french vanilla sundaes with ground hazelnuts and aquaponic berries had three takers but by far the most popular dish—the one I'd designed myself—was the triple-chocolate SS-F molten lava cake lathered in fudge and peanut butter, drawing admirers from hundreds of miles.

The topsy blonde waitress was juggling our towering tray, when I got a call.

What now? I activated my interface. Shit, it was Mom. "I need to take this." I walked away from the towering ensemble, weaving between congressmen, actresses, and models, and slipped into the back hall.

'Hey, Mom.'

'Oh, E... I'm glad I got you.'

'What is it?' I asked. 'Everything okay?'

'Everything's great, really great. Other than my hip. It's been bothering me but, oh well...'

Really? 'When was your last treatment? Two years?'

'Mhm, no. It was, let's see... before our New Zealand trip maybe. So, three years.'

'New Zealand? Mom, that was almost five. Have you not come in since?' I shook my head. Good thing she couldn't see.

'Five years, has it been that long?' she said. 'If you say so.'

She'd always been scatterbrained. 'Okay, Mom, look... I'm going to set up a treatment next week. Tell me a time.' Why she chose to live in the middle of nowhere was beyond me. It had taken her ten years to let me buy her a halfway-decent place and arrange protection. That had been a shitshow.

And she insisted on doing her own online shopping, every Wednesday, even though her groceries never deviated. Old habits...

'How about this,' I said. 'I'll pick you up for your treatment and take you to the Lif once it's over. We'll get grilled peanut butter sandwiches. I gave Luigi your recipe.' It had been ages since she'd made those for Bobby and I, every Tuesday and Saturday night. Seemed like another life.

She agreed after a little cajoling, as always. Why she was so stubborn about LE?

A message appeared as the call ended. It was Jones.

I'm sorry, boss. I won't be in tomorrow. Something's happened to Malea.

Oh, no! Was everything okay? Jones had never missed a day.

I called her.

SAM

Officers were coming and going in the bustling police station, victims in small queues as voice-based AI receptionists questioned each new plaintiff. A burly man in handcuffs with two black eyes was dragged past us, and in the corner, a baby screamed.

A call. 'Hello? What? Who is this?' My brain was racing.

'Jones, are you there?' It was Ethan. What'd he want? Didn't I work enough hours?

'Yeah, Ethan?' I said. 'I mean, sir. I mean Mr. Anderson, sir.'

'Skip the formalities. What happened? Everything okay?'

Ethan had connections, right? Maybe he could help.

I signaled Daron to shut up. 'Malea's missing. We don't know what happened.'

He didn't say a word until I finished. 'So, they're thinking kidnapping?' he asked. 'How can I help? The lab has sequencers and we've got plenty of drones. Actually, take the company VTOL. '

Was he serious? Was this the same sharp-elbowed boss who crushed competitors and wasn't afraid to bite back? 'The analysis should be done any—'

"Excuse me, Mr. and Mrs. Jones, please come with me." A young

Asian officer beckoned us towards the interior of the station, past two armed guards and into the chaos.

'I need to go, sir. I'll let you know when we hear more. And thanks for everything.'

We turned the corner, passing two bunkered desks into an open office of busy blue bloods. Harrelson was by the automatic espresso machine. "Coffee, anyone?"

We shook our heads. My stomach roiled. Just tell me! "What have you got?" I asked.

"Good news! We've got a beat on our perp and are grabbing him as we speak."

Daron's face brightened, and my heart caught. "She's okay?" I asked.

"If she's there, we'll find her," the detective said without smiling. "Perp was a neighbor of yours, Freddie Tripp, two streets over on Welch." It didn't ring a bell.

"Ah, looks like he's here." Harelson led us through the array of hand-gesturing cops and hurried reports that went into keeping Atlanta somewhat safe to a deserted hall of one-way mirrors. "Stay here." He gestured to a small waiting area with several half-cushioned chairs. "Budget cuts."

We did, and he hurried to the last door on the right, knocking and disappearing inside.

Daron grabbed my hand. "She's going to be okay, she's going to be okay."

Time slowed to an unbearable crawl and after ages, the door opened. Harrelson trudged out, exhausted. I leapt to my feet and hurried toward him. "What happened? Where is she?"

He held up a hand and silence enveloped us. "I'm sorry."

My chest tightened. My stomach knotted. Raw acid grief.

No! No, it couldn't be...

ETHAN

Jones's makeupless eyes were pale and sunken, shoulders slumped. She looked horrible—surprise, surprise. Textbook repression, at wit's end.

I'd let her work yesterday to get her mind off things, anything to cope with the loss of her daughter. But now, Rogers said she was a liability. The cops weren't sure which underground clinic the girl been sold into, only that the junkie had been high as a worthless trust fund kid. He'd taken the ten grand her body fetched and blown half on dope.

There was a two-and-a-half percent chance she'd ended up source material at one of our facilities. If she had, it wouldn't be pretty. It was against our policy to source black market, but things happen... Some employees were more *enthusiastic* than others. I shuddered as Jones entered the kitchen in a zombie shuffle. Poor thing.

"Jones, have a drink with me." Reaching under the handmade cabinet, I drew two ancient snifters the Earl of Zetland had given me after *that* stag hunt. That was before Botswana, face to face with a bull hippo. Talk about re-evaluating things.

Jones propped herself on a stool, empty eyes staring into her snifter. I had to do this just right. Women were so delicate. What levers to pull... "Want to talk about it?"

She said nothing, downing her drink with a toss. It was nine a.m. "Jones, you should go home, get some rest. Be with your husband."

She didn't so much as blink. That bad? Uncorking the aged Kentucky bourbon again—a royal thank you for an expedited procedure—I slipped the pill into her drink. I'd hoped not to need to.

She swallowed hard. "She's gone, and it's all my fault. I should have been there..."

Passing her the drink, she downed it. We slid her carved body to the floor, one less headache to deal with.

"Get her home, Boris."

* * *

"First time visiting our facility, Mr. Anderson?" the pimple-faced Asian with the olive-green prison guard uniform asked. He stuck out an unwashed, callused hand and shook mine, probably hoping to make an impression. Eww. He flinched when Boris stepped forward. Not DDI material.

"It's been a while," I answered.

The lad smiled. "I'll give you the tour till the warden's ready—"

"That's okay," I cut in. "We'll wait in the office."

He led us away from prisoners, through an uncleaned hall that echoed of lost souls to a small waiting area with triple-bolt locks, no windows, and several folding chairs facing *Certificate of Excellence* awards on the barebone walls.

No one was getting in here, not with Boris and Rogers on either side of the door, hands to rival a rattlesnake.

Hwang sat next to me and opened his mouth. So much for quiet contemplation. "Did you know there's over three million Americans in prison and 200,000 on life sentences?" he said like a Girl Scout rattling off flavors. Actually, it was two hundred and twelve thousand, but I said nothing.

"Pa says too many damned blacks and Hispanics is the problem," he continued. "He's right, at least about the blacks... Hispanics are okay though."

I tried to tune out the pitchy Southern drawl that didn't fit his face. It didn't work, but there was a knock on the door and it opened. Thank goodness.

A rag of a man walked in, the warden's sloppy-haired attendant. "He'll see you now."

We rose and made our way next door, losing the peppy redhead and entering the warden's inner sanctum, which looked like a cross between a cheapo IKEA and an old folks home.

Fresh-pressed shirt, pristine desk, and his paper notebook screamed conservatism. He jumped into pleasantries, and I played ball for two minutes, before saying, "Let's make a deal."

He eyed me. "GDC's partnered with Beyond Human for all our death row inmates. Why are we having this conversation? You asking us to break our word?" His eyes flared.

"Not at all." I leaned back in the cheap folding chair and pretended to survey the office. "I always felt public servants and defenders like yourself deserve better. If you were to reconsider your contract, what kind of price per head we talking?"

His eyes narrowed. "You mean when our contract runs out next year?"

I nodded. Worked on these suckers every time.

We ironed out details as we cut the legs out from under our Big Apple-based competitors.

* * *

Gonzalez radioed ahead to disable her missile systems and whizzed over the endless pine trees and tennis courts nearest her front porch to land. I hopped out, waving at the frizzy-haired woman in embarrassing blue and try-hard Oakleys and 90's All Stars. She never did have a sense of fashion. "Mom, surprise!"

Her custom racket clattered to the ground, blue eyes sparkling. "Ethan, I thought—"

"What, a son can't pick his mother up?"

She smiled, sweaty arms enveloping me. "Come here. You look good."

"You too," I said. "But you got to stay on top of your treatments."

She promised. We left, but not before after a quick snack of peanut butter Oreos, a throwback to the old days. The occasional cheat meal wouldn't kill me.

"What's on your mind, E?" She set aside the mid-morning margarita I'd never been able to get her to kick and put her hand on my shoulder. "You look tense."

What was it about moms? She could read me like a book. "It's Penny Wood, the murder. The Board's pushing for a resolution to the whole thing." And looking to seize control however they can...

"You're in charge, honey. Just tell 'em you're handling it."

I sighed. Life was so simple for her. "I have. But they have investor protections too. Bastards. It'll work itself out, always does. It's costing us a fortune though."

"Money isn't a problem anymore," she said. "Life is, and living it." She gave me the *remember the important things in life* look Bobby and I had always hated. Damn, I missed him.

I groaned. "We solved that." We'd been over this before.

"There's a difference between life and living. You never take time to enjoy the moment, E, you're always going a mile a minute. That's all I'm saying."

I didn't respond. She was right, of course, but I could handle it.

Sam

Out of booze *already*? I'd bought another four bottles last night. Or was that two days ago? Three? Closing my eyes, I slumped on the sweat-stained couch, eyes heavy and shoulders worse.

Fuck, it was Sunday, four days after my world imploded and Detective Harrelson broke me. Daron wasn't much better. For him, it was wine, and shitty detective shows. We were a mess. I had no idea where to turn, or what to do. The rock we'd built our life on had been swept away, casting us to float aimlessly until our inevitable end. And in terms of drowning, I was putting in my best effort. Anything to stop the pain.

The image of some sick doctor carving open my little Malea clawed at my soul. I couldn't get it out of my head.

Another swig of knockoff Jameson. Another. And still, I could feel. Dammit, it hurt. Her face kept coming back... *"Mommy?"*

A knock. Someone at the door. I could care less, but Daron didn't move his lazyy ass.

"Daron? Sam? Open up!" Who was that? What did they want?

I shuffled to the door, the wall a guiding friend as I stumbled twice. It was Harrelson, again, but not in uniform. Jeez, not him... "What now?" I groaned.

He took a whiff but said nothing. "We tracked the supplier to a high-end clinic in North Druid Hills specialized in controversial extensions."

Sunlight blinded me. When was the last time I'd stepped outside? "What's that mean?" My head hurt. North Druid Hills...?

"It means," he said, "whoever bought your daughter and used her tissue for treatment—an illicit treatment at that—was quite rich, think a million-plus per procedure, and well-connected. Quasi-legal at best, but they won't serve jail time."

"Wait? What? Who?" No jail time? The news slow motion sucker punched me, my clouded brain reeling.

"They're not saying. The clinic—whose name I'm not at liberty to give you for obvious reasons—wipes their databases every night, and have no records or proof whatsoever. Their clients, who include presidents, senators, dictators, trillionaires, etc... demand it."

Oh... "So, no leads?" Eff that. I'd find out, somehow. "You *have* to do something. This is my daughter—"

He shook his head and I grabbed the doorway for support. "The investigation is over. Even if we could go further, I don't want to." His eyes fell. "You don't mess with these types unscathed, if you catch my drift." I did, innocent until proven poor. Pussy.

My head throbbed. They couldn't get away with it. They couldn't... Her lifeless face thrashed me again, the doctor's heartless scalpel. My hand fell to my scarred abdomen. They'd cut her out of me again... I'd let my little girl down.

Back to the fridge, anything to dull the pain.

MIKE

They should be in Rome by now. I'd been so tempted to go, but if Ava only had a few months... We'd have fought—like always—and spoiled everything. And she didn't want me.

So, here I was, home alone, reading Senator Warren's bill. It was a mouthful, even for Congress. That was saying something. Did she think this would propel her to the presidency? With President Nguyen's second term coming to a close, all the familiar faces were out in force. At least I wasn't part of *that*. Media appearances, backstabbing, outright propaganda... I was more than happy as a simple senator. But how could I twist this BS bill to make it work for Georgians?

A new window, the BBC. Inspiration might strike, and the Brits were more impartial. Plus, the female anchor had dirty eyes, wild hair, and a sexier voice.

'In startling news, median age and life expectancies throughout Africa and Asia continue to decline as donor stipends tempt third world economies decimated by automation in the West. A full twenty million last year in China alone, more than double their natural deaths to fuel China's health craze.'

Click, Google News.

Were they still making noise after the anti-trust break up a decade earlier. That'd been a fight... A protest outside DDI, donors fighting for a slot and a reasonable payout. It's not like they could unionize... But, they deserved their fair share. This could be a big opportunity to get in front of people and win some air time. With Rodriguez pushing for my seat, why not?

Wallace hated the idea, but in the end, agreed, if he could bring Reggie and a few other guys to manage security. Before long, we were in a governmental black-tinted Tesla, racing through the city. If the cops shut down the protest, I'd miss my chance. And with Megan Larson hounding me, I wouldn't mind DDI taking a hit.

On the short ride over, I checked email. It still hadn't been replaced, despite what people claimed. The chip embedded in my palm verified my biometrics: genome, blood type, genetic age... the basics, before allowing access to my encrypted Amazon account.

Four messages. My email bot cleaned up every morning, flagging ones worth my time. Two arrival confirmations for Jamie's flight stung. I should have been there.

But they needed mother-daughter time, especially if Ava... Jeez.

I opened the third for some much needed distraction. It was Phil, my wealth advisor. Dude was a genius, introduced to me by NVision's CEO five years prior. They'd needed help after the company's miniaturized augmented lenses had a record hundred billion-dollar IPO. Where do you park that much dough?

A few great investment opportunities. Fourteen percent IRR, guaranteed. Call me. —Phil

I made a mental note and closed the message.

BAM. Something smashed into our windshield, another rock. Holy shit.

The driverless car accelerated, zipping past bums lining the long-abandoned cemetery. Both guards stiffened, fingers twitching.

We passed the last of the slums, the car filtering out the stench of shit and unwashed bodies. It hadn't been so bad ten years ago. What can you do?

Five minutes later, a frustrated army of peaceful protesters marching outside DDI's gleaming highrise campus, carrying signs and yelling, taking videos and posting to social. Several fearless reporters mingled with the displaced and from above, dozens of drones from Google News, Fox, CNN and the Times hovered, getting their shots for the evening news. A few angry Hindus and Christians—holdouts from pre-LE times—shook Bibles, shirts emblazoned with disgust for the assisted suicides, hell, wrongful reincarnation... You'd think they'd get with the program. It didn't look like they could afford death insurance.

Two armored male and female guards approached our vehicle, drawing weapons to create a human shield. Reggie opened the door, and I stepped into the crowd, beelining for the impromptu podium set up outside the double helix building, infinity logo obscured by the masses. It had been a few years since I'd last been in. I was probably due for another treatment. Gregori would know. He'd have my records and suite of tests he'd want run, always did.

A ponytailed hipster with a *Shut Up and Die* hoody and an older blonde who could have been his mom emerged from the crowd, blocking our way. The mob must not have noticed the pro-aging pair. Freaking Agers... how decrepitness was anything but awful was beyond me. Some people...

At least my parents hadn't deteriorated like a used drivetrain. Damn those early VTOL days and Dad's optimism. I'd been nine when they'd died. Why hadn't he listened to me?

From the stage, a woman's voice boomed, amplified over air speakers spread around us and echoing down the traffic-restricted road. "THERE'S A CONSPIRACY BETWEEN THE LE COMPANIES AND THE ELITES. HOW MANY OF YOU LOST YOUR JOB, OR FAILED TO FIND WORK? TRIED TO BECOME A LIFE DONOR AND BEEN TURNED AWAY? WERE YOU OFFERED BELOW MARKET RATES?" Not this again.

Jeers and cheers as people quieted.

"APPLIED FOR DEATH INSURANCE AND BEEN DENIED?" Another wave of fidgeting shouts as people began to push, getting rowdy. Where were those cameramen?

"THE GAME'S RIGGED. THE RICH GET RICHER, AND WE PAUPERS BEG TO OFFER OUR LIVES TO FEED OUR FAMILIES... I SAY, NO MORE." She was right.

Security personnel emerged in black graphenite vests and riot masks, fiberglass shields and sawed-off shotguns at the ready. Shit, these LE guys meant business... A statuesque pale soldier with ruthless eyes headed for the ringleader. "DISBAND AT ONCE. YOU ARE IN VIOLATION OF FEDERAL DECREE 105.61C. RETURN TO YOUR HOMES."

"We don't have any!" another woman yelled.

The rebel on-stage writhed as two guards slammed her into a headlock. A rock flew and struck the big guard's face. Crap.

His two comrades turned and fired. Holy shit! Where was Reggie?

Gas canisters arched through the air and smashed the screaming crowd, smoke billowing as heavy projectiles crashed into bodies. Madness.

People ran, some storming the stage, others fled. Another contingent sprinted for DDI's starship doors. The empty-eyed brunette next to me said, "Might as well get the money," and took off after this last group. What was happening?

I stood there, stunned until someone yanked me.

Another wave of gunfire.

Shrieking men charged us, but Reggie dropped them with pistols to the face, smashing their noses as they crumpled to the concrete.

At last, the Tesla doors opened.

A ragged little girl appeared, arcing a stone towards us. No...

Time froze. One of the temp guards fired as she grabbed another. Her innocent face exploded in a crimson spray, falling forward, dead before her teeth shattered on the cement.

Someone shoved me in the car. I tripped. The doors slammed. My ears pounded.

We raced off.

This wasn't happening.

She was just a girl...

Was this downtown Atlanta?

SAM

'Daron, call me.' Where was she? He wasn't at home, hadn't shown for work, or messaged me in hours. Deep breath. This was his way of dealing with things. It made it hard, us being so different. And war didn't compare.

I contemplated the half-empty Jack on the cluttered coffee table. Maybe later. My stomach was sloshing. Hungry too. Trudging into the kitchen, I opened the creaking fridge and grabbed eggs, activating the news in the background. Malea loved eggs...

'Protesters hijacked another body disposal truck outside DDI's headquarters—' *Click.*

'Only six months to become certified—' No thanks.

Not another 'career-in-plumbing' infomercial. Everyone shits, doesn't mean I want to deal with it. Actually, "Play podcasts."

NPR's: A History of War continued where I'd left off, *The US-Mexico Border Crisis.*

'Following actions of the Trump administration, relations soured as rising global temperatures demanded ever greater cooperation. An influx of refugees and migrant workers...' Cracking the eggs in the olive oil coated scratcher, I turned on the old induction burner. I was filling old faithful when a 'high priority' notification buzzed. Now what?

An email. *Account Deposit Notification: $27,000*

Damn Nigerian princes... Dele—Wait, it was from sales@ddi.com. A bonus? Bullshit.

Choking, I sat. That was more money than we'd had since Daron's mom dumped her shit on us. I paused to reread the subject before opening it.

Account Deposit Notification: $27,000

We have received the following transfer:

* * *

I tem #: *364718491*
    Amount: $27,000.00
    From: Defying Death Industries, Inc.
Fee: $0.05
Receive Date: 05/28/2055
Service: Same-Day

* * *

No notes? No explanation? I forwarded it to Daron. *Know what this is about?*

I mean, I'd take it, but... Wait, what was that smell?

The eggs were burning.

ETHAN

S till no Jones? It had been a week. Did she need *more* time? There were plenty of vetted bodyguards out there, men too. I'd have to talk to Vlad about a replacement, or maybe he knew something I didn't.

I leaned back in the Tutankhamun recliner at the head of the Egyptian table and took a strawberry ketone sip as the holograms of the Board watched Omar outline what happened. "Good news is, no one died." Thank 'god'—I loved a good religious pun. "And we got FOX and CNN to pull their coverage. Their leadership are DDI subscribers so we upped their spots in the queue." People were so easy.

"We have a PR nightmare on our hands," Garrett, our crafty-eyed Head of PR with the Roman nose said. "What sparked the outburst? Was this organic, or spurred by SLI, or someone else?" That was the question, but no one had answers.

"Come on, people!" I snapped. "Find out. Garrett, talk to CI after this. Find out what counter-intel knows. Were there rumblings? Any darkweb contracts or hacks out there? We need a report and recommendation by this time tomorrow." What was I paying these idiots for?

He agreed, and the meeting wrapped, everyone scrambling to protect the stock. And no one had more vested in this than me, over a quarter of the trillion-dollar company and a majority supervoting shares. But the mission was what really mattered. I'd promised myself after Bobby...

Everyone filed out as Vlad entered. Speak of the devil. "I wanted to talk to you."

"Sir, we may have a problem. It's Jones."

I sat back in my cushioned chair. Couldn't this wait? "Tell me."

Vlad swallowed. Shit, he was always unflappable. What...

"Her husband, he was processed," he said.

Oh, fuck. "You're kidding..."

Vlad shook his head. "Yesterday."

Oh boy. I hadn't factored for that. That made things interesting... "Did they need the money *that* bad?"

The big Russian shrugged. "Not my job. Just thought I'd tell you."

Dammit, Jones. She'd had been with me for ages. Were there gambling debts or something? "I'll talk to her."

Vlad left and as usual, I was forced to do damage control, after hitting the weights and sauna. The sun god, Ra, gave me a knowing look as I exited the Egyptian Room. He was a god, he knew the feeling...

SAM

No... "What do you mean he was processed?" My knees crumbled on Ethan's couch in the middle of his uncaring living room as words tumbled out, mind reeling. "A donor?" Impossible. No... I was going to be sick.

Ethan nodded, sighing.

Dammit, how could that prick be so relaxed about all this? I closed my eyes and took a deep breath, still half-drunk from when DDI's limo picked me up an hour earlier. "Daron's dead?" I asked. There must be some mistake. Was this one of those *Punked* shows, or a bad VR sim? I'd kill him, I'd fucking kill him.

Ethan leaned back in his rocker. "Yes. But he also gave someone else the gift of—"

"I don't give a flipping dick's ass about someone else's life extension." I swallowed hard. First, Malea, and now, Daron... This wasn't happening, it couldn't. My stomach spasmed.

Ethan reached over and put his hand on my shoulder. I smacked it away.

He sighed. "I know, Jones. Look, it was a mistake. He never should have been processed, but he did volunteer."

And that was supposed to make things better?

"How about this?" he added. "We'll take twenty years off your death insurance wait period and add you to the company policy now. It'll be like he gave his life to save yours."

I didn't reply. Did he think he could buy me off? Extend a life not worth living. The arrogant prick... Why not just kill me. It'd be more humane. And it's not like Daron and Malea's policies mattered any more... If anything, he'd come out on top. He always did.

Ethan rose like a coward, eyes flicking to Boris in the hallway. "I've got a phone call." Any excuse to leave.

The soldier in me took over. Pull yourself together. I'd handled worse. "I'm fine, sir. I'll be back on the job Wednesday. Thank you, sir."

Was he really gone? Daron... My lips quavered. No, no... I was fine. I had to be.

Ethan sighed, relief crossing his face as he darted away. I sat for who knows how long, head in my shaking hands as around me, life continued, and Maria yelled something to the automatic oven. Seemed unreal.

Two lives, twenty-seven-thousand dollars and five extra years for me. Was this a joke? What if I just killed myself? I had the gun... I wasn't some handbag bitch that needed pills... But Lieutenant Crowders would chew my ass out. "Never give up, never surrender!" I was a soldier, dammit. I was a soldier...

Ethan's limo drove my lifeless body home, playing cheery music with flowery scents as we raced through the crowded city. As if AI-derived neuro-cues would make things better. The alcohol wore off, my mind brewed.

The system was corrupt, everything was fucked. I worked for a freaking life extension company, and my husband's life hadn't been saved, but stolen. My daughter too. All so some rich dickhead could go on accruing interest, enjoying life and banging underage girls. No one cared, no one said anything...

Politicians, boob-jobbed blondes, CEOs... everyone was in on it, everyone with means anyways. Was this my red pill moment, drenched in alcohol, half-dead in this fancy-ass limo? Why was I here? If I was a failure as a mother, as a wife, why be born at all?

We pulled up to our little house—my little house now, I guess. I dragged myself to the door.

Inside, I headed to drown my sorrows, reaching for the latest bottle. What did it matter? No, they deserved better than this. My hand stopped trembling and I grabbed the cheap rum. Popped the cork, I walked to the window by the sink. My reflection was terrible: bloodshot, hair a mess, days-old mascara blurred.

Peering down the throat of the bottle, a convulsing wave of grief shook me. "Dammit!" I smashed the glass cabinet that held our cups, fragments scattering everywhere. Crystal shards in the sink glittered with sunlight as the blood dripped from my fist. Squeezing the bottle, crimson fell, blood and booze mixing as I dumped the poison with a satisfying gurgle.

I collapsed to the floor, anger and grief wracking me in convulsions. It hurt so much I could scream. Tears came. No more emotions, not that. It was too painful to feel. Better to feel nothing, or be dead. Dead... they'd killed them so they could live.

No more feeling sorry for myself. I was done being a victim.

My rage needed a target.

One way or another, someone was going to pay. An eye for a fucking eye.

Mama bear was back.

Revenge would be sweet...

* * *

Seven a.m. sharp, I pulled into the compound. Quinton—the new guy on the team, straight out of SEALs, and with the scars to prove it—did a double-take at my blood red lips. "Looking good, Jones."

A quick scan for explosives or biochemical weapons, and I was in, thirty minutes early, and that was after hitting the weights and showering.

I checked in with Vlad in his command center. Must be nice having a place onsite, what with the facilities and chefs, the good life. He was in the middle of a pod-shaped area, eyes darting between permanent monitors on the walls and invisible screens on his ARlenses. How he could take it all in was beyond me.

"You're back, Jones?" He raised an eyebrow..

"Felt good," I lied. "Ready to get back."

"Bullshit," Vlad said. "You were fuck all and needed a healthier way to drown the pain. I get it. But if you're back, you better freaking be *back*. Can't afford any eff-ups."

"I'm good, boss, I'm back," I said with forced confidence.

He gave me the Stalin eye, sizing me up without an ounce of perv before nodding his approval. "Upstairs, Subbasement One. Get on it."

I left at a trot.

Ethan was on the phone when I found him, in the Machu Picchu Room, pacing. "We'd love to have you here, Senator." He held up a finger and I was distracted by the Incan Ruins lining the walls, table a designer's dream with steeped levels and everything. "Think about it. It will be the party of a generation and would be a shame…"

The call ended and Ethan looked my way. "Perfect. Things are coming together. Oh, Jones, you're back. Is it Wednesday already?"

Waiting until Wednesday would have killed me, alone in that dinky memorial to happier times. "Was ready to be back, sir," I said. "A party?"

The billionaire smiled. "It pays to have friends in high places."

MIKE

I t had been three days since the riot and my stomach was in knots. I hadn't slept that night, or the one after. That girl's face... it was gone. Her life ended before my eyes. And it was my fault. If I hadn't been there... I'd called Jamie afterward, had to hear her voice. It helped, Reggie's scotch too, but I couldn't shake the broken emptiness.

Protesting an LE company these days... It was unheard of. And so much hate. I'd been thirty seconds from the front of the crowd when the guards opened fire, thirty seconds from just another casualty. Death insurance wouldn't have helped me, nothing would. And yet, I'd gone to the rally. Why? It was a political opportunity, a chance to capitalize on others' suffering. Was I *that* narcissistic? My stomach roiled.

Was that what these companies were, stains on society? Stealing from the poor and giving to the rich, literally... trading time for money.

The oven dinged. *'Your filet mignon is ready, Michael.'* Talk about ironic.

Heaving myself from the couch, I trudged to the kitchen. Reggie was there, as always, sipping a spiked americano—omega-3s, zinc, and cinnamon, his latest kick. Try hard. He had five more years before the security firm I'd contracted him and Wallace through made good on his death insurance. He was doing everything in his power to stay healthy, and made me look like a chump.

I should do better but couldn't bring myself to sweat it out at the gym, eat like a monk, or ditch the occasional booze. Ava had thought I was nuts, she'd done everything right: early morning yoga, organic smoothies, the ancestral diet, the whole nine yards... Then again, it hadn't worked out for her, had it?

"Smells good," Reggie commented as the oven seared the steak one last time. When I didn't reply, he added, "Everything okay, boss? You've been off."

Ugh... "The protests." What else could I say?

Reggie nodded. "Pretty brutal, huh? But that's life for some folks. Got to get by somehow."

His words struck me. "You ever considered becoming a donor, of checking out?"

"And deprive the ladies?" Reggie laughed. "I think not. In all seriousness, I've had friends go that route, classmates too. Economy's shit, no jobs, and the education system is a joke." He grabbed his fork and plate, carrying it to the table as I hurried after him.

We both skewered our juicy steaks.

* * *

handwritten invitation sat in the entrance of my apartment when I woke the following morning. Sturdy cardstock design. Fancy.

You're cordially invited to DDI's Midsummer Fest
Join us for the party of the decade
June 21st, 2055 | 7pm-midnight
The Anderson Estate—007 Anderson Drive, Marietta, GA

Interesting. Somebody was full of themselves. I checked my calendar, and shuffled a few minor appointments: Georgia's Attorney General, the enhanced meat lobby and RSVPed at once. Normally, swanky corporate donors were a drag, but a DDI party... Ethan Anderson had a reputation. Oh yes, he did...

SAM

W as this right? The seedy back alley of overflowing dumpsters, shagging pups, and a flashing neon titty bar was the last place you'd put a LE clinic. I checked my GPS again. But this was it, *101 Wood Valley Drive.*

No sign out front. The windows were broken and crushed antidepressants littered the grimy asphalt alongside a slew of needles. The old-fashioned handle creaked when it opened, a dark split level wooden staircase greeting me. I chose up, never one for dungeons after Saudi and made my way as my pulse quickened. Cobwebs lined the grimy windows and chipped white walls. A light flickered and I reached for my gun.

This was stupid. There was no chance in—

Shit, what was that? Footsteps.

A door opened, and I retreated. "Follow me, sir, this way. The doctor will see you." Footsteps faded into the distance above me. The doctor? In this shithole...

I waited, holding my breath before resuming my silent climb. Was *this* it? At the landing, I slid against the wall and peered in. The place was empty, but spotless, bright halogen lights illuminating the white tile floor, lazy-boys in the far corner and an automated reception desk dominating the middle of the room. This was Health Services Unlimited, HSU, the clinic that robbed me of my baby girl? Are you kidding? Deep breath. This might be my one chance.

Opening the door—again, a metal handle to avoid suspicion—I hurried in. Everything was brand new. Even the floors squeaked.

In the center of the room, a high-res greeter bot materialized, a beautiful Asian woman in a yellow kimono, hair pulled back in a bun that screamed precise professionalism. *'How can I help you?'*

Saying nothing, I touched the minuscule black mole-like devices stuck to my face, glad I'd bought the facial recognition distorters. They emitted UV light at programmatic angles to fool surveillance cams and scramble video feeds. As long as I didn't say anything, I should be fine. Where was the hologram's source? The small console was on the far wall and I checked the serial number, making a note and picture, and went for the door.

I made it to the dreary alley without seeing a soul, and hauled ass. If they had database backups, Amir would be able to hack them. On the way to Tech's campus, I called him.

'Hey, Amir, you busy?'

A flustered half-Pakistani voice answered, 'Sam, Sam Jones! That you?'

'I'm in your neck of the woods. Want to meet for coffee?'

We agreed and soon enough, were sitting in the campus' Starbucks in the shell of the old football stadium, abandoned almost twenty years, since the ban.

It had been ages since we'd seen each other, busy with kids and all. Amir hadn't aged a bit, other than a balding patch above his always furrowed forehead. He was just as skinny, just as jittery and still wore nerdy unattractive polos—albeit fancier. I couldn't help but smile. It'd been too long.

Fancier than I remembered. AI-assisted baristas, an assembly line of automated espresso machines, a room in the back to roast your own beans. Busy students spread like cicadas across the library-esque tables and comfy chairs.

"How's the research going?" It had something to do with alternative general intelligence, whatever that meant. There's a reason he'd finished high school and university and I'd jumped into the military, but he'd always been good about it, had a crush for the longest time.

"It's going well. We're about fifteen-to-twenty years from true AGI." It was *always* fifteen-to-twenty years with these guys, as long as I could remember.

"You mean Skynet?" Wait, that's not what I'm here for. Before he could bite back, I said, "Actually, Amir, I need your help."

"Sure. If I can. Owe you for that heads up about the DOD's honey pot. If it wasn't for you, I'd have a nice orange jumpsuit for my scrawny Indian ass."

I told him, stopping for the occasional caffeinated hit. His sharp brown eyes never blinked, fingers twitching like always when he analyzed a hard problem. Ms. Whittle would have lost it.

"Let me get this straight," he said, "you need a handheld device to break an encrypted network's security protocols—without flagging the sys admin—and bypass a greeter bot's virus and malware protection—"

"Can you do it, or not?" Even as a tenured professor, he overcomplicated everything. Why did guys think girls liked a showoff?

"Sure. You can buy one off the dark web and modify it. Give me two days. But are you sure this is a good idea?"

I shrugged. "If it was your family, what would you do?" He winced, biting his lip. "Don't worry," I said, "if I get caught, I'm no rat."

He laughed. "Remember that abandoned church, damn autopilot programming. Can't believe you took the heat."

We both had a laugh at the cops who'd investigated that one.

* * *

Amir finished the modifications in a day, and we met the next night at a Salad Express, like old times, when we'd both been broke as hell. I wasn't sure if he'd chosen this place for the memories, or because I couldn't afford much better. Either way, I was glad.

Leaning over the counter boasting *Cheap and Healthy*, buffet-style trays in hand, we weighed our options. In truth, we both knew what we wanted: same as always.

"Spinach and lettuce, tomatoes, ground chicken, and chickpeas," I said as the robotic arm prepared. "With walnuts and a side of avocado slices." My reusable tray was loaded and ready before the words left my mouth, facial recognition pulling my order history.

Amir stepped forward but the robot was slower this time, waiting for his order—in essence, a Caesar salad with mutton, no croutons, and three layers of onions. It was disgusting.

Food in hand, we grabbed an empty plastic table under the cartoon carrot mascot and sat with a squeak, opening our trays. He slid the circular device to me under the table, and I dropped it in my bag before touching my food. I was starving.

"It's been forever, we should toast." He lifted his lemon-flavored water—he hadn't gotten the memo on artificial sweeteners—and said, "To old friends, good health, and better times."

"And to mischief and mayhem," I added with a smirk.

He flushed, and we ate. Talk turned to his family. "It's been hard on Emily and her aunty, her grandma is stubborn as an ass and her mind's been set ever since Emily's grandpa died. Now she's refusing treatment, says she's done with LE and ready to expire, to meet her Kurt in heaven. Really believes all that. Says she's seen the world and had her ride. How selfish, right?"

So, that's why he was looking so good. "They can afford it? How old is she?"

Amir smiled. "I got lucky, married into it. Both her parents came from money, her dad's side is in pharma, and her mom's, cheap outsourced coders. She's 102 and had three treatments, but tests say she's got six-to-twelve months. Emily's worried about how the kids will react, great-grandma dying and all..."

I was speechless. It was so far outside my reality... Did he expect sympathy? "Isn't that her right?"

Amir winced like I'd slapped him. "I mean, I guess. But dying? It's not like money is an issue."

With nothing to say, I changed subjects. "Any big plans coming up?"

"We're doing the Nordics in two weeks for Midsummer's Eve. Then ten days in Buenos Aires, and a tour of the Alps and Central Europe in late fall. It's beautiful that time of year, and the kids haven't been yet. You only live once, right?"

Yes *I* do. That was a ton of vacation time, not to mention the flights. "What about work?"

He shrugged. "The job's more of a passion. We have a handful of rental properties and money in the markets..." He'd moved up in the world...

Conversation turned to me, and things got more awkward. Our lives had diverged, and the more I learned, the larger the chasm grew. What happened to two broke kids hustling for a hamburger?

It was like the world had left me behind, or at least Amir had.

* * *

I had a big night ahead of me. After this shift, I'd find Malea's killer.

Ethan was in the middle of an intense rowing workout, pushing himself against the simulator as Boris roared encouragement. Standing in the corner of the gym, hands behind my back, I checked the doorways again.

It had been three days since Amir gave me the device but with Ethan's party preparations, I'd been too busy to do much. Sounded like there was an announcement coming, but I hadn't the slightest idea. And Ethan being Ethan, he wasn't saying.

During the last sprint, magnetic rower screaming as Ethan's legs fired, shirtless back muscles exploding with force, he stopped, tapping his temple. He never cut training short. Never. Must be important. I caught myself listening.

His eyes darkened as he rose. 'Lee, is that you? You bastard.'

A pause, listening. 'You poached our top scientist. He had a noncompete.'

Ethan's eyes blazed into SLI's president. 'Screw you, Sun. I'll see you in court. And yes, we've got connections to try your ass in China.' He signed off and slammed the 100-lb heavy bag, display panel registering 1350 psi—not far off a competitive heavyweight. "If that's how he wants to play, fine."

Ethan stormed out, and Boris shot me a confused look. "SLI." Boris never was the sharpest, but a world title in Krav Maga will do that to you. I caught Ethan at the elevator. "Anything I can do, sir?"

"Short of killing that fucking Chinaman, no!" He sighed. "Things were going so well in Hamburg. R&D was close to a breakthrough. This will set us back six months."

"What now?" I asked.

Ethan's brow furrowed. "We hit back and regroup."

The next meeting was straight out of a spy film: Ethan wanted intel on our assets in China and a shady woman in sunglasses and all-black Armani outlined potential countermeasures. Ethan smiled as she highlighted high ranking SLI members we'd turned or had compromising material on. Looked like we were playing for keeps.

Ethan came to me afterwards and put an ominous hand on my shoulder. "This meeting never happened." He didn't have to say more.

MIKE

"I'm sorry, Senator Warren, I'm not going to be able to join your coalition," I said without any of the usual niceties. She'd dressed up for the meeting at my office, but she'd miscalculated, her clingy Hermes blouse and Chanel skirt having no effect on me. I wasn't *that* easy.

Warren's face soured before freezing in that perpetual politician's smile, tentacled fingers around her armchair the only thing keeping the lioness from mauling me. Reggie's hand moved to his holster, his eyes tracking the tension from post at the door with an alert smirk.

"Mike, are you sure? There's a lot of—"

"Positive, Quincy. It's not what my constituents need." Not that you care...

Warren shrugged. "Very well. We have more than enough bipartisan support. Thought you'd want to be on the winning side..." She didn't have to say more. I'd just pissed off the odds-on favorite for the presidency. Oh, well. It was a good thing I was happy with my senate seat.

I escaped her honeyed fakeness with something about another meeting, relieved once I was free at last.

Another knock. Wasn't I done for the day?

Surveillance cams showed a gorgeous woman in Prada heels and a power suit, equal parts fashion and force. Her black eyes were impatient even as her gorgeous face remained calm. My system identified her at the same time I did: Tammy Wood, daughter and heir apparent of media mogul Penny Wood. She was closer to sixty-five based on the tabloids I'd read. A quick search confirmed it.

Reggie buzzed her in. "Ms. Wood, what can I do for you?" Her company was headquartered in New York, not Atlanta. What was *she* doing *here*?

Her eyes narrowed before noticing me. "Ah, Senator, you are here. Good." She gestured to the seat with a practiced dominance.

"Yes, please, have a seat," I said. "Anything I can get you?"

"A fat, sweetener and sugar-free macchiato, if it wouldn't be too much bother." And what if it would?

The espresso machine in the far corner roared to life, grinding as nutty aromas filled the air. The beautiful woman smiled as a second nozzle descended, a slow drip and foamy milk filling the glass. I carried the mug to her and she gestured to the messy card table like she owned the place.

"So." I sat back down. "How can I help you, Ms. Wood?"

"It's about censorship, Senator."

Interesting. "Tell me more." The First Amendment was democracy's last defense...

When she was finished, I was shocked. "You're saying DDI threatened you about covering the protests?"

"Not DDI, but their PR people," she said. "Or an outsourced legal firm. Deniability. We'd been working on a story on the appalling conditions in their Ethiopian and Kenyan internment camps where they keep donors for emergency treatments. The bodies have to be fresh. Awful stuff, à la factory farming before lab-grown put them out of business."

It sounded over the top, and after the unproven London metro bombing and overdone Porn World stories, her company had a reputation. "You've seen the facilities?" I asked. "The holding pens? How'd you find out?" Actually, that was a good question. The damn hackers these journalists employed.

"They don't try hard to hide them. Over there, people are desperate. Their Kenya office has tens of thousands of volunteers a day. They turn most away, of course, health and quality issues..." Tens of thousands... And I thought Atlanta was bad.

"And what do you want me to do about it?" Probably special treatment or the like. That's what happened when they were raised at the nanny's tit.

"Freedom of the press is one of the most important tenets of democracy. When a rich billionaire or corporation violates that..."

She was right, but I couldn't let on, so I raised an eyebrow. "Isn't that what your organization does every day, use your reach to sell your products and services? You and your mother wield as much power and influence."

Mad someone beat you at your own game?

Tammy shifted in her chair. "Not exactly. We stand by what's right and true—"

"And DDI doesn't, at least in their eyes?" They were all the same.

Her eyes narrowed, and I added, "Why'd you come to me?"

"We saw you at the protests, what happened... And DDI's based here in Atlanta. We thought if anyone could rein them in, it would be you." She raised a challenging brow. "Perhaps I was wrong."

How should I play this? "Are you saying you're against all LE? Have you had a change of heart?" I grinned. "You look great for *your* age."

Her face flushed and she stood, hands on her perfect hips. "This isn't about me or my individual choices. If I want to stay young so I can keep fighting for what's right, that's up to me." She stormed out.

It's always about 'what's right...'

Some people.

SAM

F inally.

Rounding the corner into the dim alley, I hurried to the rundown clinic door to avoid being seen. I'd deactivated GPS earlier, applied the facial scrambling marks to my cheeks, and had a mask in my pocket. As long as I didn't run into—a siren blared two streets over and I froze, waiting. Nothing happened. They turned the corner, windows open. I crouched lower as they passed.

After two minutes, all clear. The pockmarked street was deserted, scarcely a window lit. Creeping to the door, I grabbed the rusty handle. The door was locked, but I was ready.

I inserted the plastic lockpick gun and L-shaped tension tool into the bottom of the keyhole, jamming it to the rear like the video said. Turning, I squeezed the trigger. It jarred the tumblers free as the door swung open.

Shit, the alarm. I thrust the device in my pocket onto the door seconds before the buzzer sounded. Get it together, girl. No more slip-ups.

Hurrying in, I tiptoed up the steps.

The main lobby was unlit and empty. Lights came on to greet me, as did the greeter bot—a Vietnamese woman this time. These rich men and their Asian fetishes... I said nothing so voice recognition couldn't pin me to the crime.

Taking the silver device from my pocket, I placed it on the bot's drive. Nothing happened. Then, a light blinked, blue, red, blue... Amir hadn't said anything about any light. I checked the doorway. Wind blew in the alley outside and sent a shiver down my spine. Worse than the streets of Saudi, that was for sure. Pull it together, soldier.

A beep, another. A green light flashed.

Green meant go, right? I held the small chip in my hand. Did it work? No alarm, but it could be silent. Cops could be on their way.

Outside, a siren blared. Shit.

A sprint for the door. This better have worked.

A shadowy figure emerged from the basement. "What are you doing? You're not supposed to—" I slammed my palm into the man's throat and he crumpled to the floor.

"What was that, Douglas?" another yelled.

I ripped the door open and darted into the night.

* * *

I didn't want to get Amir more involved if I could help it. No sense ruining his life. Pondering the device on our rickety kitchen table, I took another acidy sip.

Had it worked? Could I access the data? If there was even data to access... Detective Harrelson said they wiped their servers every day. Bullshit. Data was king. Who'd waste that power?

So, here I was, sipping coffee, pushing one in the morning, using encrypted TOR networks to learn everything I could about the trojan. It would take one call to Amir.

Not if I could help it.

I found a manual for the pocket trojan. Said each device created a private server repository. But where? A serial number search revealed it was Amazon Basics which got me to the access portal. An imprinted code granted me access, and a file downloaded. BINGO.

I opened it: names, numbers, and procedure lists. Even contact information, but no addresses. Wouldn't matter. My crosshairs were closing in. Sorting, I went far back as I could. It ended at midnight the morning prior. Twenty-four hours.

"Dammit!" I smacked the table. All that for nothing. I scanned the list again. Nothing. Downloading the file again didn't help.

I threw my coffee in the sink and went to bed, furious. So much for progress. Man, I could use a drink. Felt like a junkie. Wait, could that junkie bastard Tripp know? At this point, it was worth a try.

* * *

The prison was a featureless rectangular behemoth in the middle of nowhere, surrounded by barbed wire and concrete, watchtowers and cameras enough to power all of Hollywood. The car dropped me off at the front entrance, an imposing gray gate with MP-5 armed guards behind bulletproof glass, drones overhead. I felt exposed, no idea if this would work. It had to...

An official sign read *State your name, business, and home address.* I did, fidgety rednecks eyeing my gun and chest the whole time despite the normalcy of the situation. I dare you...

After inspections, I entered the enclosed processing bay, which ran full-body scans and diagnostics before I entered the room. At the end, a heavyset guard with a combover and mustache to match his glare, guided me to a metal table bolted to the floor. There were five others spread in a circle throughout the room. "Sit down. Place your hands here."

I did and spread my fingers on the outlined diagram, palms on icy steel.

"Don't move," he commanded with a Yankee's twang.

Something jabbed my palm. "What the heck was that?"

"DNA test."

Things had changed since my days. Talk about invasive.

"Hold on." The guard tapped his temple, eyes darting between invisible interfaces. "Looks like you're clean. So, Tripp. Why'd you want to talk to him?"

"He owed me money and I need it," I lied.

"Good luck. Perp could barely walk when we brought him in, let alone tie his shoes or access an account. Come on." The big man stood, and I followed.

The door on the far side of the processing room opened as he approached and we passed into the dreary heart of the prison. The colors were duller, the corridors danker and sweat permeated the place, empty hallway ending at opposing steel doors. There were noises and yells from the left, silence to the right. We skipped the one marked *PHC* and went right, opening *VHC* without so much as a touch, and entering the silent cell ward.

It could have been a morgue, rows upon rows of entombed bodies, lying flat and inserted into miniature caskets. I recoiled. "Are they dead?"

The guard—Landry was his name—laughed. "You kidding? They're probably banging some celebrity model or scuba diving the Great Barrier Reef." Ah... VR.

"Thought that was banned."

"Is, mostly. There's an exception for prisons. Makes our life helluva lot easier, and it's cheaper too. Run a nutrient IV and you're set. Doesn't matter if it's two years or twenty-five. Plus," he added with a grin, "they earn points which go to our bottom-line as well. They don't know, of course."

Made sense. Prisons got a cut on the donor signups as well. It was fucked up. It was business after all. "Tripp?" I asked.

"Over here. Ward three, row fifty-one, unit seven." He pointed to a white stencil on the nearest pod, *51*. Tapping an interface, he entered a code and the system scanned his face for confirmation. A second later, a black tube slid from the wall, lights activating on the front and sides as it tilted vertical and came to rest on the floor to my left.

A seal clicked, and doors swung out, a gaunt face appearing. If Freddie looked bad before prison, he looked awful now, down at least twenty pounds in the short time since he'd been caught, bloodshot eyes sunken, cheeks gaunt, head shaved. Served him right.

A glazed shock. "Where am I? What happened to—"

"Quiet!" the guard snapped. "Follow me." Landry dragged the staggering Freddie to an empty visitor room without calling for backup or restraining him. The sickly man needed Landry's help to stand, atrophied legs incapable of walking.

A table and chairs in the visitor room doubled as an interrogation booth. Cuffing Freddie's hands to the table, he turned to me. "I could use some coffee. Want some?"

This was my chance. "Sure."

He left the room in a clueless, lazy amble, happy for a break from monotony.

I sat across from the dead-eyed junkie, taking in the cockroach who'd robbed me of my family. "You killed my daughter."

A spark of recognition across his face. "That was some good dope."

My fingers trembled. It took all my training not to crush his throat. Instead, I said, "Who'd you sell her to? How'd it go down?"

He shrugged. "HSU and I got an arrangement. I bring bodies and they've got the hook up."

"Who was your contact?"

"Fuck you!" He spat on my face, and I slammed his head on the table, jerking it to within inches of mine.

"You messed with the wrong mom. Who was your contact? Who bought my daughter? Malea, the eleven-year-old black-haired girl."

He clawed at my face, and I snapped his pathetic fingers. He screamed. "Who?" I yelled. "Give me a name?"

I was running out of time. Jumping up, I grabbed my chair, and jammed it under the handle as Landry's furious face appeared. He hammered the door as I sprinted back to Freddie.

"You have two seconds." I jerked his collar.

"Fine, fine. But you didn't hear from me. It was Don, Don Smith." The name rang a bell. Why? I'd look him up later.

"Why'd they need an eleven-year-old?" Were younger cells better?

"Please, I don't know," Freddie whimpered.

The door thundered. "Open up!"

Hustling over, I let the red-faced guard in. "I won't tell anyone if you don't," I whispered with an icy stare. He'd lose his job if his boss found out. "Bastard slept with my sister," I added.

Landry's jaw twitched. "Get out of here. And don't let me see you again."

I hauled ass out of there.

Don Smith...

* * *

Dammit.

A week since I'd gotten the files, but despite everything —and all the dark web could offer—I hadn't made progress. Twenty-four hours of names, no more. And Don Smith was a dead end, hundreds in metro Atlanta alone.

Sitting on the inconspicuous bench in the little ex-lot park, I waited. It was pretty empty for a Friday afternoon. Three double-duty shifts the past week had bought me the day off, and Amir would drop by on his lunch break. He taught mornings, spending his afternoons with an army of grad students who were "less of a pain with a meal in them."

I was losing hope of ever finding the culprit. Every day my chances dwindled.

"How's it going, Sam?" Amir strode towards me in a casual long sleeve and slacks, signature messenger bag over his scrawny shoulder. "So, it didn't work?"

"Not entirely." I explained what happened. "Look, I don't want to get you more involved, but I don't know where else to turn."

He laughed, taking me back to better times. "You always were afraid to ask for help. So, I did it anyways."

My jaw dropped.

"I had access to the server all along," he explained. "Checked it last night when you asked to meet."

"And?" My body was shaking, fingers twitching an invisible trigger.

"I got names. Not sure which is your guy, but..."

Words failed me. I pulled him into a hug. "I, I owe you."

He nodded. "Yes, you do. Just don't get caught, and don't bring my name into this."

After promising, small talk about the upcoming World Cup, and a confusing complaint about some rival professor's work on random neural networks, he left.

I opened the compressed files and got to work, flipping through patients from previous days, working back to *that* day. Six names, six possibilities.

Saanvi Bhati@adityabhatirejuv + STEM insert12 Y.O. white

Bao Wang@baowang6transfusion + STEM insert11 Y.O. asian

A'isha Hajjar@aishahajjarneural machine interface9 Y.O. black

Penny Wood@pennytransfusion + STEM insert11 Y.O. white

Zach Jordan@zj11rejuv + brainSTEM insert14 Y.O. white

Megan Larson@mlarson1brainSTEM insert15 Y.O. white

Eleven-year-old, white. Had to be Malea. It was the only one that fit. Penny Wood, founder of ISG, the In Style Group?

Daron had been a loyal subscriber to *Better Home* and *Fall Fashions* since before we were married. Their obnoxious ads followed us everywhere. And this was how that bitch repaid us... An eleven-year-old's life to add five-something to some ninety-year skank. My head pounded before I even saw Penny's pictures. Didn't look a day over thirty. Bitch. Talk about beauty being skin deep.

A motivational speech she'd given at Stanford's commencement a decade earlier appeared. If it was possible, she looked younger now. 'You've got your whole lives ahead of you, so much promise, so much to offer. Don't waste your time, don't waste your life. Go make your mark. Believe in yourself, and *you* can change the world.'

Burning acid torched my stomach, nails cutting my palms. Everything red.

That hypocritical bitch was going to die. I'd see to that.

ETHAN

Everything was ready, finally... It had been a hell of a few weeks. But the DJ was here, two of the finest restaurants in town catering—plus the Lif—and Vlad had quadrupled security for the night, bringing in vetted contractors to work the bars and crowd, keeping the hundred or so guests fat, happy, and safe.

And safety was a big issue. There'd be more influence and wealth at this party than any in the history of the world. All the players were invited, and for once, most were coming. And it was all thanks to me. Me. They'd ALL remember this night, as long as they lived. At least a couple hundred years for most, and at least for a night, the lonely compound would be brimming with life.

Several DDI higher-ups would be working the crowd as well, finding which senators and governments could be bribed and swayed towards loyalty, and which to avoid. And there were business partnerships to consider. Onboarding Penny's company to DDI's death insurance could spell fifty million a year plus the premiums. Plenty of bigger fish too. I could close a half billion in contracts before the night was up.

It was time to hunt.

"Jones." She'd been looking better the past week or so, alive again.

Sexy. I pointed to the stage. "Where's Silverspoon?" The battle of the bands would be a hit, the five top groups of the past decade slaying it on stage as elites mingled and the party raged.

Jones blinked, distracted. "Not sure, sir." She looked uncomfortable. Pre-party jitters? "I'll find out." She hurried across the pristine lawns toward the main house. Band was probably hitting the booze, and it wasn't even six yet. Artists... As long as it wasn't the Zoloft, *again*. Bloody rockstars popping SSRIs. Pathetic.

VTOLs and limos started arriving a few minutes to seven, several older and more formal guests, like Japan's prime minister, Eiko Hirota, or India's Minister of Commerce, Rohan Laghari, striding to the main gate with a calm reserve, talking to one another as they waited. I was inside the entrance, ready to greet the newcomers.

Their images were magnified on permanent screens embedded in the walls, computer scans checking and verifying the identity of each. Seemed excessive, given the five thousand facial recognition cameras onsite, but Vlad had insisted and so, a line built up which I enjoyed, smiling to myself. These people weren't used to waiting for anything.

The guests came through with bows and handshakes, and before long, the grassy main was teeming with life and noise, an R&B contemporary group captivating the dancing crowd as a retro funk shook the various dancefloors.

I walked over to the luau-worthy bar, complete with imported palms, fresh coconuts, and golden orchid leis for the ladies, cannabis tea in hand, curious what most folks were drinking. Smoothies seemed popular, spiked with shots or cannabis or whatnot.

Someone bumped into me. "Ah, Penny. I've been looking for you." She was looking stunning, a slinky black dress and simple diamonds, styled beyond what even her magazine models could manage, a branded purse at her slim side.

"Ethan," she replied with icy eyes.

"How are things? You look great, new treatment?" That would get her going.

She ignored me and gave me a tongue lashing over pressure we'd put on her magazine. "You think you can tell us what we can and can't publish?" she snapped.

I raised an eyebrow, feigning confusion. "I don't know what you're talking about. Maybe someone in legal. Either way, it's just business, Pen. You know that." Like I'd get my hands dirty.

Her eyes flared. Nobody called her Pen, least of all some hotshot young billionaire. I didn't care and got down to business. "What if we could offer you a better death insurance policy?"

Her brow furrowed. "I'm listening." She was a shark, an ancient predator with a nose for blood and money. It was a wonder her parents named her Penny...

Outlining my pitch, I ended with, "We can help each other out, you and I." We agreed to meet later in the week to discuss terms. Fifty million big ones... Cha-ching.

It was going to be a good night.

SAM

There she was, Penny Wood, dolled up, as always. My hand went to my holster and froze. Cool it, soldier. Not here, not now.

Her eyes flared and she snapped at Ethan who had dressed to impress in a fitted blue sports coat and tan slacks. I waded through the crowd toward them to get within earshot. Tonight I was backup, mingling, and seeking out potential threats. Not official duty. Even though everyone was scanned and vetted, I was glad to have a gun, and not my 'official' Glock. You could 3D print anything these days, and I didn't want someone tracing this one..

"...it's just business, Pen. You know that," Ethan said. Penny's hard eyes flared, but her brow furrowed at the next thing Ethan said. The conversation warmed, and I slipped behind the pair, searching Penny's guards.

A brief check revealed no one, no hidden watchers. Might work after all...

I waited in the corner by the sushi and tapas samplers. Tesla's CMO and Canada's president-elect both chatted me up, before realizing I was just a hot security guard. They moved on to bigger fish. Fine by me.

Penny and Ethan disengaged. My mind raced for ways to confront her. I'd been thinking about it all week, and while it was risky, I didn't see an alternative. Her house and the ISG headquarters were fortresses, and she travelled with three or four bodyguards. They must either be home or drunk, not feeling the need in such a high security atmosphere.

Research said she was card-carrying NRA and had taken karate for twenty years. She was no slouch, not after the assault on her seventieth, some disgruntled ex-employee. The dude had vanished. Police found nothing. Yeah, Penny Wood had a reputation.

Penny headed away from the party toward the bathroom. My breathing slowed. This was my chance. People everywhere. My heart pounded.

Dipping my fingers into my dressy purse, I thumbed the facial distortion moles, and popped them on my face. I pushed through the crowd. The space between the roped off party area and the main house was dark, the sun having set hours earlier. Bright solar lights lined the cobbled walkway and Penny's heels clattered the stone path. I slipped on gloves and activated the signal jammer in my bag. All connectivity within fifteen yards died.

In my dress's pocket, I flipped on noise-canceling, and the area was flooded with a white buzzing noise that blocked out everything, except my frenzied thoughts.

Penny looked up as I clamped my hand over her mouth, and my arm around her throat. She threw a frantic elbow and smashed her head into my nose. I held firm, squeezing until resistance died. Lifting her unconscious form, I dragged her off the path to the dim, enclosed herb garden filled with Maria's spices.

Shoving her on the iron bench, I produced a set of zip ties and hooked her pale hands behind it. A rag stuffed in her mouth and hooked behind her head completed her getup. Once I was sure she'd couldn't speak or cry out, I smacked her several times.

Her eyes blinked open, surging as she threw her body against the industrial-strength ties. They didn't budge. Stricken eyes bulged as she bloodied her wrists on the cutting bands.

"Do you know who I am?" I asked.

She shook her head, quivering.

A light on the path we'd come from. I froze.

Someone was coming.

A rowdy pair passed our secluded cove, hand-in-hand, and continued towards the tennis center. He grabbed her ass, and she spun but didn't see us. Seconds later, they were out of sight.

Penny jerked on the ties again, a muffled yell.

"Shut your trap!" I snapped. "I'm going to take the rag out. If you scream, no one will hear, and I'll put a bullet in your head. Got it?" I lifted my gun to make sure she got the point.

She nodded, and I pulled it out. "You killed my daughter."

"No, no." She shook her head harder, tears coming.

I smacked her pretty fake face. "You're lying. HSU. My daughter was the one they harvested for your workup. She was eleven, dammit. Eleven."

Penny sobbed, body shaking. "What do you want, money? Power? Anything. I can make you rich beyond your wildest—"

A brutal slap. These rich fucks would never get it. "I want my daughter back!" And my husband...

An arrogant half-smile. "Everyone's got their price. Twenty million, fifty? A hundred?"

I reached for the rag and jammed it into her mouth. Shocked dread flashed across her face. "Wh—"

Unholstering my pistol, I screwed the untraceable silencer in as she threw herself against the straining bands. Nothing happened. The bench didn't budge.

One last thing. I pulled the 3D-printed brand from my pocket and spun it. The finishing touch, the icing on the cake, the truth behind all the pain and lies.

"Hold still." I forced the iron against her forehead and hit the switch on the rubble handle. The induction heater swelled red as her face went from confusion to writhing pain in an instant. The nasty gag muffled her screams.

Before she passed out, I turned off the searing brand and leveled my pistol.

Tears filled her hideous eyes. Good.

This one's for Malea. I fired.

MIKE

Damn, what a party... What'd they put in those brownies? Must have been filled with laughs and giggles, because everything was freaking hilarious. I'd never had such a happy dessert before, and *needed* more. Where were they?

Oh, Mr. Anderson himself. "Great party, Ethan. Thanks for hosting." The billionaire raised a wine glass that reeked of cannabis. So, he was human...

"Enjoying yourself, Senator? Have you met Tammy Wood?" He gestured to the intense blonde in navy blue and powerhouse heels at the flickering tiki bar.

She walked towards us. "Ah, Senator, nice to see you again." She stuck out a manicured, firm hand. "I'm glad we're on good terms again, Ethan. My mother told me about the arrangement."

Ethan nodded. "We'll talk later. I'll leave you two to it." He disappeared into the throbbing crowd, headed for the stage.

"So, Mike, have you considered our conversation?" she asked.

Uh-oh. Talking shop? Wait a second. I raised an eyebrow. "Didn't you say—"

"DDI's dirty, I know it. Hypocritical bastards..." She put on an innocent smile which made me feel funny for some reason. "So, will you help with the investigation?"

"Will you help with my campaign?" She didn't need to know I'd help her anyways. Don't say anything dumb, Mike. Wow, she was pretty...

"How about a profile or story every month in our southeast-focused publications?"

I laughed but wasn't sure why, a strange tickle in my tummy. Where were those brownies? "Sounds good." We got down to details and set an appointment to meet their profiling team. God, I felt good.

There were a few other chats as well, Senator Jordan from New York—dark horse Democrat proponent of low-cost housing—and Julie Murphy, ex-Olympic skier who'd parlayed her career into a business empire.

Senator Jordan, in particular, was interesting. He had connections. "Coming to New York anytime soon?" the green-eyed man with the gotta love smile asked. "Several things I'd like to discuss, away from prying eyes," he added.

Was I moving up in the world? I almost laughed, damn brownies... With his New York firepower and my Georgian semi-conservative morals, we could make a good team. Vice President Michael Schmidt...

We agreed to meet Monday morning. My assistant would set things up.

The band started, "Live Like You Were Dying."

Could tonight get any better?

* * *

A murder? At the Anderson estate? My omelet clattered to the floor, spilling the lab-grown mess all over the gleaming hardwoods of my kitchen. Ignoring it, I opened the story.

A female reporter's face materialized. 'What's been dubbed the party of the decade has risen to new levels of notoriety as sources within local law enforcement tell us a woman's body—Penny Wood, founder and CEO of *In Style Group*—was found this morning, dead, shot in the head. If that wasn't crazy enough, the ninety-two-year-old appears to have been branded, a silver dollar scorched into her forehead, hands tied in a calculated act of hatred. Mr. Anderson and DDI have yet to release a statement.' I cut the video before the usual "stay tuned" spiel.

Murder? No way... I talked to Penny's daughter, didn't I? Things were a little foggy. What happened?

How about the Times? Same story, more gory details. My gosh. Who could do something like that?

Coffee dinged. Finally!

"Hey, boss, you want any?" Reggie gave me a nod from the fridge.

"Have you seen this, the murder?" I asked.

The big man shook his head. "No, what?"

I told him.

"Oh, snap!" he said. "You're not leaving my sight again, Mike. I don't care what some fancy ass playboy says. From now on, we're rubber and glue." Whatever that meant...

He was right though. That could have been me. But I couldn't think like that.

Too many people fell down *that* shithole and never returned.

Damn SSRIs.

ETHAN

"What the fuck happened?" I barked.

Vlad, Boris, Jones, a pair of detectives, two emergency private eyes, and half a dozen other guards were gathered in the Amazon Room, walls covered with real-time video of the lush rain-forest I'd never had the chance to visit, looking at their hands. "What happened? And how do we not have anything?" I snapped. This many people and no one had any answers.

Vlad shook his head. "Whoever they were, they were good. They're not on camera anywhere. No facial recog hits either. Audio sensors didn't even pick something up."

So, an inside job... The lead detective, Jessica George, sat straighter, looking at me. Her hard face, simple attire, and experienced eyes should have given me confidence... but they hadn't found finger-prints, DNA. Nothing. "Nothing new to report, Mr. Anderson," she said.

As expected, the stock had taken a huge hit, dropping four percent the hour the news broke. ISG's situation was even worse.

It was costing me a fortune. "We have no idea who, how, or why?" I asked.

Silence. I closed my eyes, wishing I was anywhere else. Diving a nice wreck would do. Penny had plenty of enemies, it didn't make sense to go through a list. "Anything I can do to help?" I said. That would get rid of them.

Detective George shook her head. "We've got everything we're going to get, unfortunately. If we have further questions, we'll follow up with Vlad. And you don't have to hire outside investigators, Mr. Anderson. We've got this."

"With all due respect, Ms. George, our stock's dropped over $35 billion since eight a.m. this morning. Every. Second. Counts. So, we'll run a separate investigation to get this over with."

She didn't have anything to say, what could she? Thirty-five billion was inconceivable for grunts like her. I'd dropped three spots in the billionaires' snapshot, to number seventeen. Unacceptable.

Sun Lee—who was number seven—was going to have a field day with this one. Talk about bad luck, a hit—and it definitely was a hit—at *my* house. Of all places... Dammit, Penny.

I stood. "If you need me, I'll be at my place in New York. Business to attend to." Out of sight, out of mind... that's how the media operated.

The detective didn't bother trying to protest, despite telling me earlier not to leave the area. She knew where her bread was buttered and how things worked.

At least we'd hit the city. It'd been too long.

* * *

T he New York skyline was something at night. We soared over the Hudson, concrete jungle alive with bright lights, and passed a highrise with a *For Lease* sign scrawled in red: contact information and rates—one of many foreclosed properties.

Central Park materialized below us, half the park dotted with faded tents, small fires burning as outcasts cooked whatever half-edible morsels they'd found, or more likely stolen.

The west side of the park was better at least, a massive barbed wire fence running the length of the wild treescape, preserving the beauty for folks who could appreciate it. The VTOL landed on the roof of 15 Central Park West and two of my New York-based guards—what were their names again?—hurried to greet us, along with the housekeeper and butler.

I missed New York. Even the air smelled of promise. Jones grabbed the one suitcase I'd deemed necessary to bring, and we crossed the breezy underpass, entering the waiting elevator. *'Welcome back, Mr. Anderson,'* the building said with a sexy British purr, my favorite algorithmic option. *'The ladies will be here soon.'*

We went down to Home Base Four, the five-story, six thousand square-foot penthouse on the 64th floor with two extra levels of blast-proof protection designers assured me could withstand another 9/11.

My eyes went to the new fountain across from my favorite AI-derived Chagall, another new addition of subtle humor, a school a four-legged starfish. A knight-adorned medieval tapestry covered the entire northeastern corner and blocked 'Sir' Larry Page's obnoxious apartment across the way. It was two stories higher than mine, and he was number six. Bastard.

SAM

Monday morning, I got Ethan's updated itinerary. It couldn't have worked out better. A ten a.m. brunch with Senator Zachary Jordan, the hard-nosed contender from the big city. I'd done some digging and found, he was @zj11, a patient of HSU the same day Malea had been murdered.

After the party, I'd been mulling things over. Something still burned inside me, a need for justice, or maybe revenge. In some ways, Malea had been vindicated. But in so many others, it hadn't meant a thing.

Malea was gone, the bitch Penny Wood was dead... and nothing had changed. I was still alone, and the world was a cold dark place, where every day tens of thousands sold their lives for so little.

These titans weren't innocent. Whether it was Malea or some other family's suffering, HSU's self-centered clients broke the law and did terrible things. Every freaking one of them was just as guilty. And they'd all get away with it...

My stomach roiled. No, no they wouldn't. I wouldn't let them. That's what I was, my purpose. Justice. Death and taxes... they'd paid for their crimes. My fingers tingled.

A picture of Ethan climbing El Cap by the walk-in fridge caught my attention. Back before the incident. I couldn't imagine him free-soloing anything these days.

The fork slipped from my distracted hand and shattered the crystalline glass, water spilling everywhere. "Sorry." I grabbed an embroidered napkin and mopped up the mahogany table. I needed coffee.

"Everything okay?" Boris's hard eyes locked onto me in a worried stare, despite the wild night he and Ethan had had. These girls had been screamers.

He had no idea... "I'm good. Rough night, that's all." It had been easier than I'd expected. I'd got back a little after four a.m.

Boris shrugged and stabbed another biscuit as Ethan appeared, none the worse for wear. "Ready for a big day?" He'd hit the gym and was sporting his signature gray t-shirt and jeans. He thought they made him look cool. Men... Grabbing his waiting smoothie, he licked his lips and sipped the icy brown slop.

Boris said he was ready. Me too.

Time was ticking. No turning back from what I'd done.

MIKE

I stopped in the lobby of his building off Union Square and sat on a velvety couch next to security, catching my breath. Why had he invited me here? My mind reeled, fighting to slow the chaos as I crossed Persian carpets to the Capone-style lifts, elevator taking me to my preassigned floor.

His office was something else, floors carpeted and textured in a rich green felt, small holes and divots punched at random intervals, white flags marking various targets. Reggie stepped onto an incline as the ball rolled towards him. "Heads up!" a voice yelled.

Reg dodged as it rode the edge of the lip and dropped into the hole. "Yes!" Senator Jordan strode towards us, golden putter in hand. He was a tall man, with a broad back and chest, clean-shaven face, and a smile that smelled of Hollywood and fine wines, putting anyone at ease. On a lesser man it'd have been excessive, but on him it fit.

"Mike, you made it." Switching his grip, he stuck out a tanned hand, shaking both ours with practiced sincerity.

"Thanks for inviting me."

There was a plush feel to the place, despite the mini-golf course and posters of his kids' championship moments covering the walls. He plopped at his hickory desk, an ashtray away from a pre-century ad exec.

"Please, take a seat. Coffee, tea, anything?"

"Coffee, please, black."

A pretty staffer hurried off down a maze of hallways.

"So, Mike, I hear you met with Warren."

So, that's what this was about... I nodded but didn't elaborate.

"Think she's got a chance?" His eyes twinkled. Was he milking me for the scoop?

"Probably," I said. "She's the Speaker of the House. She has connections."

"What about you? What are your aspirations?" he asked with genuine curiosity. "Well, after you keep Rodriguez from stealing your seat..."

"That, and find a way to fix the widening gap in the state."

He raised an eyebrow. "Think it's doable?"

"I hope so. I'm going to try." What else could I do?

"I respect that. I invited you here to discuss Warren's new bill. It should fail. It's not constitutional, or legal for that matter."

Plus you'd love her to get a big fat black eye. But the enemy of my enemy...

"You know, I'm planning on running," he said.

I froze. This was the moment I'd been waiting for. Vice president?

He cleared his throat, the build-up killing me... Was he going to ask?

"So, I was wondering—" *BAM.*

His chair exploded in a ball of flame. Reggie tackled me to the floor.

Alarm bells rang, my ears too. *EEOOOEEEOOOEEE.*

Reg yanked me to my feet, smoke billowing and pulled me toward the door, drawing his weapon. "This way, sir!" he yelled in a hushed voice.

Dazed, I stumbled forward. Reggie spun into the hall, gun leveled. There was no one. "Let's get out of here." Was that a bomb?

I turned back to Jordan, what was left of him at least, which wasn't much. The room was a scorched mess, walls covered in soot and soft felt carpeting sparking with flames. The desk was in pieces, scattered everywhere. It must have been built like a tank and was the sole reason we survived.

Reggie shoved me into the concrete stairwell and we pounded down the echoing steps. Holy shit, holy shit.

Was he really dead? Every corner, my stomach tightened.

We made it to the lobby, panting. Where was the parking garage? Security materialized, fanning out.

Jeez. Did he have family, kids? My heart hammered, brain in shock.

So much for the vice presidential nomination.

What just happened?

ETHAN

Nothing beat New York in the summer. The weather was perfect, the people happy and every manner of cuisine, art, and experience a person could hope for.

Senator Jordan's tower didn't have a rooftop deck, something to do with building codes, so we took the Bugatti. I'd retrofitted it myself some years back, switching the conventional metal frame for graphene-laced lightweight bulletproofing. The glass paneling had been done as well, and I'd increased the motor for power. I'd have killed for a steering wheel as we raced through busy streets, whizzing past electric scooters and bikers, avoiding the slums as I practiced my pitch: a floating spa in the middle of the Hudson. It was bold, it was audacious. I was both, and going to make it happen. Talk about an upsell.

We turned onto Madison Ave and traffic gridlocked. Someone even honked. What was going on?

'There appears to be a roadblock causing a delay between fifty-first and fifty-second,' the car announced. 'It may be faster to walk.'

Jones leaned out the window and opened her door. "It's backed up all the way to flashing sirens."

"All right," I said. "Let's walk."

We exited the car in an exposed area, and hurried to the sidewalk, Jones and Boris flanking either side. "We should have brought more guys," I commented.

We hustled faster through the hectic city, past Thai street food vendors and a Jewish bakery with *New York's best apple pie!* The senator's building loomed above us in the distance. As we neared, it became apparent, the building was on lockdown. Police tape blanketed the exterior and fire and EMT crews milled about, talking to one another, sirens blaring. Something must have happened.

The guards tensed. What was going on? Both grabbed weapons as we pushed through beggars and druggies to the barricade. "Officer, what is this?" I asked.

She must not have recognized me because she didn't let us pass.

"A bomb," the ditz replied. "Somebody killed the senator."

Holy shit. My jaw dropped. "What?"

The pudgy broad nodded. "Looks like a hit."

We would have been there five minutes later... My pulse quickened. Was I the target? Doubtful, the timing was off.

Drones buzzed toward the building, CNN and Google News jostling to break the story. To our right, a news van skidded to a stop, lining up a shot—FOX.

"Let's see if we can set a meeting with the mayor," I said to Jones who was watching the reporter.

"This just in..." The black newscaster gestured to the building. "Sources are saying New York State Senator Zachary Jordan was just assassinated, a bomb in his office." A finger to her ear. "Wait... We're confirming a silver dollar was found taped to the bottom of the senator's desk."

What? Not again. Were they about to dredge that up? The stock would take another hit. Here come the Penny Wood profiles... I'd call Garrett, do damage control.

When she finished, I strode over. "Are you saying what I think you're saying?"

"If you mean the vigilante's struck again, yes."

Shit. I grilled her on the details, but there wasn't much to her story yet. If it bleeds, it leads... details and truth be damned. Time to make the call.

'Hey, Emma,' I said as soon as we connected, 'I need you to run a patient search for me. Tell me Senator Zach Jordan was never a client of ours.'

'What do you mean? Why would—'

'I don't have time to explain. Just do it.' Couldn't people follow simple orders?

'Yes, sir,' she said.

I turned to Jones and signaled to move out. 'Let me know once you hear something.' The Bugatti pulled up and we hopped in.

Time to call an audible.

SAM

It had been so easy. For an ultra-secure office building home to a senator and numerous Fortune 50, a few distortion moles and a stolen Whole Foods delivery uniform had been all it took to gain access. I could even choose which floor to ride to.

I hadn't been IED in the force, but we'd handled enough explosives. Plenty of DIYs online. A quick trip to Amazon Home & Garden for urea, cotton balls from 7-Eleven, and Home Depot, one of the last places still selling diesel, and I was set. The detonator hadn't been hard either, a Mickey Mouse *I Love New York* wristwatch with a little wiring.

The senator had the weirdest office, real golf nut. To each their own, especially if you could afford it. The newscaster touched her ear and turned to look at me, eyes narrowing.

I froze, heart pounding. Shit, had they found something?

She tapped her ear again, and started talking. Phew.

A lifeless numb enveloped me. I was clear. And another goon down. Yet what did it matter? Four more on my list. And once that was finished? A question for another day...

We hopped in the car.

A quiet trip back to the penthouse. No one said anything, I avoided eye contact. It wasn't hard. The city was breathtaking every time. I ran through the list once more, visualizing each. Saanvi Bhati, Bao Wang, A'isha Hajjar, Megan Larson…

Megan Larson was the obvious next target, or maybe Saanvi, whose company had a second headquarters in Atlanta. I'd scout both.

Saanvi's story had been all over the tabloids, a slum escapee who'd founded India's largest e-commerce player, EZ Rupee, two decades earlier—driving force behind the world's fourth-largest GDP.

And Megan Larson, corporate lobbyist. The dirty underbelly of our perverted democracy. She deserved a painful death. I'd focus on her unless something presented itself.

We didn't meet Mayor Richmond that day, or the following. Ethan was furious. "Who does he think he is?"

In the end, New York was a wash, at least for DDI.

Couldn't say the same for Senator Jordan.

MIKE

Finally back. I met the pair at Hartsfield-Jackson's revamped International Terminal Two. It wasn't bad trafficwise. The Tesla dropped Reggie, Wallace, and I at the door and parked. I paid extra to keep it until the girls arrived. The fact we had a quick escape helped me relax. Since the bombing, I was on edge and having trouble sleeping. No one knew what was happening. Two murders, and I'd been there for both. Me, why me? It was hard to believe the cops hadn't come knocking.

Walking to the automated espresso machine, I grabbed a coffee to kill time and the jitters. Plus, lazy night was a doozy. The guys grabbed cups as well, and we sat at the table which charged my account.

Had it been a month since I'd seen her?

Wallace and Reggie chatted, but my mind was elsewhere. Ava had cancer, and I'd almost died. Jamie would have been alone... She'd never been close to either grandmas, and both Ava's and my dads had passed away before LE treatment got legitimized. It was too bad. She'd have loved Pops, and him, her. Damn. Why'd it have to take fifteen years to go mainstream? Ten more minutes.

The terminal of the world's third busiest airport was busy for a

Tuesday. Were that many people flying in from abroad? All the VTOL traffic and long haul domestics would be on the other side.

Reggie tapped me on the shoulder. "Here they come."

I jumped up. "Jamie!" Crossing the autotrolley-lined courtyard, Reggie and Wallace struggled to keep up and I threw my arms around my sunkissed daughter. She shoved her face into my chest, squeezing back. Must have been a good trip.

"Did you have fun? How was it?" The questions poured out.

Jamie said nothing and started crying.

Ava gave me a look. "Slow down, cowboy." *She saw the news,* Ava mouthed.

Oh, shit. "Everything's fine, Jame, see! I'm here, and everything's okay." Luckily...

She looked up, bleary-eyed and puffy-faced. "Why didn't you tell me? A bomb? The Silver Dollar almost got you."

"The Silver Dollar?" Why'd they always have to name these nutjobs. "I didn't want to ruin your trip."

She sniffled. "The tabloids... whatever. Don't ever do that again." She threw her arms around me. "I missed you, Dad. You wouldn't believe Rome."

Wallace caught my eye, and gestured towards an unsavory pair by the far wall. It didn't look good and my heart rate quickened. "Come on." I put my arm around Jamie. "I can't wait to hear all about it."

"Wait, Dad," Jamie insisted. "I got you this, it's supposed to be good luck." She reached into her sweater pocket and pulled out a pressed penny of the Roman Forum, Emperor Marcus Aurelius' stoic face staring back at me on the other side. She must have had it done outside the Colosseum.

"Thanks, Jame, but I don't need—"

"Keep it, Dad. Please. It's important." Her eyes were desperate. What the heck, it couldn't hurt. I put my arm around her.

"Come on, guys." Reggie cut the moment short, rushing us to the waiting car

It was a good thing I'd kept it waiting.

SAM

Megan Larson. 201a Grandview Avenue, Buckhead, next to Buckhead Theatre. It overlooked Frankie Allen park, which boasted gilded columns and statues, an Americanized Athens ideal. Not a bum in sight. Cops though, seven by my count, and it'd been five minutes.

The buildings were towering storefronts, all the best brands. Even Fish Market stank of money, both old and new. These were the areas DDI thrived, where rich and well-off mingled and partied in penthouses, parks, and "public places" that required chip verification to enter. I'd passed thanks to my job with DDI. Otherwise, I wouldn't have stood a chance. So, this is where lobbyists lived...

I passed the formidable private tutoring center where a dozen kids aged two-to-five sat in a circle, a Chinese woman holding complex characters and practicing pronunciation with the little prodigies. Holographic images hovered as the kids recited words, walls plastered in far Asian art.

Megan must live upstairs, in the highrise. The door was guarded, two men, both armed, and suited up. Smiling, I continued on my way as the first checked me out. So, that's what I was up against.

Crossing the countertop-clean street to the small Viennese cafe, I grabbed a seat, leaning back as if it were the most normal thing in the world. Horrible coffee made me wish I had my fifteen bucks back. There was no guarantee she'd show. She could be anywhere...

The cafe was busy. Did no one have anything to do? Judging by their fashion sense and the health nut soups and salads, they weren't hurting for cash.

The door opened. My shoulders tensed as Megan Larson emerged, the tall brunette dressed in black shorts and a running shirt, a leashed yellow lab at her heels. Lunch break run. Two soldiers ran after her, covering her rear. Both had the air of seasoned killers, and the smaller guy had the winged skull of the Berets on his shredded shoulder.

I rose, stopped the table tipping itself twenty percent, and followed from a distance on this side of Grandview. She was fast and fit. I had to jog to keep up, which made staying inconspicuous all the harder. My gut told me the spec-ops guys would notice if I tailed them much longer so I fell back.

This would be harder than I thought.

In Frankie Allen park, I caught a break. Megan dropped down, alternating between squats, monkey bar pullups and explosive push ups. Impressive. The two guards hit the playground too, cranking out pull ups with competitive jeers as Megan did calisthenics.

So, runs were out of the question, unless I was willing to take her out from distance. Might have to. But even the bomb bothered me. If they didn't know what was happening, or what they'd done, the meaning was lost.

With time to burn, I opened the news for cover. No one reacted as I sat scanning headlines. Culture & Entertainment was counting down the *Top 50 Thrillers of the 21st-Century*. I loved a good thriller.

Not a bad list, some real classics. Number forty-nine was one of my favorites, *Zodiac*, the 1995 Fincher film: notorious San Francisco serial killer terrorizing the West Coast with ciphers and bloody letters to the newspapers. He'd gotten away with it too, only to be caught decades later by a chance DNA test. Idiots had been so loose with privacy.

Wait, could that work? Letters and ciphers... Made life so much easier. And it would put people on their toes, get powerful elites shaking in their designer shoes. Mhm…

The trio rose, and left. My mind whirred. Things just got interesting, and doable.

A call from Vlad. 'Hey, princess, where are you?'

Was he tracking me? 'What's up? What do you want?'

'I know what you're doing, Jones,' he said. I froze.

'Didn't you get my message about the ping pong rematch?' he added.

A sigh of relief. Cryptic Russian prick. I'd beat his ass again. 'No. What's up?'

'Boss says we got to go. He'll explain later. Get your ass back here.'

'Yes, sir.' I hung up, and hailed a ride, ticking my mental checklist. Everything was packed at the compound, but where were we headed? Daron had hated these last minute trips, Malea too.

The low grade Tesla rolled up and I hopped in alongside a tired woman with sooty clothes and forlorn eyes who was talking to herself. She got out ten minutes later, across from SLI's recruitment stand. I gave her what I hoped was an encouraging smile. She'd lost her way, like Daron, and so many others. If only I could help. I couldn't. Instead, I turned my focus to Megan Larson, and the upcoming hit.

Where? When?

And most important, how?

ETHAN

Where the hell was Jones? We were all waiting...
It had been a long morning, night too. Between talks with Africa and Eastern Europe, and Mom calling to see how things were going—which led to a roundabout story, some rich lady she'd met at the country club considering checking out on life—I was tense. As long as Mom wasn't popping Zoloft... Fucking drug companies. As it was, I had to go to Cape Town.

Ah, there she was. She ran along the cobbled path leading to the second landing pad, where the five of us were waiting.

"Sorry I'm late," she said, panting.

I gave her a look but said nothing. Now wasn't the time. Bigger things to think about, and I didn't need interruptions. Sliding my eye mask over my face, I reclined my inversion chair to lie flat and relaxed, concentrating on my breathing. It had been two days since I'd meditated. I needed it. The world fell away, and all the bullshit as I followed Master Swami's advice: "Inhale, exhale... Focus on the space between the two."

Ding. Sixty minutes.

My eyes opened. Everyone in the sixteen-passenger cabin was asleep except Boris. Sitting up, I gestured him over. He sat across from me, nursing a caffeinated nutrient blend, eyes sharp. "What is it, boss?"

"First time in Africa?" I could never keep these guys straight in my head.

"Yes, sir. Jones was the one who went last time, and the time before."

"Be careful with the locals." I told him about last time, about the rogue hitman. Starvation would do that to you.

He grinned. "Spetnaz training would eat the Africans for breakfast and shit them out in time for a Stroganoff lunch, sir."

I nodded, not paying attention. Damn special forces guys, they were good to the point of arrogance, especially Russians.

"What are we doing there, sir?" he asked.

"Beating SLI to the punch." A call came in before I could elaborate and I shooed him away. It was Christiaan Smuts, just the man I needed to talk to. 'Yeah, what is it?'

'They're here, sir, the chinks, a whole army of 'em.'

Chinks? What century was he living in? 'You gotta be kidding me. Where?'

'Halfway between the Cape and Stellenbosch. We've been watching them since they landed.'

'And?' I asked. Were they on to us? Had Sun Lee played me?

'And nothing, sir. They arrived four hours ago, flew in on an unmarked jet without filings or flight plans. We happened to have people on payroll who saw their delegation before they drove off.'

Maybe they'd just gotten lucky. 'We'll be there in eight hours,' I said. 'Keep them under surveillance until we show up.'

Kelvin stretched his long arms and opened his eyes. "Did I hear right, SLI's onsite?"

Jones blinked awake as well from across the double-wide aisle.

I curled my lip. "Yeah."

"Think we have a leak?" Kelvin asked.

Doubt it. "Lee's smart. If you're sourcing cheap whites with 'better' ancestry, South Africa beats Croatia, or even Albania. Many backward Europeans consider Balkans to be dirty people. They're not. It's all nonsense, but people pay more for Prada than Basics and it's all produced by the same bots in the same factories."

The rest of the trip was uneventful, filled with sleep for most and contemplation for me. We landed at seven a.m. local time, and, as soon as the doors opened and Boris gave the *all-clear*, I strode out of the craft feeling like a trillion bucks. I'd get there, it was a matter of time.

It was chilly on the private runway with views of Table Mountain. My assistant better have packed warm. We headed for waiting black Humvees with South Africa's wild-colored flag as waiting Boer officers saluted us. A tanned, hard-nosed General Kruger shook my hand, calluses from his big game rifle as pronounced as ever. Christian was nowhere in sight, probably damage control. "How was the flight?" Kruger asked. "All well, I hope?"

I'd had worse. "Gerhard, the Chinese, really?"

His crooked eyes widened. We'd been friends and business partners long enough for him to know he couldn't fool me. Heck, we'd hunted cloned rhino together. "It's just business," he said.

Boris had reached for his weapon and Jones braced herself.

"What does that mean for us?" I asked. I'd almost been expecting this.

Kruger smirked. "You Americans. There's more than enough desperate whites and blacks in South Africa to go around. Come on, it's been awhile. Relax, let me show you around."

"Why the Humvees?" Jones asked, as if it wasn't obvious enough. The local recession...

Kruger ran a hand through his Aryan blond, sighing. "It's gotten worse, RPGs. The locals don't take kindly to VTOLs, the South African air force, or foreigners..."

The South Africans were chill about things, too chill. But that's why I was in charge and Kruger, my pawn. I'd play this one close to the vest.

Electric engines revved and we zipped from the airport, passing rows of long-useless Uber drivers fighting progress in any attempt at a livable wage. Two of their 'helpers' sucked bananas, beckoning towards their beat-up wagons and sedans. I wouldn't make *that* mistake twice.

Coasting along, the townships seemed closer than last time, larger too. Massive sprawls of shacks and hovels, discarded paneling, rotted drylines, and dirt roads stretching to the battered highway. Thin, shirtless blacks and whites watched through the dusty haze. The racial mixing was new.

You see ribs, desperation rampant.

I could smell the dollars from here. Business would be good.

SAM

For a trip to Africa, things were pretty smooth. Three days of meetings with governmental heads, including the president, several advisors and two other generals Kruger had recommended, and we had most of our bribes—I mean encouragement—dolled out.

They needed our help and our jobs. The city's homelessness bordered on anarchy. I had to pull my weapon twice, but never used it. Boris, on the other hand, shot a scrawny Zulu. Smuts wasn't too worried. "The cops have enough on their plates as it is." We'd left it at that, his blood pooling in the sewer across the old Iziko Slave Lodge, a hundred yards from Parliament.

Ethan rented the top three floors of the Taj with beautiful views of Signal Hill, Bo Kaap and Bree Street below, despite General Kruger's offer to stay at his villa. He didn't trust him after the Chinese deal, and we visited several prospective towers where Ethan and Christiaan compared notes. They settled on a fifteen-story resort-esque building overlooking Sea Point. "If you're going to stay young, you might as well enjoy it," Smuts said.

And we did, Boris and I both chest deep in the icy surf. It was the first time I'd been happy—or at least, distracted—in weeks. My skin crawled with goosebumps as the salty waves reminded me of better times. Malea riding the surge when I'd taught her to bodysurf... The happy memory wrenched me from the picturesque moment back to painful reality. All that was gone.

I hurried to shore, suit sagging, freezing and empty inside. So much for a day at the beach.

The afternoon was filled with more meetings—and training, of course. Ethan hit weights or cardio at least six times a week, and it showed. "The science is clear," he'd say, "everything works better and stays sharper when you move."

Who was I to contradict? He had three PhDs. Besides, it gave us guards a welcome respite.

I had yet to find a good way to get to Megan. Her security wasn't up to our level, but it was darn good. When was her next meeting with Ethan? The pair had calls every quarter but met face to face less often. She was responsible for much of DDI's lobbying efforts, at least in Atlanta. Could I convince Ethan to invite her over? Too obvious?

ETHAN

A call buzzed as I blasted out of the hole. Locking the final rep and racking the weight, I tapped my ear. "Yeah, tell me."

'It's SLI, they showed up at the office, boss. Sun Lee's there.'

Dammit. "We'll be there in ten." Fucking bastard, I'm gonna kill him.

"What?" Boris asked.

I told him as I jogged into the immersion showers—cold and hot blasts alternating in thirty second bursts. Shit, I hated this part.

Three minutes later, we were in the tankproof Humvee. I was sandwiched between two South Africans in the tinted back while Boris and Jones sat up front. No one said a word as we sped through the streets, blacks flocking to our car, hoping to wash the windows or scrub the all-terrain wheels for a chance at a few Rand. What was Lee doing here? He never left China.

There wasn't much traffic, but a fistfight broke out between bums trying to spray our hood. The car stopped, programming kicking in. It couldn't harm a human life, not without override. Screw that. We were in a hurry. Motherfucking Lee… "Nudge them out of the way!" I snapped. We didn't have time for this. "Activate override." If they're stupid enough to get in the way, well, survival of the fittest…

Did Lee have something up his sleeve? What was I not seeing?

The engine revved as wheels gained traction, crushing a scrawny man and pinning another as we raced away. They got the message.

Halfway to the clinic, we hit a roadblock, a solid barrier erected across the M61, soldiers at attention, AK-47s at their sides. Come on, were the tribes rebelling again? What was this going to cost? I reached for the window.

BANG. A rocket smashed into my side of the vehicle, sending us bouncing.

Holy shit!

Two more slammed our left, wheels blowing. Fuck, we were surrounded.

'Commencing evasive maneuvers,' the car announced. We shot backwards as an 18-wheeler sped from a waiting alley to cut us off. The AI stopped inches short as two more blasts rocked the road next to us. What was going on?

Men appeared on the buildings to either side, chinamen. Bullets whizzed towards us, ricocheting off the car. It had to be Lee.

Jones and Boris sat there helpless. Why weren't they doing something?

"Triads?" Jones asked as the car shot forward, angling for a side street as crossfire intensified. Another RPG slammed us into a shop as everything slowed down.

Head pounding, I nodded. "Working with SLI, probably. Get us out of here!"

Another barrier appeared. We crashed through it, tearing the front half off our vehicle and shattering the window. Shit. We were exposed. Jones leveled her gun and fired. The nearest gangster's face exploded in blood, but she was already on to the next, our car shaking from a damaged tire.

Shit. Above us! Too late.

Bullets exploded into the floorboard in front of me. I ripped the seatbelt from my pounding chest as more bullets thudded into the vehicle, grabbing the knife Boris had convinced me to wear.

Cars passed us again. And there were people everywhere, scooters too. We were safe for the time being, maybe. Wait, how had they known we were—

The pale Afrikaner to my right twitched. It hit me: he knew. My hand shot out, blade tearing into the man's stomach. Blood spurted everywhere as Jones fired, the other soldier's shoulder exploding in a crimson plume that punched him into his seat. Jones pointed her weapon at the man's face. "Don't move."

I stabbed the pale man again, and again, twisting and jerking to make sure I'd finished the job. My heart thundered, grip tightening, eyes never leaving the traitor to my left.

Were we safe? That was close.

The Humvee died in the middle of Strand Street. A VTOL took off from somewhere behind us. "Let's go," Jones said.

Boris jumped out, a Tesla pulling to the curb as I ripped the pistol from the dead soldier's hands, feeling the power at my fingertips. Jones grabbed the tan Afrikaner by the collar and dragged him towards the waiting car.

Head down, I sprinted for the car as a gunman appeared in the doorway across from me. I fired and the man's head imploded, blood frescoing the window behind him.

I dove into the car, ducking. "Drive!"

A pair of gunmen sprinted into the street, spraying the clunker. We rounded the corner and disappeared. Shit, why were we going this way? "Boris, not the hotel," I said. "They know we're staying there."

"Shit!" Boris swore. "But—"

"We need to get out of here, out of Africa. Call Sea Point. Find out —" A VTOL passed overhead, headed for the Taj. At least they hadn't identified our car, yet.

I turned to the prisoner and smacked the good-for-nothing shit. "Who are you working for?"

The man said nothing. Boris smashed his fist into the man's thick jaw. "He asked you a question."

The soldier held strong. "We don't have time for this," Jones said.

"Boris, check him for trackers and strip him. Car, take us to the Waterfront."

Impressive. Was she a step ahead of me? Boris ripped the man's camouflaged jacket and pants from his body and threw the gear into the street.

Boris pulled a black glove from his pocket, put it on, and ran the scanner of some kind along the man's arms, torso and hairy back. No beeps—no implants or transmitting devices.

"Don't forget to scan his feet and give him a good one-two," Jones added with a smile.

A one-two?

Boris winced, and cupped the guy's junk, hurrying on to the feet when his balls didn't register on the sensor. "Clean," Boris pronounced. The man must not be worth much to whoever was running him.

Boris smacked the man in the groin. "That's for making me touch your sack, piece of shit. Who are you working for? We can dump you in the ocean if you prefer. Heard Davy Jones got the finest rum." Since when did Boris have a sense of humor?

The South African bent over, groaning, squeezing his shoulder as blood dripped down his naked arms and torso. "Please."

"What's your name?" I asked.

"Erik, Erik Van Niekirk."

"Did you know about the ambush?"

He shook his head. "Only that we were to tell... oh, what's it matter? We signalled General Kruger when we left the Taj."

So, it was Kruger. I knew it. Greedy pig. He'd pay for that. We raced along Beach Road toward my favorite part of the city, Victoria Wharf, the glassy mall and highrises overlooking the pure blue waters and colorful sails.

No time for sights, we needed a ride. I called Casey. "Get us out of here."

A siren blared and I clenched the gun tighter, the dead soldier's face flashing before my eyes.

Had I killed a man? Two, actually... My adrenaline was pumping. So much for remorse... If anything, I felt great.

Tucking the gun in my waistband, I whispered my motto: "A Boy Scout is always prepared."

Maybe there was something to carrying.

MIKE

After Rome, everything was different. How could it ever return to normalcy? Why'd it have to be bronchial cancer? The past weeks had been filled with appointments, second opinions, naturopaths, anything... "The science isn't there yet. If it was lung cancer or diabetes, even Alzheimers... that'd be a simple set of gene therapies, but..."

I leaned towards the curly haired doctor, crushing the foam arm rests, waiting for the magic cure or silver bullet. She didn't have one. Dammit. What was the point of this fancy office in this fancy-ass hospital filled with millions of dollars of fancy equipment, hundreds of doctors and surgeons and stupid cheery posters, if she couldn't help us?

"Have you considered ozoning?" she asked.

We had, and Ava had been through it all. Nothing helped. Not even goddamn pure-as-poison chemo. She'd lost her hair, and hope, and gained little, except mounting bills. We'd tried everything. Our insurance covered it—the best money (or political favors) could buy.

The complex anatomy on the walls and esteemed doctor's fake smile were driving me nuts. Her foot kept tapping.

Stop! I had to get out of here, to do something, anything... Ava nodded. "Thanks for your time." She pulled me from the chair and took Jamie's hand. The three of us left the oak-panelled office, more united than we'd been in years—not that that was saying much.

Ava had given up hope long ago, even Jamie's resolve had faded. For some reason, I couldn't bring myself to give up, not yet. I *had to* make things right.

Jamie had to go back to school and hopped into the waiting ride after assuring both of us she was okay.

Ava grabbed my arm. "Let's get coffee, Mike."

Good idea. We walked a few quiet blocks, past some crazies screaming about the Taxman—whether the IRS or the supposed serial killer, I wasn't sure—and into a quaint off-brand cafe.

Ava surveyed the place, her kind of place: cozy bean bags, mismatched tables, and beer bottle ceiling lights—feng shui, she called it. Whatever that meant.

We sat and ordered, black for me, and a low-sugar caramel macchiato for her because, "you only live once, right?"

That was one thing I missed about her, the vibrant liveliness she'd brought to my otherwise bland life. Who knew how long that'd last. The cancer was a ticking time bomb with an accelerating shot clock. And when it came to basketball, I'd never been good under pressure.

How had it come to this?

ETHAN

Fuck. This was a disaster. Was the Cape Town team compromised too? A hit, in broad daylight no less. This changed things. And so, the plot thickens... 'Casey, are you there? We need a ride.'

I gave her coordinates and within the hour, an unmarked VTOL landed outside the dilapidated island prison Nelson Mandela been imprisoned in for twenty-seven years for protesting the apartheid government. The Robben Island tour group visiting the rundown place ran to the iron-gated window slits and peered out.

Gonzalez' backup—Casey Ingram, an ex-navy extraction pilot with laser eyes and impossible reaction times—touched down in the dusty courtyard where Nelson and his fellow inmates had spent what little outdoor time they had, exercising or discussing politics amongst themselves, out of earshot of their Afrikaner guards.

Jones grabbed my arm and we ran for the waiting craft, landers scarce stiffening before we ascended again. People shouted, and Boris and Jones's eyes darted around the compound.

"Happy to see me?" Casey asked from the front. We raced away, towards mainland and our eventual extraction in Windhoek, Namibia. I couldn't get off this damn continent soon enough. Africa, every time, every goddamn time...

About halfway through the flight, Mom called. I almost didn't answer, but something about the attack made me reconsider. Maybe time was finite... 'Hey, Mom.'

'Oh, Ethan. I caught you. Good. How's life? Now a good time?' she said in her half-flustered voice.

Even after everything, I smiled despite myself. 'For you, Mom, it's always a good time.'

'It's Betty Sue.' Of course it was. Short, chunky, blonde hair, always baking... She'd made the best brownies. 'Her husband, Ted, yesterday was the twentieth anniversary of his passing.'

Ted had been like a father to me: teaching me basketball, how to chase girls, and to "rub some dirt in it" when I was being a bitch. Other than a few professors at Tech, he'd been my biggest male role model. His death had been a shocker. I'd been eighteen at the time... I took a tired sip of my fermented kombucha.

'How is she?' I asked. We'd been over at their house for enough game nights for me to guess: putzing around, adopted a puppy, or something...

'She's good, all things considered. Sad, but she made peace with it years ago. Anyways,' Mom said in her roundabout way, 'she's thinking about checking out.'

I spit the effervescent green tea out, blanketing the plush carpet and real hardwoods with a prebiotic bacterial spray. 'She's what?'

'Says she's tired of living without Ted. To be honest, E, I've been considering it as well.'

'No!' I snapped, louder than I'd intended. Boris and Jones turned to look at me, faces creased. Even Casey tilted her head. I lowered my voice. 'Let's not talk about this now, okay. Just don't do anything rash. Promise me.'

She did and we signed off, my stomach in knots that had nothing to do with the kombucha. Checking out, why? She had so much life to live. She was the reason I'd started the company, her and Bobby. I couldn't lose her, I couldn't...

What would I have left? Who would I have left?

I closed my eyes. What was the world coming to? People deciding to die for no other reason than they were bored of life. Goosebumps rippled down my tense arms. It made no sense.

Death? Nothing was worse than dying, nothing...

The water sparkled below us, but even the glistening seas and inevitable wonders beneath couldn't lift my sinking spirits.

Checking out? Was she *really* considering it?

Jones caught my eye and handed me a beer. My hands were shaking.

Shit.

SAM

Home at last. When our wheels touched down and we skidded to a stop on Ethan's private tarmac at Hartsfield-Jackson, it was a relief. I'd forgotten how stressful traveling was. Time zones didn't help. And this trip, we'd dodged a bullet, literally. We'd effed up, and almost paid the ultimate price. And Ethan had let us know it, although, in fairness, he'd acknowledged most wasn't our fault, but Kruger's.

Through the grapevine, we learned Kruger's body was found floating in the Cape. Whether that was Lee's folks, or our doing, I wasn't sure. Ethan kept a straight face, and told us the news with a mixture of surprise and contentment, a brief grin touching his lips.

I knew the feeling. Yet, revenge didn't change anything. Speaking of, whisperings of "The Taxman" had died a bit. The heat—and fear—was off, which was fine by me.

We disembarked in the lofty hangar under DDI's logo, triple our usual guard standing watch. Ethan was shaken more than he cared to admit, especially after the call with his mother. His eyes darted with nervous tension. He'd never raised his voice to her like that, not once. She was the one person he deferred to, the one person capable of taming the tamer. Something was up…

They flew back to the Anderson Estate while a car took me home. My shift was over, and I needed a break, which didn't bode well for Megan Larson.

Unfortunately, I hadn't found anything more about HSU's leadership. Despite staking out the place three times, I'd come away empty. And nothing in the public record: no state or federal filings, no website, nothing...

They were real though. I'd seen the lab with my own eyes, no amount of conspiracy mongering would change that.

I spent the next three days scouting Megan's neighborhood and routine. It never varied. Leave the house at 12:15, the same paths and park workout, a post-run smoothie at *Frozen Aging*, a trendy, stool-only mini bar two blocks from her home. Then back to the apartment.

The park was my best bet, and Wednesdays were quietest.

After a quick breakfast of coffee and eggs in my empty kitchen, I changed into nondescript clothes, attached my moles and wig, and packed the gear I'd need. I'd bought and refurbed an old rifle from the consignment shop Daron had pawned his mom's engagement ring at four years ago to make rent. I'd added a scope. The rounds were one-off, untraceable thanks to a street dealer and dual-encrypted payment. I wasn't taking any chances.

A car dropped me a mile from the park. Black Basics duffel bag in hand, I walked with my hood down and eyes lower, heart pounding despite the normalcy of the situation. I'd done this half-a-hundred times in Riyadh and Medina. What made this hit any different?

Reaching the park two hours before the trio was scheduled to appear, I played the scene in my head. Setup in the heavy woods on the far side, wait for their superset rests, and take the shot. I veered left of the bathroom, eyes down as I avoided the two obvious cameras patrolling the doors. There'd be hundreds more throughout the park, but the facial algorithms would eff their search anyways...

Stepping over a rotting log, I knelt, woody shirt melting into the murk around me. I pulled on gloves and dragged pine branches over my legs, obscuring me from even the most prying eyes.

Laying prone, I screwed the silencer onto the old Remington. I'd fine-tuned the scope east of Forest Park two nights earlier, and though I wasn't sharp as I'd been, I could still tag a Qu'ran from a quarter-mile without breaking a sweat.

I lined the crosshairs on the swingset's beam and followed the double-decker playground to get a feel for the balance. A deep breath. I was ready.

In the army, I'd been a hammer for nails. But I'd changed. Things weren't so simple anymore. I'd looked into Larson's sordid affairs. She represented some of the cruelest and vilest industries, anyone who paid top dollar. Morals never entered the equation. She wined and dined senators and congressmen, seeking tax cuts, preferential treatment, and perks for her employers, most of which hit working classes hardest.

No semblance of remorse or charitable acts, other than herself, of course: weekend trips to the spa, rejuves every three years instead of the recommended five. A string of apartments and penthouses from here to Monaco.

Megan Larson was guilty... And I was a hammer.

* * *

At 12:47 on the dot, the first guard—who I'd taken to calling Red, for his ass-ugly farmer's tan—appeared in a red t-shirt and shorts instead of his usual graphenite. He'd regret that. Megan emerged a moment later not two hundred yards from me, running hard before dropping to the rubbery floor. Pushups first this time. She cranked out twenty and leaped to squatting position. Hairy —nicknamed for all the obvious reasons—grabbed the multi-colored monkey bars, and started his lat-pumping routine.

I slowed my breathing, increasing the holds.

Megan dropped from the bars and stood panting. Lining up the shot, I inhaled, centering the crosshairs on her chest. A ten count to keep still. Now.

I squeezed the trigger.

Pht. The rifle bucked a touch and the bullet covered the six-hundred feet in under two-tenths of a second, her body twitching as blood sprayed from a wound above her left ventricle. Still got it. She collapsed to her knees as her guards spun, reaching for weapons, eyes searching, helpless.

Folding the barrel of the collapsible Remington, I shoved it into the empty telescope kit in the duffel and stood in a seamless motion, guards backs to me. I zipped it, and slung it over my shoulder, marching through the wooded forest toward the street.

Sirens blared, growing ever louder. My step quickened, pulse too.

A minute later, I hit the busy street, crossing the intersection and melting into a group of burrito-sporting Atlanta Arsenal shirts and animated costumes. I split off by the eSports creeper arena three blocks later, and went another five, past an animal shelter nicer than most homeless ones. A flock of Atlanta PD drones zoomed from the precinct two streets over.

I hailed a ride across from Amazon's North Atlanta shopping center, and was home thirty minutes later to watch the story unfold. They hadn't found anything by the time the rusty Tesla reached our street, and it wasn't until I was at the kitchen table, cleaning the gun and replaying the scene that it hit me: I had to write the note.

ETHAN

Damn. She was one of our best lobbyists. I sipped my post-workout and shook my head, disgusted. We were *this* close on the Georgia deal. The tax break would have been huge. Did we have another Georgia lobbyist? I wasn't sure, and fired a quick message to Kelvin to deal with it, and possible fallout. It wasn't like DDI was her sole client, far from it. But we couldn't afford any backlash, not with the South African debacle so fresh. At least the press hadn't picked up on that, yet...

"Oh, shit," Boris said from across the kitchen table. "Taxman struck again." He was wearing a brandless t-shirt and sipping coffee, having devoured three Preeta's whey chocolate croissants—Maria's pastry perfect counterpart—and was reading his Cyrillic newspaper, Rossiyskaya Gazeta. Old habits die hard... the bad ones too.

Not again. "What happened?"

"Bastard sent a letter and everything." Boris shook his head. "Some people..."

Closing out the ticker tracking our cap relative to SLI, I jumped to the Times.

Taxman Delivers Ultimate Toll - 3rd Victim Found.

Megan Larson, age 29, was murdered yesterday at 12:51 in Frankie Allen park. Police say the shooter was caught on camera but face ID and FBI databases are coming up blank.

This morning, the Times received an encrypted message from the supposed murderer that authorities have been unable to trace or authenticate. It reads as follows:

'Megan Larson and the others before her have been found guilty of murder, corruption, black market LE, and using uncompensated minors as donors. Any society that tolerates the murder of its children to benefit the rich ought face a reckoning for its sins.

I am that reckoning. Justice is served!

—The Taxman

That wouldn't be good for business but wasn't surprising. When you trusted government to do hard things better left to markets and free enterprise... Show me any startup or VC who'd let that slide?

And who the hell was this 'Taxman' anyways? I'd like to meet him, give him a piece of my mind. Who did he think he was? Life extension had saved and bettered more lives than anything since Salk cured Polio in 1955. Anyone that said otherwise was ignorant, born again, or peddling drugs...

Now, if he went after Google Life or freaking Sun Lee, that'd be another story.

I called Kelvin, who was at headquarters. 'Seen the news?'

He sighed. 'Just now.'

'How should we respond?' Public relations was the one thing I couldn't stand... Why couldn't they all get in line?

'Silence,' he said. 'People aren't associating the story with us. Our employees and clients aren't involved. Our name hasn't been dragged up yet. Putting out a statement would lend credibility to his ridiculousness.'

Made sense. We'd done the same with Cape Town. No one outside top management knew. We could pull the project and no one would know the difference. We'd have to up our Croatian and Albanian footprint in core Caucasian markets. If SLI was going to flood the market with cheap South African whites, we'd need to be ready.

Kelvin signed off and I kicked back, eyeing Jones. Seated in the corner, she'd been lost in thought since we started breakfast. Something wasn't right with her but I couldn't put my finger on what.

MIKE

Ava deteriorated faster than doctors anticipated, a month after returning from Rome, her ribs were visible. We'd spent more time together, the three of us, since they'd got back. It had been a hard and happy time. Like old times, but *so* different. I was touched she chose to spend her last months with me. Maybe things hadn't been so bad after all.

And there was the matter of final arrangements. Ava wanted a funeral, she wanted to be buried. "I don't care what everyone else does, Mike. I want a plot, somewhere Jamie can visit when she's older and remember me."

What could I say? I didn't know a single person who hadn't been cremated, and hadn't the slightest idea where to begin. Buried? In the ground? Like wormfood? "Umm... Okay, we can do that."

While I was busy preparing my sad excuse for a home for Jamie, buying all her favorite foods, toys, and things she'd loved as a girl, Ava worked the other end. She called a mortician—which turns out were a real thing—and we visited two different cemeteries. The first wasn't so bad, but the second was enough to kill you then and there.

We exited the car and the spookiness started. I hadn't set foot in a cemetery since I was twelve, a traumatic night of hide and seek. And today, decades later, it wasn't much better.

Headstones scattered everywhere. Treading on the remains of long dead lovers and kids... It was creepy, and the wind whirled just so, a strange echoing *whoosh* surrounding us, eerie over the entire place. My stomach was in knots.

Flowers and bouquets, roses, letters and love littered the lifeless graves. It revolted me in a spine-tingling way. Why bask in death? The headstones made everything worse. Such short, unremarkable lives. Eva Beth McBride lasted seventy years. And Barry Manson, a mere ninety. I shuddered.

I'd never been good with death. My hamster, KC, had died when I was nine, eaten by our robo vacuum. Amazon had apologized, and my parents bought me a new one, but it wasn't the same. The squeals tormented me to this day, the *brrrr* of the compressor squelching any further sound.

This felt like that...

Ava surveyed the horrific scene with a brief sigh of content. "Isn't it beautiful, Mike?"

What did she see in this place? Even the funeral director looked dug up, something between a skeleton and a zombie, eyes deeper than Everest.

A nod, not trusting myself to speak. This was her thing, for her and Jamie. I wasn't about to ruin it. She'd been getting spiritual and stoic lately, reading Marcus Aurielius, the Buddha, and other death-accepting philosophers. Downright counterproductive. If she was going to fight off the cancer...

But we'd had *that* salvo of an argument, *twice*. "I can die how I damn well please!" she'd snapped the two times it came up. I'd avoided the topic like the plague since and things brightened.

We passed a blue-eyed woman with auburn hair and a stylish demeanor, carrying roses and a pan of brownies. Two years earlier, she'd been profiled in the Post, as had her son, the notorious Ethan Anderson.

She stopped at a headstone and set down the brownies. "Oh, Betty Sue." She shook her head. "I hope you found your Ted."

I looked away before she noticed, and she disappeared into the drab rows, engulfed by towering monuments to death and sadness.

Talk about a place to spend eternity. A perpetual pool of sorrow to wallow away your days...

We left not long after.

SAM

The next few hits were smooth, little more than the cough of the suppressor or a dying last gasp to alert even the most attentive guards their client had expired. I got more creative with my letters as well, sending elaborate ciphers and messages to the news agencies, hoping to scare rich bastards shitless.

It worked. Every day, the Taxman was top of mind and tip of tongue. From Ethan's guards to the other diners at the cheapo Italian place with the fusilli by my house, the murders were all anyone wanted to talk about. In a strange way, I liked it.

And there were hundreds of names in HSU's database. It was overwhelming, and yet, each time, filled me with a sense of purpose—and dread—at the prospect of playing god. But what else did I have? Malea was gone, Daron too. And when I'd pulled the trigger and ended that bitch's life, I'd felt a spark. Not living, per se, but more alive than I'd been since, well…

I was training again too, which was good. No more lazy shit all-night bingers. The Taxman gave me something to live for, something to kill for.

And there were billions of people in the world, billions. Eight I think, but I was never a big reader. Eight billion, no one advocating for the poor, the weak, the downtrodden.

Africa was worse. The poverty had been unimaginable this time. It'd always been bad, a shithole since the slave trade and failed unification, but this time, homelessness was rampant, and desperation, more contagious still.

Enjoying my prime rib, Ethan trimmed a fine slice with Michelin star finesse, the gulf between my two worlds never more apparent—five stars for lunch, Ramen for dinner.

My death insurance policy would come into effect at the end of the year: Ethan's attempt to buy my loyalty and forgive everything. But he'd commercialized life extension. Without his innovations and dogged tenacity, we'd all be equals, at least in theory. Beneath the fame, riches, and rugged exterior, he was a decent guy though; cutthroat in negotiations and hard choices, but his mission was a good one, and his means almost always lined up.

"What do you think, Jones?" It was Ethan. Boris and Maria looked across the dining room table at me. Ethan had taken to taking meals in the illustrious Renaissance room, lofty engraved ceilings, fine reds, and finer da Vincis blanketing the walls, matching lab grown diamond chandeliers at either end.

"Sorry, what?" I said. "Must have gotten distracted."

"The Taxman, this serial killer? What do you think?" Ethan asked.

I was taken off-guard. Uh-oh... Do I take the bait? "I mean, it's awful, and okay at the same time. Murder's never right, not in cold blood. And yet, punishing people for crimes they'd never see justice for... there's something poetic in that."

Ethan nodded but his eyes darkened and for once, he said nothing. Whether he secretly agreed with me or couldn't care less, I wasn't sure. He'd been moody as of late, holed up in the compound, taking more calls, and avoiding travel at all costs. He'd had his mother over twice in the past two weeks as well, a record according to Vlad. He'd been tense both times.

Something was off.

The luxury of when to die was stressful... The irony almost made me laugh. I'd have lost my job though, and maybe my life. Was I being dramatic?

Another harsh sip of ketone coffee. Ethan made us try it two years back, and I was hooked. Why'd he always have to be right?

But last night was rough, I needed the energy.

Tonight wouldn't be much easier. The game was afoot.

MIKE

What a day. Two speeches, three podcasts, and a meeting with Georgia Tech's president on the future, viability, and direction of the prestigious university. And I had to meet Speaker Warren, at her lair for drinks. "We can't talk in public." Those had been her exact cryptic words when she'd called me earlier.

Why not? What was so pressing, so secretive, she'd risk a scandal... after what had transpired between us? I'd vowed off alcohol after that binger of an eff up... lasted all of three days.

But if a reporter snapped a pic of us, or worse, got wind of what had happened that sloppy seconds night, I'd be screwed. And yet, she was leading the Democratic primary. I couldn't afford to piss her off, not after turning down her last offer. Her claws were sharp and she wasn't afraid to use them.

We left the office at quarter-to-six, and, after Wallace cleared the parking garage, whizzed to her Midtown place overlooking Piedmont. The weather was great this time of year, and at night the harsh humidity was replaced by a cool calm. But we didn't feel any of that as the air-conditioned car rounded the corner and stopped at an ivy-covered midrise with a pricey view of the monument.

Security waved us to the underground bunker, vetted our IDs, and directed us to the nearest lift with the efficiency of an underpaid Amazon foreman. "Wallace, Reggie, wait in the car," I said.

Reggie's face hardened like I'd insulted his mother, a dangerous proposition at best, given the guns on that Georgia broad. "Like hell," Reggie replied. "We're coming."

I shook my head. "I'm fine. The building's locked down, and the senator requested it." To be honest, it was odd, some CIA shit, meeting in a locked apartment... Something had Warren spooked, or conspiring, but what?

Negotiations took two minutes, but in the end, I won and climbed out of the butterfly doors. The lift beckoned me as it opened and I strode into the mirror-ladened square, screens transforming from a reflective nothingness to beautiful landscapes before the doors shut, Beethoven's Fifth: my favorite. Must have my data from somewhere. Who said dystopia was so bad...

The lift dinged seventeen floors later, the top floor, and I exited. The building was decked out, a world away from the place Ava and I bought so many years earlier. Hallways of repurposed elmwood and handmade rugs, antique lamps and miniature tables every few feet. Speaker Warren's was the door on the far side, past the Sistine replica ceiling and sweeping views of Midtown.

At the mahogany door, I knocked, not that I needed to. It opened, and a bald guard with a hefty nose and tailored black suit appeared, gun drawn. "Senator Schmidt?" His brow was furrowed, fingers twitching.

"That's me, last I checked."

"Take a seat." A humorless face gestured to an endless couch by the two-story fireplace—lit, despite the season—and gave me another once over. The place was nicer than I remembered, more spacious too. Presidential portraits lined one side, a sweeping watercolor of the White House, the other.

"Would you like anything to drink?" the Midwestern cowboy asked.

I said no, and he sat across from me on the matching ottoman, big hands ready at his sides, eyes intense despite a feigned indifference. He could use a chill pill, or a cold brewsky.

"Do you know what the Speaker—"

He shook his head, saying nothing. So, that was how it was going to be.

Sinking into the plush foam, I closed my eyes. I should meditate. Ava and Jamie had been encouraging me. I could never bring myself to just sit and breathe. Seemed dull, so pointless. Who had the time? And good luck keeping this mind still.

A polished grandfather clock tolled. Footsteps.

"Oh, Mike, you're here." Saved by the... well, speak of the devil. Warren strode into the room, clad in refined elegance, dashing, yet professional, black dress showing off toned arms and a competitive nature. "I've been meaning to talk to you."

No shit... About? Before she said anything, she motioned to the front door. I opened my mouth but she shook her head, touching a finger to her rosy lips for the briefest of seconds.

Her eyes spoke volumes and froze the words in my throat.

We slipped into the hallway and walked to the elevator in silence. I opened my mouth again, but she *shhh'ed* me. We rode to the second floor, got off, turned left and headed for the emergency stairwell. The stairs? She opened the fireproof door and we descended, her pace quickening in the dank stairwell with stains from last year. Who took the stairs?

We hit the busy street and she turned to me. "Sorry about that. I think I have a mole, Alex's people," she added.

Ah, Diaz. That's what this is about? We hurried down the sidewalk, rounding the corner and grabbing a cozy booth in the far corner of *But First, Coffee* without saying another word. The place was dead except two loud couples two booths from ours debating IVF and intelligent design and a bloodshot barista with no name clothes ready to end her double shift. She'd be automated any day... Poor thing.

"So," she said once we had our bitter brew, "where to begin? I need your help," she said.

"Mhm..."

"You're on the committee for Homeland Security and Governmental Affairs. It's about the Taxman." Her eyes darted to the doorway. "I'd like for you to propose a special joint task force to investigate the Taxman killings. This is a serious issue—"

"Why a committee?" I cut in. "The FBI are working on it." Something of the sort had crossed my desk. "And why me?"

"There's not enough resources on the investigation!" She looked to the door again and spilled her latte, hands shaking. Was this the same sweet-toothed, blade in your back Warren who owned the hill? "We *need* to find this guy."

What had her spooked? "You know something I don't?"

She winced, leaning closer. "I got a message two days ago from a LE clinic I used once, it doesn't matter which. Let's just say, there is a pattern. *All* his victims are ex-clients."

Ahhh... "And you're worried your name's on this hit list?" The hunter had become the hunted... how poetic.

Her eyebrows flared.

Oh, snap. Wait... I gestured to the trendy cafe. "Why are we meeting here? Your place is a fortress..."

"One of my guards might have been turned," she said. "You never know. And I can't afford for this 'mistake' to become public knowledge, if you catch my drift."

A blackmarket clinic, eh? And she's sharing it with me? Short of one drunken tango five weeks ago when... Oh no!

My stomach tumbled as she leaned closer. "Mike, I'm pregnant."

Shit! You gotta be kidding me. It was one time, one. I closed my eyes. This couldn't be happening. There'd been cannabis, shots, maybe some coke... How could—"Are you sure?" I asked.

Her eyes narrowed. "Yes, I'm sure. Idiot."

Duh... that was a stupid question. "And it has to be—"

"Yes, it's yours!" she snapped. "Or, it was. I aborted it."

Aborted? "You what?"

She rolled her eyes. "Please, it's a fetus. Come on, Mike. Don't pretend to be so high and mighty or sentimental."

An unexpected torrent of emotions: my stomach, my head, every-thing spun. It was a lot to take in. Aborted? But— Wow...

"Anyways," she continued as if we were discussing the weather, instead of ending a human life, "it's not a problem anymore."

A problem... is that what a baby was? Jamie, all those years ago, holding her for the first time... Aborted?

"Then why'd you tell me?" Was anyone watching us? Was this a setup? The place was deserted, and the coffee wasn't *that* bad.

She shrugged. "Seemed like the right thing to do. And by the way," she added with venom, "I've got more than enough dirt to bury you, even without this. So, if I hear a whiff in the press—or anywhere—it won't be pretty. I want a joint task force." She stood and left.

Dazed, I sat there for a moment before jumping to follow her. My brain reeled. Was it a boy or a girl?

She entered her marbled building as I caught up. A quick scan, and we strode to the lift. She never looked at me, not an ounce of love or motherly tenderness in her cold eyes. What was this creature? Had I really...

We got in, and a curly woman with hard shoulders, a harder face, and black leather gloves fell in behind, eyes shrouded by shades. The door closed. There was something not quite—

Her hand shot out and a ceramic knife twisted into Warren's torso. What the fuck?

She ripped it out, and with a cutting motion, slit Warren's throat. The Speaker collapsed to the floor in a splash of blood, spraying the mirrors with crimson. The figure spun on me, leveling the blade.

Jamie... I didn't want to die and raised my hands instinctively. This was it. "I don't have any money. I—"

She laughed, pressing the button to stop the elevator. We were four floors from Warren's penthouse. If I yelled...

"Don't even think about it," she said with a distorted, semi-mechanical tone. She lifted the bloodstained white blade towards me. "What's your name? Why were you meeting Warren?" Good question, shit...

Was Diaz desperate enough to kill? I hadn't seen her face, and forced my eyes to the floor, not that it mattered. There were cameras everywhere, but that's what they did in the movies. I was going to be sick.

"Mike Schmidt," I said in a shaky voice. "Senator Michael Schmidt, from Georgia."

She ignored the second question and flicked through her interface. "Schmidt, huh?" She paused. "Looks like you're clean."

Like an idiot, I said, "Clean? Clean of what? Who are you?"

The killer's robotic voice cut through the air. "Speaker Warren broke the rules, took the lives of innocent children. I'm here to level the playing field."

Oh... My mouth dropped. "Wait, are you the Taxman?" A woman...

Her gloved hand punched a button on the lift and the elevator resumed, stopping at the next floor. She pushed me out and I braced myself for the blade. It never came.

"I know where you live, *Senator*. Let's keep this conversation between the two of us. Don't let me see you again."

Speechless, I nodded, stomach contorting. The doors closed, the lift descended.

What just happened? Could I turn around?

I clutched my thundering chest. Any second she'd reappear and finish the job.

Any. Second. Now.

SAM

Holy shit, holy shit… Why was this rat box so slow? Come on. I exited the guard-lined lobby with a forced ease and had reached the chaotic street when the alarm sounded.

EEOOOEEEE.

Hurry. Walking faster, I kept my head down as scooters swerved and restauranteurs beckoned.

I couldn't hitch a ride this close. Cops would pull transit records. Speaking of, wailing cruisers screeched past, VTOLs, and drones too. Pulling my hood tighter, I continued on, one of millions headed home from a long day's work, panting beneath veiled terror.

Sparing Schmidt was a gamble at best. The cameras were easy enough to fool when cops thought them foolproof, but human judgement was something else. Thank goodness I'd bought the voice box…

Now they knew I was a woman. But he was innocent though… I'd done the right thing.

Good, my fake nose was still there. Wig too. Senator Michael Schmidt, what was he doing with Warren? He'd always struck me as a straight shooter, a man of the people, the opposite of power-hungry Warren. Had he been her darkhorse running mate? I'd do some digging.

Was she following me? Turning, I pretended to peer into the fancy department store at Chanel's latest line. As if... The woman strode by, disappearing around the corner.

I was getting paranoid. But I'd been impulsive, stupid... What was I thinking? Stick to the plan. Case the joint, see what her security and daily protocols were, and go from there. My hearted pounded as a pair of patrolmen zoomed past on e-bikes. I slipped into an alley.

Why had she left the building unguarded? That was a surprise. Talk about arrogance. Power was the ultimate invincibility, I guess.

Either way, another one down.

A week ago, I'd been lost, without a purpose. And here I was, putting my life—and freedom—on the line. Felt great, more alive than in months. But even I couldn't keep up with the everyday atrocities. The treadmill was too fast.

I dropped the ceramic blade into a recycler a mile from her building. A satisfying crunch calmed my nerves as it was pulverized, to be picked up and repurposed by city maintenance bots for some Starbucks mug or Amazon-to-Go spork. Ironic.

A car dropped me a quarter mile from HSU's lab. Why hadn't I come here sooner? They were the real problem. The almighty dollar. Was it fear?

The street was as eerie and lifeless as ever. Only bums came here, and they never left. The smell of urine and blood assaulted me.

Hurrying to HSU's unmarked door, I reached for the handle, listening. Something made me stop, but what? The back of my neck tingled, and I took a step back. Come on, Sam. What was wrong with me? I stepped forward and gravel kicked up to the door.

It exploded in a sea of sparks, a beeper dinging. Basic training took over as I dove, the door erupting from its hinges with a deafening *BOOM* It smashed the far wall with a ringing *thud* as my head nailed the ground. Smoke filled the air as soot and concrete rained.

What happened? A bomb?

Everything went black.

MIKE

I couldn't believe she was dead. From one moment to the next...
My arms were shaking and covered in blood. Warren's guards
were holding me and the police had questions, but I kept my mouth
shut as best I could.

"She broke the rules and took the lives of innocent children..." The
words haunted me. What had the killer meant? She hadn't seemed
crazy, quite sane actually. But looks could be deceiving.

"Mr. Senator, can you describe the perpetrator?" the heavyset
officer across from me asked. He put his hands on the now grimy
armrests of Warren's plush sofa and leaned forward.

It wasn't easy. It all happened so fast. "She had curly hair and
glasses—sunglasses. She was strong too, especially for a chick.
An automated voice. Don't you have video footage?" From the
corner next to Warren's small army, Reggie gave me a
thumbs-up.

"Not your concern," the other officer with the lisp said. "Tell us
what you remember."

"About how tall?" the AI sketch artist asked as holographic images
mish-mashed to match my description. Science could do that?

"Hell if I know." Each time I replayed the scene in my head, it got cloudier. After a while, we had to stop for coffee. It was getting late, nothing was making sense. The coffee didn't help.

"Did she say anything?" Wallace asked at last. The cops looked offended but said nothing. They should have asked ages ago. Not exactly Scotland Yard material. But in a high-risk field like policing, who could blame them?

That knife, it'd been inches from ending my life. I shook my head, weighing my options before changing my mind. "She said, 'Speaker Warren broke the rules and took the lives of innocent kids.' Said she was here to 'level the playing field.'"

The cops sat straighter. "So, it really is a chick? The Taxman..."

How much should I say? Was it safe? If they caught her I'd be fine. But if they didn't... Swallowing, I clammed up, and soon enough, was allowed to go. Wallace and Reggie dragged me to the car. I wouldn't be getting out of their sight anytime soon.

They were right. I'd been stupid, and gotten lucky. Next time, I might not. It was a long, sobering ride home. They were quiet, neither saying anything.

The killer's words danced through my head as we bypassed the city's rougher parts and sped along the tolled highway. Reggie wasn't taking any chances.

What had she meant? And who was she?

"Level the playing field?"

Wow, Jamie. She was one wrong move from losing both parents. What was it about this killer, why'd she keep appearing in my life? Did I know her? Should I say something? What drove a woman to such extremes? I wasn't sure.

In many ways, she was right. The system was broken, the poor were screwed. But a vigilante couldn't be the answer. It couldn't. We had a political and judicial system for a reason, rules and norms. This should be solved through proper channels. But how? What could I do? Probably nothing, but it was it worth a try, wasn't it?

Brainstorming, I ran through possibilities before settling on one I hated. It was political suicide. No, I couldn't do *that*. It would doom me in the long run. I shook my head. What a dumb idea.

Reggie gave me a sideways glance.

"Nothing," I said. "Just thinking."

Mind your own business, Mike. This isn't your fight. So why was my heart pounding? At least I hadn't peed myself.

We made it back, and I slept like a choppy storm, drenched, writhing, and sick to my stomach in my big privileged bed above the suffering city. Talk about a night.

The morning was worse. I felt awful and had to go for a walk. "Hey, Reggie, I'm going out."

"Like hell you are!" The big man hurdled from the chair and hurried towards me, eyes flashing a challenge. "I'm coming."

Whatever. "Come on." I slipped on my sneakers and they tightened as I walked towards the door.

Two minutes later, we were on the street, strolling north as I soaked it all in. Tall buildings and cars, people headed to work on scooters, dodging drunks plastered across sidewalks. It was worse than normal. I stared into their downtrodden faces.

A frightened mother with pleading eyes and half her teeth, young redhead clutched to her chest, ratty blanket pulled tight, begged without words. I saw her, as if for the first time, and winced. Was she always here, every morning? What kind of life was that? Had I never noticed, never cared? Activating my interface, I touched her hand, transferring her enough for a few warm meals.

"Thank you," was all her weak lips could muster. Reggie raised an eyebrow but said nothing. He must think I was crazy. Maybe I was. She might spend it on drugs. Whatever. It felt like the right thing to do.

As I walked, overwhelming helplessness engulfed me. There were more, hundreds lining the streets. Wool fell from my eyes as the invisible underworld that had been there all along materialized. Had I chosen not to see? It was terrible, and everywhere, stretching forever. And this was the nice part of town...

Dazed, I sat on the cold sidewalk. These were my people, the people I was elected to represent, to help. Oh, god. What had I been doing all these years? I slumped forward, as lost and hopeless as these people looked.

Crowds passed Reggie and I with but a glance, just another lost soul as they sipped Starbucks and munched carb-free bagels a mile a minute. Only a young girl caught my eye, and even she looked away, the mere appearance of destitution enough to make her shudder, and clutch her mother's arm.

I wasn't spiritual, and didn't believe in fate, but something clicked for me then, something that started in that elevator and had been thundering through me since.

Everything was a lie, everything. Our society, our health, our happiness... all of it was built on hypocrisy, on invisible suffering.

No more. Reputation be damned.

SAM

Damn. My head throbbed as I limped away, grabbing a cab several blocks later.

Idiot. You should have known better. If these guys were willing to pull a public bombing, I'd have to be more careful. They weren't your average docs. Speaking of, I should probably get this checked out. Yeah right.

So, Senator Michael Schmidt. Who are you? I found his voting record, public site and social profiles. Seemed average, nothing extraordinary. From Syracuse originally, moderate, anti-pharma, anti-guns... wow, and he'd won a Georgia seat? He had the looks for it, young and experienced, eyes that invited trust and midfielder's build. Maybe in another life.

What was *this* guy doing with Warren? There wasn't an ounce of slime on him. He'd never stand a chance in the White House.

Finally, home. Sleep would do me good. A call came in as I grabbed the creaky rail. 'Yeah, Vlad, what?'

'We need you back here now!'

'Why? What happened?'

'Better yet,' Vlad said. 'Meet us at 12th and Spring Street, Senator Michael Schmidt's office.'

What the—? Schmidt? No way... 'Um, okay. Why?'

'Now!' Vlad snapped. 'Check the news.' He clicked off.

Shit. Had he identified me? Was this a trap?

I opened the news, mind racing. It didn't look good.

Holy cow. *Senator Schmidt: The Darker Side of Life Extension.* Was this a joke? Did he do something? I opened the article, unable to believe my eyes.

Is it time we reconsider the ethical considerations of LE? Senator Michael Schmidt *of Georgia thinks so.* Holy crap! It was an opinion piece, an anonymous one at that.

Every day, tens of thousands of innocents are murdered so we 'elites' may live. It went on to list the facts and controversies, even the dirty black market dealings and ended with a call to action.

If you believe murder—in the truest sense of the word—is wrong, be the change you want to see in the world. Write your senators and elected officials. Help make a difference.

The piece was signed, *Nameless, Faceless, But Not Worthless.*

I smacked myself, speechless. So, it wasn't a dream...

There were a slew of Ager articles and write-ins as well. The senator's position had the whackjobs out in storm.

And today was supposed to be my day off. Instead, things were moving. I hurried into the house, grabbed pants, and gave them the sniff test. Good enough. In the kitchen, I ordered a ride, downing leftover coffee as I did. The bitter kick helped.

A Tesla was waiting by Archie's busted up tray table, doors open. I slid in alongside an older Asian man at wits end, hair disheveled, clothes ashen. In his hand was a crumpled eviction slip.

I didn't say anything.

Twenty silent minutes later, I exited to the towering glass office building whose aspirations—like its inhabitants—reached for the stars. *I'm here,* I messaged Vlad and Boris.

Two minutes, Boris shot back.

Walking to the beggar-free bench, I took a seat, head reeling. Was Schmidt a possible ally? Would it even matter? This could be a setup...

A VTOL flew overhead and landed on the building above as Boris called. 'We're here. Get to the thirty-second floor. We'll meet by the lift.'

It clicked: Ethan was going to meet Schmidt to "talk some sense into him." Shit. What if Schmidt recognized me? I touched my face. The nosejob was gone, wig too. Stay calm. You got this.

An uncertain step towards the building, another, equal parts dread and anticipation. At the door, a whiny bot confronted me. *'State your name and purpose.'*

I did and a guard appeared, the door opening. "Right this way. Senator Schmidt's expecting you."

He is? Not good—oh, with Ethan. Chill, girl.

He gestured for my gun and I gave it to, reluctant, feeling naked.

We stepped into the lift, racing upward as my heart raced faster. Schmidt might be against LE and big pharma, but condoning murder... My hand twitched towards my empty hip holster. Stay cool.

The doors opened and I bumped into Ethan, Boris, and Rogers. "You made it," Ethan said. "Thanks."

Thanks? He never thanked me. He was rattled, or readying his nice guy routine. I fell into forward guard as we strode towards Senator Schmidt's unimposing door.

It opened, our images passing whatever facial scans his security teams ran. Phew.

'Welcome Mr. Anderson,' a Yorker-accented AI said. *'Mr. Schmidt will be with you shortly. He's on a call.'*

Two glaring guards watched us from across the room, stretching to reveal bulges at their hips. Both had killers' eyes and the stature to back it up, lightweight cotton shirts doing little to conceal a rugged life.

Ethan pulled me into the cozy, unassuming office while Boris and Rogers remained in the hallway. He took a seat in one of the two straight-backed mahoganies but I remained standing at the door. If Schmidt's guys were afoot, I couldn't let them get the upper hand.

Plus, if I had to run...

A concealed door at the back opened as a bleary-eyed, unkempt Senator Schmidt entered and eyed us. "Ah, Ethan Anderson. Surprise,

surprise. How are you today?" he asked, words more at ease than his reserved expression.

Ethan rose and offered a hand. "Senator, it's good to see you again. How goes the re-election campaign?"

"You're here about the article, about the quote?" the senator commented without beating around the bush.

Ethan nodded. "Among other things."

Schmidt's eyes twinkled at this obvious lie, but he said nothing, taking a seat.

"You're an LE patient, are you not? Don't you find it hypocritical?" Ethan asked. So that was the routine he'd play? Ethan had a spiel for everyone.

"I do. I find the whole system hypocritical. The entire industry. We're living a hypocrisy where many suffer for the benefit of few. It's the ultimate corruption."

Was he coming around? "What are you saying, Senator?"

"I'm not sure yet," the senator said. "But it's time we questioned basic assumptions about our world." He looked up and caught my eye. A flicker passed through them but he said nothing.

Shit. Had he recognized me? I fidgeted, glancing at a breathtaking watercolor of Irish coast, any excuse to look away. So, he was a painter too. Didn't expect that.

"Was there anything else, Mr. Anderson?" Schmidt asked.

Ethan shook his head, smart enough to keep his mouth shut, not even the hint of a bribe.

"Very well. I'll have to ask you to leave. I have a meeting with the AJC after this and need to prepare. They're doing a cover story on the horrors of LE internment camps." He smiled. "Maybe you'd care to give a quote. Thanks for stopping by."

No one moved or said anything.

The tension was palpable.

Schmit had some balls.

ETHAN

The arrogance of *that* prick. High and mighty self-righteous shit. We saved hundreds of thousands a year. Did that mean nothing? Nothing? And what of the innovations and progress wrought by our clients: the doctors, scientists, and businesspeople that changed the world and built things for the better? Fuck.

I wanted to punch someone or break something.

Was progress worth nothing? Were we better off Luddites? To make an omelet, you had to break a few damned eggs.

Closing my eyes to keep from killing someone, I focused on the meditation Swami Sivana Saraswati had shown me all those years earlier, high in the Himalayas when he had saved my life and stilled my soul. I could hear him now, "Live in the present breath, find meaning. Its quality expresses your life."

Did Schmidt think he could threaten our business—our entire industry—and get off scot-free? If he did, he had another thing coming. "Relax, son. Make peace..." I pushed the Swami's guidance aside.

Screw that... Two could play that game. I was going to crush Schmidt, leave him reeling on the floor. Rodriguez—I needed to talk to her. Now.

'Rodriguez, it's Ethan Anderson. Can we meet?'

'Is it about Schmidt's piece?' she asked, reading my mind.

Good, we were on the same page. 'Yes, yes it is. We need to talk,' and crush that insolent fuck.

'My place, three o'clock,' she said.

Perfect. 'I'll be there.'

It was time to declaw the yippy mutt.

* * *

Our landing gear touched down and I tapped Jones's shoulder, impatient. The whole morning had been a wash; no one had dirt on this joker. But I never left anything to chance.

Little had changed on Rodriguez' inferior estate, other than the leaves. It was beautiful this time of year, oaks and elms turning rich shades of crimson and gold. Why'd Schmidt have to ruin it?

Fall was always my favorite season, I'd never known why. Perhaps it had to do with dying, or more precisely, pausing death. Because that's what hibernation was, escaping the inevitable, living to fight another day. It was a time of preparation, a time of work.

That's what I needed.

Mom had instilled that in us boys from a young age: from maintaining the lawn and cooking dinner during her many double shifts to competing to get ahead. Not that school was much competition. Sure, we'd battled each other for the best grades, but our slum school hadn't had the best students. Hungry stomachs, swollen eyes, and constant nightmares would do that to a kid. But not us, not Bobby and I.

Mom hadn't been herself since Betty Sue's funeral. I hadn't been able to bring myself to go. Funerals freaked me out. Why celebrate death in this day and age? It was so old-fashioned, so quaint. Who wanted to be buried, alone forever?

"All clear, sir," Jones announced.

We headed for the lift, reaching the main house two minutes later.

Rodriguez was on the sweeping southern-style porch, feet up, enjoying the cool fall breeze. "I was wondering when you'd show." In her swanky silk and fitted red sweater, she looked good as ever, and fit the season.

"You always were direct," I said. "I like it. So, what do you think?"

She grinned, a political viper preparing to strike. "I think my leverage just went up. Come, sit with me." She gestured to the matching Adirondack rocker on her picturesque wraparound, dark wood contrasting well with the pale floorboards and ornate columns.

Climbing the crooked stone steps, I took a seat.

"Coffee?" she asked. "Tea, water..."

"Water, please." A few moments later, a butler arrived, bowtie and everything, carrying a silver tray. She'd either come from money or was desperate to look like it. "It's absurd, isn't it?" I said, to return to the matter at hand.

She nodded, smiling. "And you're ready to play ball, and help me take his seat."

I raised an eyebrow, letting her read between the lines. The ball wasn't *only* in her court.

"I see," she said. "The elections are in little more than a month. You could swing the polls that much?" She sounded nonchalant but her tense shoulders and burning Latin eyes gave her away. She wanted this, bad.

It was true. But that's why we were having this meeting. She was down ten points in the latest polls. It'd be a piece of cake. "We'd been planning a few rallies and fundraisers for Schmidt, but you're more our type of candidate. Smart, sophisticated, just what Georgia needs."

She gave me a look that screamed *And?* These politicos were so needy, so easy to manipulate...

"And," I continued, "a few million in Super Pac funded ads to announce the five thousand job facility DDI was bringing to Atlanta would show your commitment to the economy and local prosperity."

She beamed greed. "That's more like it. I'll be in the ads." Vanity, such an easy weakness to exploit.

I nodded. She'd ask for more and I'd have no choice but to accept. Forcing a smile, I held out my hand. "Do we have a deal?"

Of course we did, but she played hard to get, biting her over-plumped lip as if the decision was ever in doubt. We needed each other, and both knew it.

Keep your friends close, and your enemies closer. But if it came down to it, she was no match. She was pushing a 120 IQ at best...

"I think we do, Mr. Anderson. I think we do."

Good. Let's get the hell out of here.

MIKE

The next three days were a whirlwind of absurdity. More death threats—and fanmail—in those three days than my entire political career. Even *physical* letters. Who'd have imagined?

I slid the eight-inch stack onto my cluttered floor and moved on to the next. Good thing I wasn't a neat freak.

And the reporters were hounds. From one moment to the next, I'd gone from backwoods nobody to national spotlight. No one had ever been stupid—or arrogant—enough to take on the LE companies. Journalists from here to LA, NY, Hong Kong, and London had all called, all in the past two hours. Plenty more had left messages or requested interviews. Everyone wanted the inside scoop, their piece of the action.

"Why was I doing this?"

"Who was Mike Schmidt?"

"Who was funding my campaign?"

It was anal probing even the IRS would have balked at. And I'd stuck my neck out there for what? It was crazy. And that was one opinion post, one quote on one controversial topic...

Shit was about to get real.

Shoot, I was running late. Time to go. One last letter.

Dear Mr. Senator Mike,

You're a terrible, awful man. My dadda says your gonna rot in H.E—double hockey sticks! I love my momma, not you. If you're so angry, why don't you donate your life?

Sincerely yours,

Jade ~~Smith.~~ Just Jade

PS. Go die.

Reg gave an encouraging look. "Stop reading that garbage. You've got a date with primetime."

I fortified myself with another sip and stood, stretching my aching back. Grabbing my jacket from the chair, we headed for the door.

A top-of-the-line VTOL picked up Reggie, Wallace, and I from the roof. The sleek craft was fitted with turbo boosters, a stocked mini-bar, and a plush leather interior. Why'd we have to fly... The door closed the second we sat and the Hollywood-looking backup pilot welcomed us aboard.

Oprah was in town, filming a GoogleFlix special on the Colosseum set to open next spring. The whole endeavor was a mistake in my opinion. Humanity had had its Rome, and its games. But some billionaire was funding it, said the people needed a purpose. And for many a struggling athlete, the bloodsport prize was tempting—unlimited death insurance and all you could eat Whole Foods. For many, it was the only way out.

It sickened me, but wasn't the first of its kind, and wouldn't be the last.

We landed and Oprah's boytoy patted me on the shoulder, drawing a menacing look from Wallace, whose hand was halfway to his weapon before I stopped him.

So much for a good start.

We exited onto a rooftop bar fit for a prince and were escorted by four Armani-suited guards, all packing heat, faces a mask of professionalism. I swallowed. Oprah's people hadn't told me what to expect. I knew the basic concept, and format, but she'd been known to throw a curveball or two in her illustrious—and endless, literally, endless —career.

There'd been rumors she'd run for office. That never happened. Must be skeletons in her past. There had to be. No one got to be 101 and world renowned without ruffling a few feathers, "free cars for everyone," or not.

The green room was straight out of Jamie's teen dramas, albeit a billion times fancier. Three makeup artists, a CGI hipster at a physical workstation, a mani-pedi team of smiling little Vietnamese women. A wood-paneled bar along the exposed brick back wall, every major liquor brand—most I'd never heard of—bottles worth more than my apartment, with pungent cheese, caviar, and chocolate interspersed. No wonder Oprah had her weight swings.

I found the nearest chair and sank into it, doing my best to disappear. It didn't work.

A blue-haired hipster in a Prada smock and matching flats approached me. "Right this way, Senator. You're in good hands."

"No thanks. I'm—"

"Oprah insists." She led me past a wall of Emmys, four Oscars, and action shots with every US president since Clinton, her eyelashes as fake as her age and twice too thick.

The makeup booth was as bad as I'd expected, wraparound holographic mirrors, a dozen multi-directional lights, and five cheeky palettes, every color known to man. Cameras to either side scanned my face to create a lifelike still before my eyes, tones and colors layered like lasagna without the enjoyment.

I closed my eyes, equal parts embarrassment and jitters. What if I flopped in front of millions?

"Oprah's ready for you," a voice announced.

Shit. The room had thinned out, just my colorful stylist and a man at the door in a rippling Oprah t-shirt and tailored denims. He tapped his ear. "We're coming." Oprah must sleep with her staff...

Getting up, I followed Hitler's perfect Aryan out of the dressing room, through spotless hallways and past encouraging posters and highlights of past guests, all of whom were a bigger deal than me. We reached an enormous red door, a glowing green light above it and stopped. I forgot everything I'd planned to say.

"Good luck, Senator." He gave me a tap on the shoulder and guided me forward. "Happens to everyone."

The door opened to the dragon's den. Jeez, Oprah... younger and skinnier than I'd expected. Somebody kept DDI busy...

For a major production, the studio was bare, a pair of inviting La-Z-Boy leather recliners, the world's second most powerful woman staring me down as she stood to greet me. Stay cool. Don't let her intimidate you. Looks could be deceiving...

Despite everything, Oprah's presence pulled me in, made the two dozen producers and cameras melt away, the impossible pressure too. She flashed perfect teeth, not a strained wrinkle in sight as her form-fitting black Chanel sweater clung to powerful arms. "Senator Schmidt, thanks for coming."

Like a moth to fire, I was drawn towards her, powerless to stop, like a radioactive magnet. Was I walking to my own political execution?

She made small talk, gesturing to the seat beside her while I slapped on my best politician's smile, heart slowing to a manageable beat.

"So, you've had a big week, Senator. Why LE companies? There are so many big issues..." She folded her hands into her lap, making the moment all the more surreal.

I struggled to rehash my position from earlier without stepping on more toes. There were a lot of big feet in the arena.

"Some say with the murders of Speaker Warren and Senator Jordan, there's a void in the Democratic party," she said. "Are you tossing your hat into the race? Are you planning to run for president?"

It took a moment to register. "What? President? No, no... The entire process of LE is unethical and immoral, that's my only—"

She was already on to her next question. "Then why the strange timing? Warren died and the next day..." She bit her rosy million-dollar lips and left the implied unsaid. "We'll be back with the senator's answer following this commercial break."

A young kid rushed up, carrying a heaping green concoction. Oprah took it and had a sip. "Kale, chia, and tumeric, and enough vitamins to sing the ABCs." She rolled her eyes. "Doctor's orders. Want one?"

I declined and thirty seconds later, a holographic countdown.

Three, two, one. "And we're back," Oprah said, charm filling her airy voice once more. "So, Mr. Senator, again, your timing of the announcement, of the story, of Speaker Warren's death...?"

Talk about implied guilt... It was a fight to appear more relaxed than I felt. "It made me think, that's all," I said. "Question long-held beliefs." That was the truth, for the most part. She didn't need to know the rest.

"Like the fact you've undergone LE therapy twice, and that your daughter with your *ex-wife* also has death insurance? How's she feel about all this? How's Jamie?"

My jaw tensed. Jamie... this wasn't about her. "What's that got to do with anything? I'm happy to answer any questions you have about—"

"For a man so principled and moraled, it begs the question," Oprah cut in, again, not letting me finish a thought, "who, or what, motivated you? And where do you go from here?"

The room was shrinking, contracting around me. So, this is what a fox felt as hounds closed in. The bitch looked so innocent. "What are you saying?" I asked icily.

Something in her eyes reminded me of a clip of the last uncloned wild cheetahs staring down a springbok, cat's taut muscles preparing to strike. Oprah was lining up the kill.

"Are you in league with the killer, Mike?" she asked. "Or sympathetic to her cause?"

Stunned, I fell back in my seat. Was this a joke? Not even the hint of a smile... "Are you kidding me? No, she's a murderer. She—she killed the speaker, slit her throat before my eyes." I shuddered, blood gushing everywhere in my mind, soaking my shoes. "It was horrible..."

"Yet you want the same thing, you and her. She's even eliminating potential political rivals for you..."

This was a trap, and I'd fallen for it. The bright lights, the nice studio. I was across from a centenarian shark that crushed adversaries and could compete in any beauty pageant. What was I thinking? Dammit.

"Who do you think you are?" I snapped. "I won't be—" She cut to another commercial break. Freaking commercials, I couldn't even get a word in.

"You're doing great, Mike. People love emotions. Gets the ratings up and—"

Bitch. The nerve. I stood to shocked faces and strode towards the door. Try that on for your fucking ratings. "I'm done. We're through."

"And we're back," Oprah announced with a rushed voice. "The senator's gotten up and left the interview. Oh, dear me. He seems rattled. Are the rumors true? Is he running for president? And what about the murders?" A pause. Oprah touched her ear as I turned to leave. "Guess what guys, it's time for my roundup, the most amazing products I've found the past week. You guys are going to love this."

ETHAN

It had been brilliant, perfect. The DDI brass assembled around the Outback Room's big Timor table were enjoying themselves as the senator stormed from Oprah's studio, even the fault-finding Board members who'd been invited to the exclusive screening.

"It was just what we needed, to discredit the guy on national television," Kelvin said. "I can't believe he up and left." And Oprah's people showed the hallways too, capturing his retreat, tail between his legs as yet another host sportscasted his shameful demise. Served him right.

"What'd you'd have to give her to make this happen?" I asked.

"An interview with you," Kelvin said. "And a dozen death insurance policies to hand out at her next live event."

I could handle the crafty woman. Schmidt had underestimated her. But I was a survivor and wouldn't make the same mistake. And we'd *level the playing field*. We must have dirt on her.

Several of the Board had pressing questions, misgivings about the interview. But I wasn't worried and calmed their fears. We were back in business. Schmidt would go quiet into the night, political career in ruins like the washed-up Luddite he was.

That's what happens when you mess with Ethan Anderson...

SAM

She'd crucified him. I couldn't wait any longer, if I did, he might lose his nerve. This was my one chance. But how?

Schmidt's security team fell in line on the broadcast as they hustled to the ground floor, an executive Tesla waiting before they hit the pavement. Two seconds of exposure and they were zipping away. They were good.

It wouldn't be easy. But I had to... We needed to talk.

The daughter... Oprah had mentioned a daughter, and an ex-wife.

Maybe they could get a message to him. His emails would be screened. Nothing electronic would pass his filters. I shook my head. Oldschool it was. Risky as hell, but Malea deserved justice. They all did.

A quick search for *Senator Michael Schmidt* was anything but easy. It took a while, but eventually, social masking companies aside, I had Jamie and Ava's profiles open. No address anywhere. Mike must be a high-end agency.

So, Jamie attended Decatur Private High School, no surprise, monthly tuition more than a year's rent, and entrance exams, worse still. You had to know someone.

And her mom used to work but quit five months ago. No explanation. Did she need to work? Maybe the divorce… Or a "finding your purpose" thing. Life was too easy with money. Had to stay off the Xanax.

There wasn't much. A picture and a high school. Should be enough, as long as I didn't get myself shot. DPHS had a reputation.

* * *

The school was huge, four or five times Malea's old one for a third as many students, grounds to awe an Olympian. Brand spanking new, with all the latest in performance training, security, and surveillance, kids so rich their eyes were innocent. They'd never gone hungry or scavenged Ramen a day in their lives.

I missed Jamie at the start of the day, students climbing from armored Teslas in a frenzied surge toward the building before the old-fashioned bell—for little more than antique charm—sounded.

This time, I was ready.

Seated across the soccer field, letter in hand, I calibrated my zoom-assist. Two armed guards were statues until a piercing bell rang, signalling the end of the day. Both touched matching panels on either side of the double-doors to unlock them. Micro-turrets and anti-missile systems lined the solar panel laden roof.

Students raced forward as the doors opened, loud teens spilling into the brisk afternoon in all the latest styles. A tinge of jealousy. As a girl, I'd dreamed of going to college, maybe taking up engineering or film. But that was a pipedream. "Get a real job," that's what dad had said. School hadn't been much more encouraging. My grades suffered.

But these carefree kids had their whole lives ahead, unlimited options. Malea never stood a chance…

Jamie? A hip redhead waving to a varsity boy blocked my view. I rose and strode towards them, needing to catch her before the Nazi squad showed.

I intercepted her with a smile. "Jamie, Jamie Schmidt-Lopez?" The senator should have known it was a bad idea when the wife insisted on keeping her name. "Do you have a second? I'm a friend of your father's."

The two airheads with her raised plucked eyebrows and kept walking, rolling their eyes as they clutched Guccis closer to their padded chests.

"Are you a reporter?" Jamie asked.

Impressive. "No. Quick, take this." I handed her the letter. "Don't read it. It's important. It's for your dad." Improvising, I added, "He's in danger, especially if you read it."

Her eyes widened. "Is this because of the Oprah thing?"

"Yes, and no," I answered. Innocence bred gullibility. "Take it, trust me. Tell him to open it when he's alone."

She took the sealed envelope, eyeing me and looking around. The parking lot had cleared and her ride was waiting. "Who is to say it's not some bomb, or something?"

It was cute, the things fifteen-year-olds dreamed up. "Feel it. It's a piece of paper, Jamie, that's it." A guard headed over, hand on his weapon.

"Please, Jamie, trust me. Your dad's life depends on it." With that, I turned, disappearing into the slimming crowd of students. I jumped into the first Tesla with open doors and shocked a jock who'd been pressuring a short-skirted blonde into the car with him. "Don't do it hun." The boy scowled but didn't say a word as we zipped through the city.

Jumping out five blocks later, I hailed another cab, and another.

I gave it fifty-fifty odds. If she opened the letter, I was screwed. But I'd worn gloves, and it's not like their cameras picked up anything identifiable, not with the moles. After slipping from the third car, I yanked the new nose from my face, tossed my blue contacts, and flipped my jacket inside out. Should be good.

Time for work.

Another late night shift. Ugh...

MIKE

Jamie and I sat in the middle of the cookie-cutter Amazon cafe, staring at the white envelope hogging the table and my attention as patrons came and went with a junkie's regularity, automated espresso and latte machines cranking out withdrawal cures without so much as a human interaction. Lucky for us, not a single other table was taken, other than Reggie and Wallace nursing triple espressos by the window. Amazon wasn't known for its atmosphere.

"Some woman gave this to you?" I asked, worried. Someone came up to my daughter? First Oprah, and now, this? How had they even found her? I'd have to change identity firms.

"Yeah, Dad. Pretty and tall too. With serious arms, sharp blue eyes, and brown curls. Said you were friends and you were in danger…" Her eyes widened. "But don't worry, I didn't open it."

Who she could be talking about? No one came to mind. "Thanks, Jame. Everything's okay. You don't have to worry about—"

"You didn't see her face, Dad. She looked stressed, said your life depended on it."

Was some joker messing with Jamie? These damned reporters. "Everything's fine." I grabbed the letter and ripped it open. Let's get this over with. "Look, it's just—"

Senator Schmidt, it's your elevator buddy. We need to talk.

I froze. My heart stopped. No, it couldn't be. She'd been near Jamie, near my daughter. Looking up, I forced a smile, mind reeling. The killer? "It's nothing, just some prank from a college buddy." A fake laugh put her at ease even as my stomach contorted.

"Are you sure?" Her eyes were hopeful, and here I was lying to her. What else could I do?

I nodded, changing topics to boys, school, anything... and slipping the letter into my pocket. She didn't notice. Why'd she want to meet? Why me? Was Oprah coming back to bite me again? Who was this chick?

After coffee, I couldn't bear leaving Jamie alone. What if something happened to her? "How about dinner?"

She liked that, and we had the lambchops she loved at Carrie's on Commerce's. The trendy bistro and bar fell flat on me, even the famed blueberry crumble failing to capture my attention. Should I go? What did she want? What had I gotten myself into? Why was I freezing?

Tonight, ten p.m. The tavern on the southeast corner of Piedmont Park. Come alone. That was it. No reassurances, no context. Nothing. Did she want to clean up loose ends? That's what I was, a loose end, a risk.

But she'd brought Jamie into this, made it personal. Shit. Did I have a choice?

"What do you think, Dad?"

Her eyes flashed as I looked up from my half-eaten crumble. Had I missed something? "Sorry, Jame, what?"

"Nothing." Her shoulders slumped, looking down despite "Dancing in Time"—her continuous repeat song of the month by some AI boyband—ringing in the busy background. "It's just, kids at school, they've been saying things about you, about Oprah."

I hadn't thought how all this must be affecting her. Damn. "That's what happens when you rock the boat, sweetie. Is it okay, what I'm doing, I mean?" How could I be so selfish?

She shrugged. "I mean, it's a good thing, life extension. You're not an Ager, are you? Why do you want to ban it?" At least Reggie and Wallace were out of earshot.

"You know the old saying, 'All the best things in life are free?' Well, LE's one of *the* best things in life, but it's very much not free. People pay with their lives." That was good, I should remember that.

She nodded but said nothing. After a few moments, she added, "I don't want to die, Dad. Not like Mom is. Never."

It was like she'd read my mind. Reaching across the small table— our plates long since taken away by a cheaper-than-a-bot waitress—I took her hand. "Everything's going to be fine. You've got your whole life ahead of you."

Tears touched her moist eyes, clumping her overdone makeup. "But, Mom..." A sniffle. She came to my side of the booth, and sat next to me. I pulled her tight, holding her in my arms like old times, my eyes pooling as well. She'd grown, but in some ways, she'd always be my little girl, the one I'd loved the moment I laid eyes on her.

"I know, Jame, I know."

I had to protect her, had to go...

* * *

The bell buzzed. Not now. I didn't have time... Oh, Ava?

"Hey, come on in. What's up? Is everything okay?" I rose from my desk and hurried towards her, putting my arms around her as I sent the guys into the far room for a little privacy. Was this it? Did she have news?

Her sickness had done a number on our relationship, taking it from standoffish to friendly again, almost close. It was for Jamie's sake, and confronting her own mortality. But either way, it was good. I'd missed her after all these years, my little firecracker.

She sighed, frail in her thin pullover, skin stretched and sunken. Her eyes were weak, her face a tad flushed, makeup smeared. "I've been thinking a lot. About you, me, us... life. Any day now. Every day is a blessing." She swallowed hard. Was the other shoe about to drop? I braced myself. "I'm glad we turned things around between us, at least in the end, but I'm scared, Mike. I'm happy too, happy you'll have each other, but I'd be lying if I said it was easy."

I couldn't imagine what she must be going through. The thoughts, the emotions... "Why'd you stop by? Not that you can't just stop by," I added. "Curious, that's all." It was a welcome surprise. It'd only been three days, but I missed her.

"I saw the news. Jamie told me what happened, about school, everything. I'm proud of you."

Not a shocker she was just hearing about it. "The news is evil, designed to divide." How many times had I heard that living together? And now, older and wiser, I realized, she was right. Screw you, Oprah.

"Why?" I asked. Proud? It'd been a long time since she'd said that.

She smiled. "Because you're being bold and dumb and daring again, like you used to be, standing up for what you believe in."

As she said it, I winced. She was right, and it hit me like an anvil. I'd softened over the years. Where was the hotshot hellraiser who'd tried to destratify schools and pushed campaign finance reform? Talk about naive. Both failed, but I'd given it my everything. "Thanks," was all I could manage, emotions a tidal crest. Why couldn't I be like some guys, hard as ice.

She gave me a peck on the cheek, our first 'kiss' in years. "Follow your heart, Michael. You're a good man."

Michael, she hadn't called me that in ages either. The air was thick with déjà vu, threatening to storm. It was just what I needed—and didn't need—to hear at the moment, fuel for the internal fire raging in me.

We shared half a bottle of 2008 Puligny-Montrachet, Ava's favorite, reminiscing. It was the happiest I'd been in ages, and when it came time for her to leave, she invited me for dinner but I'd already eaten.

I contemplated blowing the Taxman off, but it seemed like a bad idea. She knew where I lived. He'd gotten to Jamie. She didn't seem the patient type.

Besides, Ava was right. I needed to do this, to be the idealist again.

Feel the fear, and do it anyway.

And this time, I might just piss myself.

* * *

I t was dark, very dark. Clouds obscured the low-hanging moon and stars, and even streetlights were blanketed in foggy gloom thanks to a recent warm front. Was I *really* going to do this? Was I an idiot?

Peering from the safety of my living room window, I watched the world turn. Nine thirty. Reggie had gone home, but how was I going to lose Wallace?

The big man was in the new recliner opposite the fireplace, eyes transfixed on invisible action. He was a diehard Lakers fan.

"I've got a date," I said with a practiced nonchalance.

Wallace scrutinized me as I pulled a Burberry jacket over my button-up before returning to his game. "Okay, one second. Let me get —THREE." He blushed. "Where's Reg?"

"He ran home for dinner but will meet us there," I lied.

Two minutes later, we were downstairs, in a car headed for Midtown. The city was alive, bright lights and life as people bounced between bars, clubs and robo-brothels. Atlanta was one of the few cities to legalize mechanical kinkiness. I'd heard it was so good, you couldn't tell the difference. No thanks.

The car stopped on 11th outside a Thai fusion bar, string lights flooding the street with warm ambiance, a happy Buddha hologram at the door, greeting passersby with a big-bellied rub. I pointed, and Wallace opened the door, reaching for his weapon.

Moment of truth.

Sliding towards him as his eyes searched the area, I inputted a new location into the Tesla's navigation contract and snatched the door panel. A quick tap of the close button and the black butterfly door shut, wheels turning. Go, go.

Wallace spun, drawing his weapon and realized what had happened. He chased us but quit after a block, our sportster pushing forty as it whizzed along Peachtree. A call came in, Wallace. I ignored it.

Four more followed. Messages popped up. I muted all notifications, disabled GPS, and sat back, watching gleaming skyscrapers above me.

One down, one to go.

It was going to be a long night.

This was a terrible idea…

Why didn't I bring a gun?

SAM

I pulled the hood tighter over my new wig, surveying the lead up to the park. Park Tavern was packed, the corner busy with folks headed to Ponce Market, and the trendy Beltline. It was the nicest part of Atlanta, and the busiest, which suited me. He'd be here any minute.

Another sip of coffee. Loud, happy people everywhere: couples of every age and ethnicity. A pitchy bachelorette party in skimpy pink jumpsuits, each one-upping the last, drinks everywhere. No self-respect.

The tavern was a local legend, rock from Thursday to Sunday, Greatest Hits albums lining the walls, to die for healthy mojitos and carb-free fries with every order. Even the local-roasted coffee devastated my paycheck.

This was risky. What if his guards showed, or the cops? Was it a setup? A million ways this could go wrong. Touching my holster, I reassured myself it was there, familiar carbon fiber lending some semblance of control.

There. He was getting out of a car. I rose, table robbing my account before I'd reached the rustic door.

There was a jerky unease to the senator's movements as he checked his shoulder and looked around, unsure what to do next. I'd told him I'd make contact, and I would. And the park was too big and unassuming to bug.

Walking towards him, I kept my head low, and activated the jammer. He looked ready for a date, slacks and a button-up. Maybe he didn't get the memo.

"Senator, follow me." I brushed past him and continued down the path deeper into the dim park. Footsteps crunched gravel behind me before we reached the paved split off. Falling alongside him, I said, "You came?"

He looked straight ahead, avoiding anything bordering on eye contact. "What do you want?"

"You came alone?"

He nodded.

"Why the change of heart about LE?" I asked.

"Sometimes it takes a shock to see what was in front of you all along." His voice was back to its normal pitch and cadence. Deep.

"It's more primal for me, but that's okay," I said. "I think we have the same mission, you and I."

Schmidt shook his head and gestured to a stone bench overlooking the artificial lake. We sat, moonlight casting dancing shadows across the still water. "We both may be against exploiting the poor for the sake of the rich, but we're nothing alike."

I had to laugh, and put my hand on his shoulder. He recoiled but said nothing.

"You have no idea," I said. "But that's beside the point. You need me, and I need you."

He scoffed. "Why do I need you? You're a murderer, a wanted criminal."

Footsteps. We both froze.

Grabbing my gun, I whispered, "Who'd you tell?"

He'd set me up. It had to end somehow.

But the mission wasn't complete...

I wasn't going down without a fight.

MIKE

As the footsteps crept toward us on the bench, neither of us said anything. Her gun appeared. Oh, shit. This was it, wasn't it? My breath caught as her predatory eyes searched the dark night.

A gay couple appeared, hand-in-hand, gazing at the stars. "I'm ready to meet your parents," the skinny guy with the ponytail said.

"I know," his steampunk partner replied as they disappeared around the corner.

My heart skipped a beat, a tense laughing gasp bubbling out of me.

The hooded killer let out a relieved sigh as well, cutting through the heaviness.

"You think you're safe?" She asked. She was doing a good job hiding her face, and I, my best not to look.

My pulse quickened, something in her semi-robotic voice freezing me. Was she threatening me? This was a public place but we were alone, and she had a gun. Heck, who was I kidding, I wouldn't stand a chance.

Shit, my signal was gone. That never happened. Was that her? "What do you mean?"

She laughed. "You thought you could disrupt a trillion dollar industry without blowback? They won't go down without a fight."

"Oprah was—"

Her laughter took on an eerie mirth, echoing across the water and sending goosebumps down my arms. "Think that was bad? I mean trained killers, not some Botox TV bitch." She paused as the enormity flattened me, like Kimmy Reinhard's roundhouse back on Columbine. "How's your security? Actually, don't answer that. You got here without them. Tells me *all* I need to know."

She was right. Where was Wallace? Was he coming for me? "So, so what do I do?" I strained to keep the fear out of my voice. A trillion dollars, fuck me, that was a lot of money…

"That's more like it. What are the chances legislation passes banning LE outright?"

Was she kidding? Today? Maybe in ten years… "Impossible. It'd be hard to find five votes, let alone, fifty-one." Did she know nothing of politics, of how the Hill worked? That many favors…

"What would it take?" she pressed. Her gun hand moved closer towards me.

Something told me my life depended on it so I thought harder. It hit me. "That could work," I said, more to myself than anything else. Maybe…

"Tell me!" she snapped.

I did, and her red lips creased into a smile. "Interesting."

She held out a firm gloved hand, seizing mine. "It looks like we're in business, Senator. I'll be in touch." The assassin stood, disappearing into the night.

My eyes craned sideways. Was she gone?

Her shoes made not a sound on the hard gravel.

After an eternity, my heart slowed. Wow, what a night.

Wait, had I just agreed to go into business with a serial killer?

ETHAN

"What the hell do you mean he's going through with it?" I was two steps short of heaving this fucking cup at the wall, only Swami's teaching stilling my hand and heart enough to talk straight.

Across the Machu Pichu Room, Yancy nodded, looking at the other department heads around the ancient ruins I'd never had the chance to visit. Fucking terrorists and tourism... "He released a statement earlier today," Yancy said. "The balls on this guy. Reaffirmed his ethical issues with LE and called for other senators and politicians to come forward in drafting legislation, called a few out by name..."

Dammit. I gritted my perfect teeth. There was no way he had the support, but it was one more thing I didn't need. The Board was breathing down my neck as it was, trying to cut me off. Cape Town had been a big setback. We'd been working that deal for two years and sunk a fortune into their African asses.

And then, there was Mom. She'd mentioned "feeling old" again, of being "tired of life." What the hell did that mean, "tired of life?" The world-renowned psychologist I'd flown in and her weeklong cruise in the Bahamas hadn't helped either.

These things happen to other people, not to me. This was bullshit. At least she wasn't on antidepressants, or so she said.

But now some two-bit senator was trying to threaten my immortality, my legacy? I slammed my fist. Dammit, I should have visited Machu Picchu. "Keep an eye on him!" I snapped. "Have intel do a full work up and have a team tail him. We need dirt on this guy, something to stop this ridiculousness."

The meeting ended, and Jones and I hit the gym. It'd been a rough few days and the brutal training session left me gassed, but great. After, we hit the infrared sauna, but Jones was quieter than usual. "Everything okay?" I asked. I liked Jones for some reason, she was a good one. Loyal too.

She nodded, shaking out of a reverie. "Sorry, sir. A lot on my mind."

"You and me both. This bullshit has the Board gunning for my balls," I said, scratching them beneath my towel. She didn't mind, although we'd still never shagged. "It's absurd."

"He's got some valid points," Jones said after a few moments. "Don't you think?"

What? No... "What are you talking about? It's the stupidest thing I ever heard. Who'd go back to a world of aging and death?" I hadn't hired her for her brains; tits, maybe...

"But what about the donors?" she said in a thoughtful voice I'd never heard her use.

"What about them?" I stood, thirsty. Damned these things are toasty. Maria better have my shake ready. "They don't *have* to sign up, but they do, in droves. Jeez, Jones, you sound like a preacher or something." A last puff dried my body as I strode into the heated locker room, fresh clothes ready and waiting. Banning LE... talk about childish idealism.

Slipping on my outfit, I let the idiocy slip from my mind.

What was on for today?

MIKE

I wanted to cry, probably would.

For some reason, tears wouldn't come this time. It always helped when I let them out. Swallowing hard, put my arm around a miserable Jamie, mascara running down her cheeks, mood as dark as her mourning dress. Seven people, seven measly people, came. And Reggie and Wallace were two of them, working. Of all the lives Ava had touched, all the people she'd worked with and supported... and five came to her funeral? Bastards.

Then again, when was the last funeral I'd been to? Jeez... Had it been *that* long? The gaunt undertaker with the thistle mop hair and false youthful cheer resumed his formalities with a southern drawl. "Here we lay to rest Ava Lopez, mother of Jamie Schmidt-Lopez, who died on the twenty-second day of October, 2055."

The cemetery was still and ominous, only our party to bother the land of the forgotten, headstones powerless against passing seasons as death stretched into eternity, repressed by loved ones afraid to even set foot. Who could blame them? This place gave me the creeps.

The others fidgeted next to the black cigarette box that trapped Ava's lifeless body, eyeing browning grass with a will to run and horrified faces. One man was unfazed. He was tall and wide, an athlete's build and army shave, sharp green eyes watching me and the casket with dull boredom. He tapped his temple, scanning something.

If you were going to come to the funeral, the least you could do is to act like you cared. Prick. Well, with five people, I'd take what I could get. No wonder I'd never seen a funeral home.

Five agonizing minutes later, it was over. The boxy blue diggers had covered the grave, a simple granite headstone all that remained of a life well spent, or lived at all. Everyone except Reggie and Wallace, had left. It was peaceful, or pathetic, depending on how you looked at it.

We'd thought long and hard about what to write on her tombstone, what to say. To summarize a life in a sentence or two... What a way to go, little more than an epitaph. *Mother, lover, teacher, friend— here's lies a liver of life who will be missed.*

And with that simple line, she was gone forever. I choked back tears despite myself. Even at her bitchiest, shattered plates and broken dreams on the floor, I'd loved her. We'd had a good ride.

Now it was just Jamie and I.

Jamie sobbed one last goodbye, kneeling by the grave as I squeezed her hand, brushing away tears. It was her first, and hopefully last, funeral. All things considered, she was handling it well.

We stood, and tears came, soaking my dress shirt in a chill. Reg saw, and gave me a pat on the back. What would I do without him?

Pull yourself together, Mike. Jamie needs you. I rubbed my eyes, blinking away tears. "Bye, baby," I whispered. And that was that.

Jamie hadn't wanted to celebrate or mourn. She wanted it to be over, to be another day. Or maybe that was me. Or was it society, pushing pain and suffering out of sight, out of mind? Either way, the four of us headed home, but not before ordering two gallons of Triple Chocolate Rocky Road from Whole Foods. It was her favorite, Ava's too. Twenty-two minutes by drone. Perfect.

I had the afternoon all planned, all Jamie's favorites. Our chick-flick marathon was ready, industrial-sized scoops and four jumbo packs of kleenex around the apartment, prepared for our chocolatey ode to pain-fueled indulgence. There was low-alcohol 'kiddy wine,' in case Jamie needed it—courtesy of Wallace's wife,—beer for the boys—and harder—plus the CannaChill Tea Ava hooked me on years earlier.

Ticking it off in my mind made things easier until Reggie broke the silence. "Who was that guy in the suit?"

I'd been wondering the same. "Jame, did you know him?"

She shook her head, batting wet eyes, her face something between Monet, modern art, and a Kindergarten canvas gone awry. "He gave me the creeps. I never met him."

Reggie nodded. "I was thinking the same thing."

Up front, Wallace gave him a serious look.

"What?" I asked, tense as Jamie grabbed my arm.

Reggie shook his head. "It's probably nothing. He gave me bad vibes is all." That made two of us.

We continued in silence until the pitched tent ghettos and crumbling nothings of Sweet Auburn. A pair of drunks threw empty bottles at us and another shook a Jesus sign, near as old as the 'supposed' prophet himself. A half-naked rail of a man leaped onto the car, wild-eyed.

Jamie recoiled, screaming. He slid off, and she said, "What was that? What'd that guy want?"

I gave her a puzzled look. "This is Sweet Auburn... What do you mean?" It's been a shithole for years.

"The tents, the signs... they look terrible," she murmured with a straight, horrified face.

Wow, she wasn't joking. "Did Mom never show you the rough parts of Atlanta?" Dammit, Ava. I stopped myself. Jeez, cursing her even in death, not an hour removed from her burial. I was a dick. Was I that heartless? Maybe that's why I'd ended up alone...

Jamie shook her head as Wallace raised an eyebrow. How had I not exposed her sooner? It was fifty percent my fault, wasn't it? Damn, Mike.

It was awkward, but I did my best to explain. How do you tell your daughter she's lived a sheltered, privileged life, a lie? How do you tell her the world's not fair, maybe broken beyond fixing, and in many ways, it's your fault?

Her expression turned from discomfort to horror, searing me inside. "You mean they live there?" she gasped. "Like that?"

Wallace shot me a disgusted look, and I felt ashamed. I wanted to sink into the seat and disappear. How do you respond to that? What do you say?

Whatever I said was wrong... Things got political and Jamie got pissed, her mother's fire lighting the tinderbox. She'd always had that 'it factor,' the force of will as psychologists called it. In the middle of a tirade, she burst into tears. "I miss Mom."

Talk about a helluva day. And with teenage hormones too... Man, I was a shitty dad. I put my arm around her. "Me too, baby. Me too." More than you'll ever know...

Times were changing. But this time, I'd be on the right side of history.

I'd been a fool.

SAM

It had been three weeks since the Oprah fiasco slammed airwaves, and things had been building since. Schmidt had been on the Tonight Show, 60 Minutes, and NPR—every major news outlet. The hawks circled, sensing blood—or a big story. For the media, either would do.

His face was everywhere, and reactions were anything but glowing. FOX was calling for his head, and President Nguyen had denounced his scare tactics. Conservative newscasters—funded in large part by DDI and companies like it—were unearthing every questionable decision he'd ever made: his divorce with Ava, every detail of his voting record, even a speeding ticket back in highschool before they'd banned personal driving.

It was like the Taxman murders never happened. Things were amped with President Nguyen's second term ending next year. Rumors Schmidt would run, that this was his ploy. They were absurd. I'd met the guy. He didn't have the sharp-elbowed, blade-in-the-back ruthlessness to win.

Around "the Oh Shit table" of the Oahu Room—another of Ethan's vicarious creations, walls a real-time view of the big island—were two of DDI's most active Board members, Nancy Collins and Ha Eun Kim, both representing their firms' interests. Collins, in particular, was prominent, given her early investment in the company.

God, Oahu would be nice this time of year. Surfing might get my mind off things. I'd always wanted to take Malea… Rolling guilt.

"Ethan," Nancy said, black eyes lining up the ambitious CEO. "What makes you think DDI can weather this storm? And where are we at with Rodriguez's campaign? Can we cut the legs out from under this guy?"

Ignoring the other nine Board members, Ethan locked eyes with the powerhouse and cleared his throat. "Yes, we can. We've survived worse, and Schmidt's little more than a bump in the road." Collins raised a cruel eyebrow but Ethan continued, "Rodriguez gained six points in the polls but is still six back. We're putting everything we can behind—"

"We're running out of time, Ethan," a bearded Indian hologram said. I couldn't remember his name. "If he's re-elected, or god help us, runs for president, he's got a real chance of pulling this off."

Ethan tried to reassure the Board everything was fine, but the titanic grumbling didn't dissipate. At last, Nancy spoke up, "Ethan, you've had a good run with DDI, but if you're not the leader to—"

"I'll handle it!" Ethan snapped, his eyes smoldering. With a wave of his hand, he ended the meeting, cutting their connections without a word.

His hand trembled as he reached for his ketone-spiked kombucha. They might not notice, but I did. He was rattled. Even his socks didn't match. I fought the smirk, straining to keep a straight face.

Ethan punched an invisible button and tapped his ear. 'Kelvin, I need you to come in two hours. That's an order. There's something I need to talk to you about.' He sent a similar message to Garrett.

What was so important it had to be face to face?

And what did we have planned the rest of the day? My mind spun, happy for anything to keep it busy.

Things had slowed with my Taxman "activities" now that Schmidt was making progress. If I derailed his efforts, I'd never forgive myself.

* * *

They arrived at four-thirty, both silent as they walked onto the full-size Hawk's replica court in the third sub-basement, complete with jumbotron. Ethan swished another freethrow, and knocked down two more, before turning to the desperate to please suits.

Neither said a word, hands behind their backs. Ethan put his foot on the ball. "Is there no dirt on this guy?"

Kelvin shrugged, and Garrett shook his head.

"Guy's a saint," Kelvin said. "Not a questionable vote or contribution to his name."

Ethan's lip curled. "Anything we can engineer? Cause some trouble in his life?" Ethan hid the corporate espionage stuff well, but he played dirty.

"Kelvin and I have been talking." Garrett gestured over at me, and raised an eyebrow.

"I trust Jones," Ethan said.

Do you, Ethan? And you thought you were so clever...

"Ethan, what are you asking us to do?" Kelvin asked at last.

"Take care of it!" Ethan snapped. "I don't care how."

Kelvin and Garrett looked at one another, and nodded, faces hardening like little boys trying to be taken serious. They could use some basic training and a screaming drill sergeant. "We'll take care of it," Garrett replied.

"Good." Ethan grabbed the ball and turned to the hoop. "I don't want to know details."

DDI's two master manipulators headed for the door.

My stomach rumbled. Time for my break too.

* * *

I passed the pair on my way back from Maria's best omelet to date: sausage, sweet peppers, onions, and a little chimichurri. I was about to enter Ethan's zen room when I overheard a single word, "Shooter."

Neither struck me as hunters, both pathetic excuses for men. Pausing in the recessed doorway, I listened.

"And there's no way he can be traced to us?" Garrett asked.

"Not according to my guy," Kelvin said. "And you heard what the boss said. Deal with it."

The hairs on the back of my neck bristled. What was—"Bastard deserves a bullet anyway," Kelvin added. "I always liked Rodriguez better. Think of the bonuses we'll get. Last year's was nothing."

"When?" Garrett asked. My stomach knotted.

"Today, at six. Called his office. There's a rally two blocks away, he'll walk."

What the hell were they thinking? Killing a US Senator? Were they fucking mad? Then again, who was I to talk? What do I do?

I couldn't let them kill Schmidt. But I couldn't compromise my cover either... Footsteps faded, and I snuck in the door, Kelvin's hushed words playing through my head again and again. Two hours. How would it go down?

Neither had the stones to do it themselves, corporate tools through and through. They'd mentioned a "shooter." But who had they hired? Shit.

Decision time. Stopping outside Vlad's office, I clutched my stomach. "Ughhh," I said, loud enough for him to hear. Another as I hurried toward the bathroom. A few fake heaves and a sink-soaked face later, I was headed for the gates to "get some rest." Like that would happen.

The waiting car sped away as I tried to reach Schmidt. No luck.

We passed Cumberland and Buckhead as I visualized Mike's building, picturing the surroundings and simulating the hit, at least how I'd do it. Too many rooftops to cover, and a busy intersection too. It didn't help buslines stopped there. It'd be rush hour.

"Pick up, dammit it!" I was running out of time. So was Schmidt. "Can you go any faster?" I asked the car.

'Sorry, Mrs. Jones. The legal speed limit in this area is fifty-five miles per hour.' Goddamn environmental regulations. It was half-past five. No luck contacting Schmidt's guards either.

We got off I-75 at exit 250 and hit traffic. A crash? Now, of all times? It'd been three months since the last one. Dammit. I checked my GPS. Half a mile, fifteen minutes.

Leaping from the car, I dodged a careening scooter, and took off down a side alley, angling for the highrises off 14th.

He wasn't picking up.

People shot me suspicious looks as I sprinted by. A few even reached for weapons, but I was gone before they had the chance to react, hurtling down Slate Street, past tailored suits and ambitious eyes.

There! The glimmering tower materialized. Crossing the street, I scoured the entrance to Schmidt's office. People everywhere. Any could be the assassin. Heck, it could be a team. Too many people.

I hurried toward the marble steps of the imposing edifice. The door opened and my eyes followed. Schmidt, his two bulky bodyguards flanking either side.

Shit.

Grabbing my weapon, I flicked off the safety, and shoved it into my jacket, beelining for him. Twenty yards.

Where was the hitman? "Schmidt!" I yelled. No reaction. No surprise.

A hooded man with a Marine's build appeared from the far side of the building, black eyes locked on Schmidt as he hurried towards him. Something about him screamed troubled. He reached for his pocket. A glint, his hand flew up. Five yards.

The guards were arguing and didn't notice us. Idiots!

I dove, tackling the senator. The black guy reached for his weapon. *BANG.*

Schmidt and I slammed into hard marble stairs, tumbling. *BANG.*

The man missed again, and adjusted his aim. Landing on my back,

I brought my weapon to bear. BANG.

The hooded man crumpled.

My head spun as I stood. The white guy dropped down to his charge, muttering something. The other shielded the pair as his gun swung, onlookers forming.

Shooter down, blood everywhere. I ran over, and kicked the Walther away. A gaping crimson hole in his Metallica hoodie as his eyes glazed.

He wasn't a threat, so I turned back to Schmidt. The other guard leveled his weapon. "Freeze!"

Schmidt rose, staring at me. His eyes narrowed before recognition dawned. "It's you."

I nodded.

Sirens sounded.

* * *

"So, Ethan Anderson's bodyguard, mhm?" Schmidt set his drink on the granite countertop of his uptown apartment, spinning a strange brass coin between his fingers.

I surveyed the connected living and dining rooms, noting escape routes, and possible weapons. Steak knives, blender.

The senator had managed to keep film crews away, and so far, my name hadn't surfaced. If it did, I was out of a job, or worse. But I didn't entirely trust Schmidt. He was a politician...

"Hired to protect the very man you wish to destroy." Schmidt chuckled. "Ironic."

Again, I said nothing, uncomfortable. Sipping the whiskey sour he'd made, I sized up his guards again. Though he'd assured me both were trustworthy, I was wary. There was a $100,000 reward for the Taxman's head, or any information that led to her capture. I gave Wallace a sideways glance but he was busy checking the floor-to-ceiling window for the fourth time, scanning the street far below.

The room was tense and quiet, a heavy, fitting silence. Jamie's light snores from the other room grounded us.

"What do you two think?" Schmidt said at last to the two guards.

Reggie shrugged. "Only reason I've got death insurance is this job." He gestured at Wallace who'd turned from the window and was eyeing us.

"My brother had to put one of his kids up, under the table," Wallace said with a wince. "His wife popped triplets. Talk about debt."

"My sister's in the same boat," Reggie added. "Her man can't find work, or the money to get married. They barely got health insurance, let alone death insurance."

Schmidt nodded to himself. "So, you think I should keep going, keep pushing?"

I was stunned. A United States senator taking input from lowly bodyguards... Sure, Ethan consulted Boris and me about safety and security, but a life-altering decision, something that could put the company at risk... as if.

Both guards voiced their support, and Schmidt sighed. "Reggie, we're going to need more guys, and someone to protect Jamie, especially with the press onslaught. An extra man or two for public appearances."

"On it, boss." He headed to the other room, tapping his interface as he did.

After a long debate, we decided I should keep my job with Ethan and DDI, the perfect position to spy on the very organization we sought to destroy. It was risky, even more than before. At least I wasn't due for a polygraph until next year.

And the Taxman couldn't disappear either. Though Schmidt never came out and said it, he was scared. He needed the killer—ie, me—to deflect media scrutiny and potential blowback. Even the mob had money invested in LE, not to mention their lives... the Godfather didn't end well.

"But let's set the record straight," the senator said after an intense back-and-forth. "I'm not condoning murder, violence, or the like. This is a nation of laws and principles..."

I could have rolled my eyes. Typical politician. At least this one I could use... if he didn't use me first, that was.

MIKE

Avery was in, Feldman as well. And we were close to getting the pair from Michigan, if they didn't flip last minute like last time with the education stimulus two terms back. Fucking politicians, but who was I to talk?

Things were moving, my numbers better than ever, and at last, we were hitting a turning point. Sure, we had fifteen votes to go, but everyday came with more commitments and increased coverage. Even the conservative, LE-leaning Seattle Times and Washington Post had featured a few prominent—even supportive—opinion pieces on our movement. The masses had spoken and were tired of human farming.

The economic climate couldn't be better, or worse, depending on who you asked. Phil licked his chops as my accounts accrued and dividends soared while the people—the ones I was elected to protect and pushing for in my bill—were hurting, unemployment a whopping sixteen percent. And that didn't include the twenty-five percent who were underemployed, some working as little as five or ten hours a week to make a semblance of ends meet, no healthcare or benefits. That was McDonald's money, good for little else.

One middle-aged ex-KPMG accountant at a rally in New York described it to me best, her clothes reminiscent of the sitting pretty job she'd had five years earlier, time leaving its friendless mark on her threadbare khakis and half-missing button-up. "We're one hard to kick cold or flu from bankruptcy." And she'd been an analyst...

Another sip of death black coffee. Caffeine! Thank whichever deity discovered the secret elixir.

It had been a whirlwind of meetings, speeches, and interview offers every day. I was exhausted, and couldn't handle much more. But as someone famous—or foolish—once said, "I'll sleep when I'm dead." The irony wasn't lost on me, or Jamie, who'd I'd been letting down big time. She needed her dad... To be honest, I needed her too. My energy was floundering, coffee or not. Why'd I sign up for this again?

And there was this freaking debate with Mayor Rodriguez tonight. Her shadowy donors had been pushing hard, her anti-Schmidt rhetoric flooding airwaves every hour like a self-help infomercial, calling me everything from communist to Luddite, ignorant to uninformed. They'd slandered me with every slur in the book and more than a few new ones, and, if nothing else, deserved props for creativity.

At least action and violence wise, things had cooled down. Who knew how long that would last... Famous last words.

ETHAN

"What do you mean we have a problem, Vlad?" Ignoring the cue ball I'd been about to strike in my game with Jones, I set my cue on the custom Monet-felted Olhausen the billiard masters had elevated just for me. It was a beautiful table, custom made, sides carved with DDI's infinity logo, ensnared by twirling helixes which fit with my laidback game room.

Vlad stood in the Pacman and pinball corner next to Jones, face a mask. Something about it terrified me, his Russian eyes, ominous. When had he come in? He was a ghost.

"Remember the attack on the senator a while back?" Vlad whispered like he was back in 'Mother Russia.' "It was all over the news." Jones set her cue by the roaring all-stone fireplace, and took a stool at the bar, listening.

"What about it?" I asked. I didn't need more bad news.

"You're going to want a drink," the big Russian said. He strode past the bar to the walk-in saloon-style liquor room and emerged with a clear-cut bottle of Killian and three glass tumblers, taking his time.

Okay, a bit dramatic... Hurry the fuck up. "What?" I snapped.

He passed me a shot glass. "We decrypted Kelvin's personal messages. Standard procedure for all employees, and we found something..." he began. Now what? "Turns out, Kelvin and Garrett got it in their heads you wanted them to 'take care of the problem, *literally*.' The assassin, the guy who tried to blow Schmidt's brains out, he was our guy... a contractor we've used before."

Jones's eyes widened, and I froze, drink dying inches from my lips. "FUCK. Tell me you're kidding, Vlad," I said. "If this is some dark ass Russian humor—"

"Sorry, boss, it's true," Vlad said. "Rounded them up earlier. They're locked up downstairs until we decide what to do with them."

My god. An actual assassination attempt?

Breathe, Ethan, breathe. Setting my glass down, I closed my eyes. Attempted murder... that was jail time, serious jail time. No way around it. None. My chest pounded.

"Me?" I said at last. "They think I ordered the hit?" Those fucking morons. And they effed it up too?

Vlad nodded while Jones looked at the signed Dominique Wilkins jersey on the wall, pretending not to pay attention.

"Sonafabitch! We need to fire them!" We have NDAs, right? Where's legal? " Get Yancy. Dammit." Everything raced.

"Sir," Vlad said in a matter-of-fact voice, "it gets worse..."

"What do you mean it gets worse? How the hell could it get—Shit! Someone knows... Who?"

Vlad lifted the bottle, turning it in his rough hands and admiring the label before pouring me another. Fuck, another shot couldn't hurt... "The senator's security team may have identified the body and made the connection."

What? Was I missing something? "Why do we think that?"

Vlad flicked a switch and a recorded hologram materialized, the senator's face coming into ultra-res at his desk, promising "Earth Shattering News," at tonight's debate.

No... No way. He was going to announce it on national television? Our stock was already down twelve percent. Did we have a choice? I couldn't afford another dip. No... it was time! "Vlad, the thing we talked about... do it." There was no going back. What choice did I have? He'd forced my hand, brought this on himself...

Jones's confused eyes flicked between Vlad and I. Vlad downed his drink without saying a word and hurried off. Gotta love KGB discipline. That's how you run a secret police. Corporations could learn a thing or two from them. Stalin would be proud.

It was going to be quite the night.

MIKE

"Are we sure about this?" I asked one last time, pacing the kitchen. Politicians and powerful figures had been put away for much less. Uncalculated risks weren't my thing. Touching the spot on my chest where the assassin had been aiming, it hit me I was playing on borrowed time. Would he have shot me?

"Look here, boss." Reggie opened his underworld Rolodex again and showed me the connections and messages between the shooter, Toran Balder—an ex-Marine with honorable distinctions and a prosperous post-military career as a gun-for-hire—and DDI. The company that sometimes needed a hush cleanup. There was no proof he'd been involved in the previous hits in Croatia, the UK, and Taiwan, but with Sam's help, Reggie had to put two-and-two together.

So here we were, burning the midnight oil—ie. local Death Brew blend—planning how to handle the news.

I couldn't believe Anderson had the balls. That fucker. It was going to be quite the night.

The debates were hosted by the Atlanta Journal Constitution—one of the few independent local newspapers left—at DDI Arena, where the Anderson's Hawks played. The venue had been moved from the AJC's headquarters ever since the national spotlight had fallen on our local election. No biggie, it's not like EVERYONE would be watching or anything...

This was the part of politics I hated most, the waiting and showboating, each candidate fighting for soundbites to hammer home their point. Like Churchill once said, "Democracy is the worst form of government, except for all the others." And he'd seen its high point...

Wallace walked over and tapped me on the shoulder, ripping me back to reality. "Thirty minutes, boss."

Okay, one last cup of death. It was fitting... The refill was half-done when an encrypted *Urgent* message pinged through my filters. Now? Of all times...

What's the big—oh, shit! It was from DDI.

--

Your daughter's rare genetic anomaly

Senator Schmidt,

Our records (see attached lab results**) indicate a recent genomic screening for your daughter, Ms. Jamie Schmidt-Lopez, failed to identify abnormality KIF5A and BNIP1 genes, putting her at extremely high risk for early-onset Amyotrophic Lateral Sclerosis, also known as ALS, or Lou Gehrig's disease.

DDI is the ONLY company in the world with the expertise to discover and patented gene therapies to treat this rare condition, which in ninety-seven percent of patients is fatal before age fifteen, none making it past twenty.

Let's talk, and don't do something you regret tonight...

Yours truly,

Ethan Anderson

**results_schmidtlopez.pdf

--

My university mug slipped from my hand and splattered to the floor, shattering. Coffee sprayed everywhere as I reached for the counter to brace myself. I missed and fell hard, a ceramic shard tearing into my palm. "Ahh!" Coffee soaked my clean shirt. My head spun.

Reggie's mouth opened in slow motion.

I slipped and hit my head.

Darkness.

* * *

"Are you ready, Mr. Senator?" The quiet girl with the clipboard and braids behind the American blue curtain beckoned me towards the stage. "They're all waiting for you, sir," she whispered.

Everything played through my throbbing head for the umpteenth time as I closed my eyes. A stadium full of cheering folks on the other side all wanted to hear what I had to say... It was lunacy. What *was* I going to say? It's not like the nation—actually the world—was watching or anything.

The Arena had been re-outfitted for the debate, a massive stage to one side, hoops raised into the ceiling, rows of folding chairs lining Ethan Anderson court where Jamie and I had once caught a game for her tenth birthday. Podium seating rose to the sides, and portable stairs led to a politico-perfect black stage, red and blue podiums awaiting us. Mayor Rodriguez flashed a devilish grin from her stand opposite mine, energy of the crowd throbbing as drones broadcast everything and the curtain prepared to drop.

Reggie patted me on the back. "You got this, Mike."

Mike? He never called me Mike in public. I must look as bad as I felt, like a deer in headlights. Everything was riding on this, my senate seat, my bill... even Jamie's life. What was I doing? What was I going to do?

Early-onset ALS? Ninety-seven percent... She was fifteen, just five more years.

A voice in my ear told me I had 'twenty seconds.' Hurrying forward, I faked a smile as the veil descended, audience appearing in droves. The place was packed: socialites and reporters, politicians and lobbyists, all awaiting what had been billed as the biggest, most important debate in any senate race. Newscasters and speculators were having a field day while companies like DDI glowered in angry silence, markets waiting to react.

No one knew what to expect, least of all, me. The lights were blinding.

A tall man appeared at the far side of the stage, striding towards us. Clad in a simple gray suit, the host, Rick Stone, a bushy-haired AJC man with a goatee greeted Rodriguez and I. After some basic formalities, he went to the circular desk in front of our podiums and got to it.

"Mayor Rodriguez," the man asked. At least he was starting with her. "What do you intend..."

I couldn't concentrate on the question. Tapping my temple as micro-cams flashed, I checked on Jamie. She was online, alive... But how much longer? ALS, jeez... It sounded awful, mental and physical deterioration at warp speed. And early-onset, at that. Anderson hadn't been exaggerating either, only DDI had the expertise to help, and the threat had been blatant enough. The bastard. What was he going to do?

"Same question to you, Mr. Senator," the host asked. "What do you intend to do about Georgia's rising levels of unemployment? States like North Carolina and Texas haven't been hit as bad, and you're proposing closing the LE clinics."

Good question...

Well, here we go.

SAM

E than had given me the night off, my first in a week. Things had
been moving, and he never stood still.

I was home, on my couch, when it happened, watching the debate
and snacking leftovers from the Chinese place down the street.
Schmidt had been holding his own, but was tentative, tense. Something had him rattled. I checked my messages during commercials for
some tech billionaire's singularity center in Austin and a Northside
LSD clinic—talk about shitty targeting. The host, whoever he was,
wasn't very impartial. You'd think the AJC would at least masquerade
journalistic integrity, but he'd thrown a couple layups Rodriguez's way
and curveballs at Schmidt—thanks to the Journal's biggest donor and
local employer, DDI.

Oh, a message from the senator. How'd I miss that? Darn filters
dinged it as spam. Mike was pushing the mayor on her dirty corporate
contributors and weak stance on affordable housing when I opened it.
She snapped off an icy reply but I wasn't listening.

No way... Health Services Unlimited (HSU's) IRS tax filings and
operating agreement. Last year's returns. One hundred and fifty
million in revenue? Ninety-seven in profit. I could use one or two of

those million. But overall, the information wasn't helpful. The old headquarters was listed too. Nothing useful.

Malea's glowing face flashed before me, that volleyball tournament in Florida. We'd practiced the night before, unlike the night she'd disappeared. The last time she'd ever asked me for, and I'd failed her as a mom. What if I hadn't agreed to work late?

Fleeing searing guilt, I scanned the operating agreement. Long and tedious. You could always count on lawyers and by-the-hour bots to increase billable time. The last page had a signature section.

IN WITNESS WHEREOF, the undersigned, intending to be legally bound hereby, has duly executed this Operating Agreement effective as of the date written above.

Veronica Hunt - 10/07/2041

Veronica Hunt, where had I heard that name? Was she involved in politics? Or maybe one of Ethan's parties...

A search yielded nothing. Another, no luck. After twenty minutes, I had nada. She was a shadow: no social profiles, no website, nothing. It took effort and money to be this untraceable, a lot. Well beyond what Schmidt had invested, and he was a senator.

I flicked back to the heated debate. The senator was fielding questions from jostling reporters, hands flying. "Senator Schmidt, are you proposing an outright ban of LE procedures?"

"You've seen the bill. You know what we're proposing," he said. He sounded better at least, voice regaining the timbered composure he was known for.

"But what about companies and individuals involved in LE?" the reporter pushed. "Would that mean jail time or...?"

"We're not looking to put anyone away, only to end a barbaric practice," Schmidt replied.

"Hypocrite!" someone yelled.

"Traitor," another screamed.

It cut to a commercial, ironically, for a life donor limited time offer. Muting it, I focused on HSU. Anything else here?

In total, there were 118 Veronica Hunts. Which though? For all I knew, Veronica wasn't her real name. The company was incorporated in Wyoming, but that didn't mean much. Most C Corps were, something about taxes and transparency. Ethan mentioned it once.

MIKE

"What do you want, Ethan?" I held my ground as the towering billionaire emerged from the shadows of DDI Arena, his bodyguards—like mine—murky specks amidst the dark marble columns overlooking the biotech hub that was Atlanta, a hub he helped build.

"The same thing you want," he replied with a false earnest, "to save your daughter's life."

My fists tightened but I said nothing as he strode towards me, hands in his jacket pockets, not a care in the world.

"You know what to do," he said in a low voice more fitting his cat-like movements. He stopped next to me and looked out over the shimmering city, soaking it all in, the lights illuminating busy streets and busier pubs on the street below. They'd chosen a great location for the Arena, all things considered.

"So?" he asked, impatient.

This was the moment I'd been—waiting for—dreading—all night. What should I say? What should I do? Millions of lives, weighed against Jamie's...

"I need to think," I said at last. "We'll talk again." I turned and left, heading for Reggie and Wallace under the lights of the east entrance arches, leaving Anderson speechless.

Try that on for size, asshole.

The air between us bristled with burning tension as my heart pounded.

Had I just murdered my daughter?

* * *

'What do you mean you need more information?' I sank onto my sofa, exhausted. It would have to wait until at least tomorrow. What did Jones expect? And after that shit show of a debate... Did she know how many favors I had to call in for those HSU documents? NSA, CIA, FBI... nobody had anything on them, or if they did, they weren't saying. Reg hadn't had much luck either.

Sam held up her hands, a shabby apartment in the glowing background. Where did she live? How much did I actually know about her?

'The sole lead I have is Veronica Hunt...' She explained everything she'd found, or failed to find. 'She's got NSA-level invisibility.'

'That's all I got,' I said. I didn't sign up to be a spy. 'And besides, I can't give you—'

'Mike!' Sam snapped. 'You promised, dammit. These bastards won't be punished otherwise.' She had a point, and I hated it. How had we built such a corrupt system? A system that paid my salary and benefits.

'Give me a week. Things here have been... they've been crazy to say the least.' Understatement of the century.

She nodded, happy for the time being, and I wondered—not for the first time—if I was making a terrible mistake. I could go to jail for this, or worse. It didn't matter how noble her mission, there was no getting around it, I was aiding and abetting a serial killer. A serial killer...

When had my life become a freaking political thriller? At least I was standing up for what I believed in.

What would Mom think?

ETHAN

"What do you mean you've decided, Mom?" I asked, equal parts anger and fear. My abs tightened, a tingle running down my spine.

"I've lived long enough, Ethan. I'm tired of all this." She sighed, gesturing from the pinewood porch of her chateau overlooking the sprawling Crane Creek vineyard, her second favorite getaway, a skip from the North Carolina border with a natural stream running down the center. She'd even hired locals—well, Mexicans, at least—to maintain it, the hardworking hands and aged casks producing some of the finest reds this side of the Mississippi.

This couldn't be happening. After all we'd been through, all I'd worked for.

"Mom, what are you talking about? You're young, you're beautiful... you've got your whole life—"

"Darnit, E. Don't make this harder than it is." She slid her rocker closer, putting her arm around me in what was normally a better-than-anything squeeze like she always used to. Today, it highlighted the emptiness...

"I know you've worked hard for all this," she said. "To keep little old me kicking, and cause of Bobby, but..."

I took a deep breath and sipped my grape-infused water, thinking. It was true. My empire... everything was going up in flames, all for nothing. And as much as I hated to admit it, she was the *one* constant in my life, the one thing that mattered. She always had been... Ever since those incompetent morons stood there helpless as Bobby died. We'd been so poor they hadn't even sequenced him... It would have been so easy, a simple blood-brain stem cell transfusion. We performed hundreds every day. Fuck.

Dinner had been so nice too, dammit, roast quail and seasoned veggies fresh from her garden. Her new chef, Marchioni, knew his way around a kitchen. And now, *this?* Was I shivering? "When?" I asked, dreading the answer.

She gave me a weak smile, sensing my pain. "I'm not sure. There are a few more things I'd like to accomplish, and to set right. But soon."

Soon? I swallowed hard. Why hadn't I seen it coming? After the incident with Betty Sue... "I—Okay..." Conversation petered out. What could I say? Good luck, have fun? Lovely weather we're having... She was quitting on me, quitting on life. I hadn't been able to save Bobby, and now, I'd be alone *again*, unable to save her. Was this fate's cruel idea of a joke?

Vlad emerged from the stone staircase and it was all I could do not to run. Death? My stomach turned. Why? The silence and finality was infinite

Standing, we said our goodbyes and I headed for the rooftop landing pad, opening my calendar—anything to distract me.

I had an important meeting with the British Prime Minister. If the US was going to play hardball, fuck 'em. We'd switch operations, simple as that.

It wasn't, not really. But that's what I kept telling myself, and what I'd sell the Board, and Nancy freaking Collins. If anyone should check out of life...

And there was Senator Schmidt, the bastard. Why'd he decide to grow a pair?

What happened to politicians you could just buy?

Dammit, was mom serious?

Alone, again...

* * *

The headlines looked good. Still nothing. Schmidt would uphold his end of the bargain. Despite training, dialed in nutrition, and extra sessions with my new kundalini master, the last few weeks had been rough, exhausting. I kept waiting for the other shoe to drop. It hadn't, at least not yet. And mom hadn't said anything.

But my sleep and HRV—heart rate variability—scores had been horrible, dreams haunted by cops and congressmen, Mom's planned suicide trumping all else. Suicide? It seemed impossible, and yet here she was, planning her death like a day at the spa—what to wear, when to go, should I get my nails done...

It was obscene. The entire assisted death industry was an abomination. Didn't people see the point of living, the value of life? Bobby never had a choice. If only...

I shook my head, and Yancy Miles—our prim and proper Head of Legal—gave me a sideways look from across the patio overlooking the tennis center and indoor driving range. "Everything okay, Ethan?"

A shrug. Even though he knew what happened with Kelvin and Garrett—lawyer-client privilege and all—he couldn't relate. It was a job for him, nothing more. And he was a lawyer, at that. If DDI failed, if the industry imploded, he'd jump ship and be fine. But this was my baby, my life... I'd given *everything* for this company, everything. It was all riding on this, the future of humanity...

A call came in and a face appeared, Sun Lee, flanked by a trio of suits. *Anyone* else would be better. What the hell did he want? At least Yancy was here.

Lee and I went way back, all the way to university, rivals, even then, at age fifteen. How we'd both ended up in the same dorm at Tech was beyond me—like the biotech gods of post-CRISPR enhancement had put their sadistic hands on the scale for the ultimate clash of good and evil.

That first day of Organic Chemistry still stung, when the short, sharp-eyed Lee had raised his hand after I'd answered a question, cherry-picking my minute error. Professor Gorich had been stunned with his near-perfect grasp of the differences between ionic and covalent bonds. He'd snarled when Gorich looked away. Age hadn't softened the brilliant, ruthless competitor.

'Ethan,' he said with a slight nod of his expressionless face.

'Sun,' I replied with equal formality, curious. Why had he called? What did he want? We hadn't spoken in ages.

'How are things?' he said with an uncharacteristic nonchalance. Was he baiting me? I wouldn't put it past him.

We hit pleasantries for all of thirty seconds before Chopsticks—he'd been shit with a fork when we moved into the dorms—got down to business. 'Things aren't looking so good for you, are they?'

I stifled a retort about his mother's conversion to Catholicisim. Sure, I hated the guy, but there was mutual respect as well, unparalleled corporate gladiators, not mere mortals. He wasn't here to gloat, wasn't his style. 'What do you want, Sun?'

His narrow eyes thinned, matching his Yakuza-esque tux. 'What would you say to a partnership?'

What? 'I'm listening.'

'We couldn't acquire you,' he continued. 'But, a merger...'

Was he shitting me? I'd run through every situation imaginable and was caught off-guard. Interesting.

How? No, better yet. 'Why?' I asked. Was this a trap?

'Your business is in turmoil, on unsure ground. And as Sun Tzu said, "Victory comes from finding solutions in problems." With our combined resources, we could weather the political storm, reroute your US clientele to our Canadian and Colombian operations and crush your domestic competitors in the process. And before you ask,' he said with his signature arrogance, 'we've run the numbers. For us, a merger beats killing your company and picking up the pieces. Ninety-four percent confidence level.'

Drumming my fingers on the iron table, I played it out in my head. 'I'll need to talk it over with my Board.' That'd buy some time. And the *all-important* question. 'Who'd be CEO?'

Lee lips curled in a victorious smirk that disappeared at once. 'I think you know the answer to that, *Ethan*. You know where to find me.' The Chinese delegation disappeared, leaving me stunned.

Shit. What now?

A merger? With SLI no less... No thanks.

Dammit, Sun. Greedy little bastard.

SAM

We were in the Maui room, surfboards and stunning crystalline beaches covering animated walls, Ethan walking the Board through the proposed merger.

My wrist buzzed three times—high priority message. Tapping my temple, I zoned out the aggressive ROI debates and legal hurdles from the team, and a message from Schmidt appeared.

Veronica Hunt

Age: 59

Marital Status: Married

Title: CEO of Health Services Unlimited, CEO of Health Holdings Inc.

Address: 7 Lenox Avenue, Manhattan, NY, New York 10065

Notable Facts: Married to founder of Beyond Human

--

Health Services Unlimited

Updated Address: Park Avenue Baptist Church, 486 Park Ave SE, Atlanta, GA 30312

Major Shareholders:

- *Veronica Hunt: 22%*
- *Beyond Human: 19%*

- *Google Ventures: 17%*
- *New Enterprise Associates: 13%*
- *Genentech: 7%*
- *SLI: 6%*
- *DDI: 6%*
- *Gates Foundation: 4%*
- *Other accredited investors: 6%*

--

My guy didn't find anything on Health Holdings Inc.

I skimmed the information again. It was a goldmine. A quick glance, but no one seemed to have noticed. Now wasn't the time. Closing the message, I tried to focus. It wasn't easy.

Ethan was arguing with one of his underlings

New York. She lived in the Big Apple and was married to Beyond Human's founder? Even DDI had invested in the company. All the scumbags were in bed with each other. Did they even realize, even care?

"I'm headed to Shanghai next week, Hangzhou actually," Ethan was saying. "Lee wants me to…" Hangzhou? China? That'd be a first. Ethan hadn't said anything about it.

Boris curled his lip from the tiki torch laden far corner. He must have picked up on it as well. A week, crap. Didn't leave much time.

How was I going to get anything done?

* * *

That night was a wash, the following one too. It wasn't until Wednesday evening I had time to plan and scout HSU's new headquarters.

When the Tesla clunker dropped me in the middle of Grant Park, I was shocked at the squalor and despair emanating from the tents and shirtless hobos lining the tree-filled grassy knolls. I'd come here all the time when I'd moved to Atlanta... the contrast was startling, almost unreal.

Making my way along the sketchy semi-suburban roads, half the streetlights out or fading, I reached the dilapidated red brick building that once housed rip-roaring Bible belters and Baptists. It was cold and dark and dreary, the houses around it abandoned and boarded up, destroyed from continuous looting. It was the perfect place to hide an illegal enterprise.

Finding the facility wasn't enough, I needed to learn more about the business, and the employees. What sick bastards worked at a place like this?

Pulling my dark hood lower, I skirted the flickering lamps to the edge of the building. All the lights were out, except one on the second floor. The door was locked, and so was the one leading to what I presumed was the schoolhouse. All these churches with their Sunday school programs. At least Dad hadn't been one of those Sunday morning swoozies.

Inside the building, a *creak*. Footsteps. Who was here at this hour, nine-thirty?

They echoed downward, toward me, as I slipped into the shadows around the far corner, waiting. Closer, closer. A light turned on, and I slunk further back, melting into the prickled bushes.

The door opened and two tall figures emerged, walking fast.

"Are you sure?" Was that Ethan? I inched closer. It sounded like... "You haven't heard anything from your sources?"

Damn, it was Ethan. What was he doing *here?*

"Like I told you, Ethan," a strong woman's voice answered. "We don't operate out East. They've got their own experimental labs and our hands are full enough as it is."

"I'm leaving Saturday for Shanghai," Ethan said. "Do you have plans tonight?" So, they did know each other... Where were Boris and Rogers? He never left the house alone... Something was up.

"Not this time, Ethan. We tried, remember?" Really? Had *they* had a thing?

A pause. My foot slipped on a leaf, making a sound. "Did you hear that?" Veronica hissed.

They walked towards me. I ducked as the silhouette of a woman rounded the cracked brick, peering into the dim recesses. Her glowing cat eyes stared at me as a car skidded to the curb. She spun on her heel. "Goodnight, Ethan."

A second car screeched to a halt as she bent into her ride. "Goodnight, Veronica."

"Sorry we're late, boss," Boris said from inside the bombproof Tesla A7.

Ethan slid into his favorite track car. He never drove highways... No VTOL?

"This never happened," Ethan said to Boris as both cars whizzed away.

I sat there, stunned. What just happened?

Flashing blue lights appeared at the end of the street and overhead, a drone was buzzing. Run. My feet froze until they'd passed. I headed off, mind reeling. Were they working together?

MIKE

There was *nothing* worse than being a parent. Jamie seemed fine, at least on the outside, happy and cheerful as a teen girl who lost her mom could be. And her grades were bouncing back. I hadn't told her the news, how could I? "Oh, by the way, honey, you're not going to make it past twenty. Sorry about that. Want to see a movie?"

Fuck me. What was I going to do?

It wasn't a long wait. Dr. Henson called me back from the dinky waiting room of childish sayings and happy posters, past a handful of angry patients whose expressions mellowed when they saw Reggie's bulk. He stayed in the waiting room. I couldn't have him or Wallace with me, not for this. I'd break down for sure...

The short doctor in scrubs and Pumas brought me back to the whitewashed room, gesturing to the simple 3D-printed chair as he took a seat behind a cluttered desk, swiping through Jamie's files. His eyes were friendly, posture relaxed. Better than the last three.

This was my fifth doctor's appointment in as many days. I was getting desperate. The small white device next to the flat examination table was the same as the last doc's, an all-in-one medkit, able to diagnose most diseases, print some custom meds and test and screen for thousands of genetic abnormalities. He was better equipped than the last two.

"You didn't bring the patient?" Henson asked after a few moments.

I shook my head, embarrassed. "Haven't told her yet."

"To be honest, Mr. Schmidt, it looks pretty clear cut. The guys at DDI are the best. We work with them all the time. It's Lou Gehrig's all right."

A familiar dull cloud cast over me, swallowing me into the uncomfy chair, hope draining like a leaky bladder. "There's nothing you can—"

The doctor raised a hand to cut me off, recognition dawning. "Oh, you're *that* senator. Trying to ban LE." He smiled to himself. "It all makes sense. DDI wouldn't—Oh!"

Unable to say anything, I nodded. I was *that* guy, the one who'd single-handedly ruined his daughter's life…

"You're stuck between a rock and a hard place, my friend. I wouldn't fancy being you." Yeah, no shit. Thanks for nothing, buddy.

I saw myself out.

God, I could use a drink.. But Jamie would be home from school soon. Every second counted. How many more would we have left before her mind started to go?

* * *

We got back home a little before three. Reggie sat down at the kitchen table with a sigh. "Want to talk about it?"

Shaking my head, I angled for the fridge. Anything to distract me. And the kicker was, things were going well with the bill. It was like a riptide… I might not be able to stop it, even if I wanted to. There was no turning back. LE was wrong, pure and simple. And yet, Jamie… Was I that selfish?

Grabbing leftover cinnamon apple pie, a treat for Jamie last night, I offered some to Reggie. He declined, grabbing a greens mix from the cupboard, and tossing it into a tall mixer cup. He filled it, blended it, and sipped. It was disgusting. No idea how he did it. Sure health was important, but at what cost?

Jamie came in a few minutes later to break the desperate ice, maybe for the last time.

"How was school, Jame?" I asked.

She rolled her eyes. "Fine, Dad. Although the injection retroviruses we were culturing died. Someone bumped the petri dishes. There goes a week of work."

Thank god I wasn't in school now. The things kids were learning these days. What happened to simple advanced mathematics and computer science? "Apple pie?" I gestured towards my empty plate. That I could get my head around.

She shook her head, reddening before heading for the living room. Huh? Turning down apple pie? What was that about? She hopped into her favorite recliner, and tapped her temple.

Today wasn't my day.

After dropping my dishes in the washer, I went to the sofa, wanting to be close to her. She was watching that supernatural romance series she loved, *Fireburn*. She should do her homework, but how could I rob her what little time she had left. It could be five more years of this agony, waiting for the inevitable...

So young, so innocent... And what about Ethan's offer? It had stampeded my head, day and night, never a rest, never letting go. If I could help her...

"Dad," Jamie's voice cut in, interrupting my misery, "know what time *Bucket List* starts?"

"Should be on now."

A holographic game show appeared, contestants—a ragtag group of twenty-somethings—assembled at the base of the Pyramids, the Sphinx welcoming them to their life-or-death showdown. Jamie loved *Bucket List*, but I hated myself for getting into it.

The premise was obscene; trade your short life—the contestants were all poor—for a shorter one filled with competition and peak experiences. Sure, for the Average Joe, summiting Everest, diving what was left of the Great Barrier Reef, and hiking the Great Wall was an okay trade, but at what cost? Had I enjoyed watching this months earlier? My stomach tightened. It was barbaric.

The little blonde was falling behind the pack, pushing her fit lungs, desperate not to finish last. She was just a girl, her Adidas shorts and athletic top, not so dissimilar to Jamie. But last place, she might not survive the day. And if not her, somebody was getting 'donated' today, hence the ratings.

She made it to the top, a mere half second after the last of them. I looked away, horrified at what came next.

The next few weeks passed much the same, little to distinguish one day from the next, except the cancer-esque growing pit in my stomach until one day, the call came.

It was Anderson. 'Let us help your daughter, Mike,' he said without preamble. 'We both want the same thing.'

Pushing aside my Bluefin Tuna, I made sure Reggie and Wallace weren't listening. Both were busy in the other room, coordinating with the secretaries and teams of my fellow conspirators. Things had been moving fast, out of control really. The NYTimes piece had been huge, *Inside America's Death Camps*. More senators and congressmen signed the bill every week, pledging support. The rats saw turning tides and were preparing their lifeboats, Titanic be damned.

I'd been thinking a lot the last few weeks, about life, about legacy... most of all, about Jamie. 'We need to talk,' I said.

'We are talking!' Ethan snapped with uncharacteristic frustration. The billionaire had been unflappable to this point. We were getting to him at least, which made me smile.

'In person,' I replied.

We agreed to another late-night rendezvous, this time at Ethan's place. I'd tell him to his face, I couldn't do it. How else could I live with myself?

"Fuck!" I swore as soon as the call ended.

Reggie poked his head in from the kitchen, smiling. "Everything okay, boss?" Despite the long hours of late, he looked good. Wallace said he'd met a girl, a Colombian. Good for him.

Had I had that look too, chasing Ava all those years back? She'd been wild. "I'm going to need you to work late tonight," I said. "That okay?"

His face fell a tad. "Sure, Mike. What's up?" Hope I didn't ruin any plans.

I told him.

He grimaced but said nothing.

ETHAN

Dang, it was good to be home. After two weeks of way too much China, brief visits to the London and Hamburg offices and embarrassing off the record negotiations with Sun Lee, I was done. Slipping off my clothes and into my wetsuit, I primed my body with deep, relaxing breaths. The tank always did me good. I remembered my first float, twenty-two years ago, New York, visiting Professor Plotka. Too bad he'd turned down the job offer. His loss.

The door opened to an empty room dominated by a black pod in the center. Semi-disoriented, I crossed the sound-canceling foam floor, isolating me from anything short of a 2.4 Richter quake. "Open."

The pod did, an oval door flipping upward to reveal still, salty water. I climbed over the chest-high sidewall and into the futuristic enclosure, lying back. Closing my eyes, the lid shut, casting me into complete darkness, not an ounce of light, sound, or smell penetrating the sensory deprivation tank.

Freedom...

Joy and life, pure tranquility, everything in-between. Thoughts of losing Mom, losing my company, failure, Bobby... all of it faded away. If I could just stay here—

A bell jolted me from my peaceful state. My hour was up. Time to work.

A demi-god, I arose from my murky chamber a changed man. No more fucking around, there was too much at stake, humanity's future... I wasn't going to let some ass-backward senator ruin it. It was time for an ultimatum.

How do you like them apples, Mikey? I could play fucking hardball too.

And if that didn't work... well, he wouldn't like what was coming to him.

You don't build a trillion-dollar omelet without breaking some eggs and burning some pans. Schmidt could use being knocked down a notch.

I'd be happy to oblige.

SAM

The senator's VTOL touched down a little after seven and wasted little time, doors flying open as Schmidt strode across the landing pad nearest the SAS-approved obstacle course and orchard to where we were waiting, flanked by Reggie and Wallace. The night was dark and the mood darker as the two foes closed ranks. Our eyes met for a moment before the senator stopped in front of Ethan, squaring his shoulders like a boxer ready to trade blows.

Ethan raised an eyebrow. "So? You wanted to talk."

Schmidt nodded, and looked at Boris and me, squirming. "Alone."

Ethan put on a laidback smile, hands in the pockets of his Corvette racing jacket. "If you insist." He led the way through the small grove of peaches and apricots Vlad kept as a hobby towards the main house, lights materializing as they went. "Don't your people know about your daughter?" Ethan asked as they rounded the corner, disappearing from view.

His daughter? What did that mean? Schmidt hadn't said anything... I trusted him, but only so far.

Wallace and Reggie stood next to the gazebo, trying to conceal the familiarity. We hadn't officially met. I tipped my head, and walked over. "How are things?"

We shot the shit, complaining about the Hawks and Europa's launch next week. I'd never been much for space, but Ethan was obsessed. Five years ago—the last restock of Elon's Mars mission—he'd stayed up twenty-four hours straight. And he *never* sacrificed sleep! Almost bought a launch company once. If Musk hadn't died on impact, he'd have done it. Men and their pissing contests.

A shout. "Fuck you, Schmidt."

"You're done for, Ethan. Done! You're never coming back from this."

The senator stormed back, Ethan chasing at his heels, face livid. "You're going to regret this!" Ethan veins bulged from his murderous neck.

I reached for my gun, and leveled it. The others did likewise. Nobody moved. A hair's breadth from carnage. But who to shoot?

What happened? Ethan had said...

The senator waved at his posse, heading for his ride. "Disgraceful. Blackmailing me with my own daughter. Heartless bastard." He flicked Ethan off as the political veneer exploded away.

Ethan's fists balled but he said nothing, fuming. Blackmail? Schmidt's daughter? What was going on? Schmidt had some explaining to do.

The craft revved and took off, leaving us stunned.

"What happened?" Boris asked at last. Good old Boris, two seconds late, as always.

MIKE

The nerve of *that* guy. Anderson wasn't going to get away with it, not for a second. I called Rodriguez. 'It's Mike. Can you talk?' Was I really going to do this? That witch? She'd near about roasted me onstage.

'What do you want?' the mayor snapped, voice sharper than a ghost pepper's bite. Our relationship had soured further, and "stealing the Senate race," as she called it, hadn't done anything to help.

'I want to make a deal,' I said.

That put her off guard. She must be scrambling and took a few seconds to respond. 'Wait, what?'

I told her what I had in mind.

'Interesting,' she said at last. 'And what will you give me in return?' And so, the greaseable wheels of Washington—and democracy—turned.

It didn't take much convincing. With the recent push to ban or at least cutback LE, Atlanta was in for a world of hurt. What with DDI's main headquarters and the work happening at Georgia Tech... the local economy was anything but stable at this point. And Rodriguez's polling numbers showed it. She needed me, and I could deliver.

'Deal,' she said. 'When?' We ironed out the details.

Things were about to get dicey.

Let Anderson suck on that in his posh-ass smoothie.

* * *

My jaw dropped. "He knows Veronica? You saying they're partners?"

Sam nodded.

We were sitting across from each other in a throw up green booth of a nondescript 7-Eleven, one of the hundreds of coffee chains dominating Atlanta's drip-addicted downtown. She sipped a small black with unsurprising regularity, marching beat strong from her time overseas, as were her restless eyes.

I'd opted for a greens latte, dairy-free. Since the prospect of LE's was waning, Reggie had been on my ass about staying healthy. "Plus, Mike, you need to be at the top of your game," or so he said.

Our booth was in the far corner, away from prying eyes, next to the penile enhancements, pastries, and the overpriced lenses—a strange assortment. But that was 7-Eleven, the beards and babes rampant, plenty a tacky tattoo or pierced nip. Kids clustered outside in the micro-lot, smoking weed and worse. Why they chose 7-Eleven was beyond me, until one entered the shop, and grabbed a VR code. Wasn't there enough porn online?

"Didn't you check the cap table?" Sam was saying.

The what? I shook my head. Did I look like a business guy? "I've been a little busy." Before I could ask what she'd found, she took a hard right.

"What did you mean, blackmail? Your daughter?"

Shit. She wasn't supposed to know. I glanced around but no one was paying attention, so I told her.

Her blistering eyes narrowed. "When were you going to tell me?"

"Why should I—"

She cut me off with a glare. "We're in this together."

She was right, and I said nothing. What could I say? "But wait, HSU?"

"I didn't find out much," she said, before sharing everything she'd discovered.

Interesting. Maybe I could bust Anderson on illegal activities, at least as an accomplice. That'd be serious jail time, nice publicity for me too. "You're sure he's involved?"

Sam shook her head, sighing. "Good luck with proof."

Damn. Rodriguez, though… that could work. "What if we called in the cavalry?" I explained what I had in mind.

She smiled. "Serves them right. How can I help?"

That's more like it.

ETHAN

I hated going into the office, especially on a Monday. It wasn't traffic, that was for the poor bastards stuck on the roads. As if... It'd been ages, and I wasn't going back to driving. But what did Omar want now? There was enough on my plate as it was.

"Ah, there you are, boss." Omar rounded the carpeted corner. "Been looking all over for you." He was dressed, as usual, in tweed and a lab coat, hair two steps from Einstein, but with a Middle Eastern black which matched his sharp eyes.

"What is it?" I didn't have time for this.

"You're going to want to see this." He led me through pristine, award-covered hallways towards our second lab—the more *experimental* of the three—without saying a word. Most folks here didn't have the clearance and I had a strict policy against open-corridor conversations. Too risky. Need to know basis.

"Good news, or bad?" I wasn't in the mood for secrecy, or waiting.

"You're going to like this," he replied.

As we approached, sensors within the vault doors verified us before we reached the end of the hall. A quick iris scan unlocked the room and we stepped into the massive lab, white coats bustling between micron-spectrometers, million-dollar sequencers, viral delivery agents, and everything that made up a state-of-the-art genetics and bioinformatics research center.

And unlike the suckers relying on government funding, our scientists had free reign and near unlimited resources to work on profitable, patentable research. It was our goldmine, even SLI couldn't touch our capacities, which was why we needed such top-notch security. The bastards had tried, twice.

"Show me."

We passed a pair running tests on four transparent, artificial wombs, another group altering blood samples with a CRISPR-Metr7 workstation and half a dozen other teams whose projects I wasn't as familiar with, each a potential moonshot

Hauser was at a bench by the window. We locked eyes and his expression clouded. I should have fired that moron when I had the chance, insolent shit. But his work on mammalian gene variants had cost a fortune and would return a hundred times that. Why was it always the smart ones? But who was I to talk?

By the sparkling window in the corner sat a beautiful young blonde with all the right traits, and a redheaded scruff of a boy, three-or-four-years-old at most. The kid was lanky and interested, eyes sharp as a drill as he took in the controlled chaos around him, scratching at his white scrubs. "Remember Project I?" Omar asked in a hushed voice.

How could I not? The prospect of intelligence, of locking down the secret to genius, of playing god... "Don't tell me... you fixed the earlier issues."

He winced, pausing before continuing as if those early autistic outcomes hadn't happened, "I'd like you to meet Ethan Jr., and his mother, Eveline."

I offered my hand. If it was true... This could be a gamechanger. "I'm Ethan. How do you do?"

The mother stood but the boy remained sitting, eyeing me. Without warning, he swung his bootie-covered feet off the chair, walked over to a lab bench, and read off the list of chemicals, eyes soaking up test tube arrays and cutting-edge CRISPR software which in many ways, had served as his father. Another worrisome glance from Hauser, but the boy turned back to us. "So, this is how you did it, how you made me?" he asked.

No way... We never expected... not this soon. He was three-years-old... Things were looking up! Damn, I was good. Talk about luck. I could see the trillions from here. Things were going to be fine.

An alarm sounded. The building went dark.

Someone screamed.

* * *

"What the hell's the meaning of this?" I stared down the burly Atlanta PD captain. Green, huh? I wouldn't forget that name, or that ugly face, nose broken from here to Florida, with a missing tooth like the Gulf. "What do you want?"

"Following orders, sir," the hotshot said in a Georgia drawl without bothering to look at me. "Kev, you locked down the building yet?" His eyes flashed around my office, taking in the awards, the pictures with world leaders, my handcrafted mahogany desk. He didn't deserve to set foot in *my* Oval Office.

Locked down the building? "Wait! Let me see a warrant." I was going to kill Rodriguez. What was she playing at?

He air transferred a file to me. "Happy."

I flipped through it. Shit.

Green touched an old photo of Bobby and I shooting hoops next to my copy of Sun Tzu, leaving a smudge. My blood boiled. "Get out of my office! I need to make a phone call. Now!" He and his men retreated, chuckling to themselves. They'd regret that.

'Yancy, get your ass here!' I said as soon as the call connected. 'The cops showed up.'

His dull monotone answered at once, 'Don't say anything. I'm coming. Anything I should know?' he asked. That was about as wild as Yancy got. Bloody lawyers. Why hadn't we automated their asses yet?

'I don't know why they're here, unless... did that bill pass?'

It hadn't. Footsteps, and a quick goodbye to his wife. We disconnected.

My next call was less pleasant. 'Rodriguez?'

'Oh, hi, Ethan,' she answered with an infuriating poison sweet-ness. 'What can I do for you?' That told me everything.

'What the hell are you playing at? The cops, here?' I slammed my fist on my desk.

'You shouldn't have pissed off Schmidt,' she retorted.

So, he was behind this. I knew it. Dammit. 'We're on the up-and-up, you know that.'

'A little birdy told me otherwise. Either way, it's not my problem. That's for law enforcement to decide.' Did she find out about Lab Two? Bitch. She'd pay for this.

I hung up before I said something incriminating. Shit. Lee's offer was looking better and better, even if I'd had to step down as CEO… if that was even on the table after this mess. They *couldn't* be allowed to get access to Lab Two, at least not to our data. That would ruin every-thing, plus the potential for future patents.

Where was Green, that shitbag? I'd get to the bottom of this and get those two-bit donut clowns out before they found something worth investigating. Project I wasn't exactly kosher, but they wouldn't realize, would they?

At least they were morons…

SAM

It was beautiful. Officers poured into the building, spreading like a virus, enveloping the massive cancer that was DDI. Ethan slammed his door shut like a little boy, and I was left in the hall with the rowdy cops. I looked down, hoping they wouldn't notice. They didn't.

The rumor mill was anything but helpful. Cops didn't know why they were here, only that the mayor herself had ordered the sting, a real hush affair. "Think we could get treated?" an older Irish guy with a touch of gray and slim shoulders asked.

"You wish," Green answered. "Costs an arm and a leg, literally."

A few cops laughed, gazing around the fancy hallways as confused white coats with wide eyes walked between offices, headless chickens amid the madness.

"Serves 'em right, damn LE companies. My sister donated a while back, lost her job." A few more guys and a chick piped up, similar experiences.

The door opened, and Ethan emerged, face a mask once more. "Green." He gestured the curly cop into his office before his eyes caught mine. "Jones, you too."

What did he want me for? He couldn't know, could he?

We stepped inside the spotless office, and I went straight for the high-backed leather armchair, waiting to sit until the ruddy-faced cop slapped his ass in a chair.

"What do you want, Green?" Ethan asked in a nicer voice. "How can I help?"

Ah, Ethan was playing his favorite game, *Win Friends and Influence People*. He'd had me read the Dale Carnegie classic once. Ethan was the master of manipulation.

Green bawked, confused. "What, what do you mean?"

"I want to help you do your job, get this routine check over," Ethan said. "What do you need?"

Green was so taken aback, he sat there, stunned. Forgot his donuts... After a moment, he said, "We got everything we need, sir."

And with that, Ethan had control of the situation. It was impressive, regardless what you thought of the guy.

The police left not long after, promising to be in touch if they needed anything. Ethan smirked to himself as they left, at least until he tapped into a call.

'Veronica, what?' He gestured to the door, sending me out.

Veronica? Interesting... I craned my ears as I ambled out.

'What do you mean they raided your office too? Shit.' Ethan gave me a look. "*Get out!*" he mouthed.

I did.

So, things were moving.

Ethan stayed in his office for an hour. Boris and I waited in the staff lounge across the hall, docs giving us uncomfortable looks and wide berths as they snuck free snacks and every kind of drink, tea, and smoothie imaginable. We sat at DDI's market cap ticker table. "Subconscious motivation," as Ethan would say. Matched the anti-Ager artwork covering the walls. I flicked my interface, and hopped to the Times.

It was the lead story. *Illegal Atlanta Genetic Clinic Raided by Cops*

That was fast.

The story was bland on details, a rushed summary at best. No arrests though. Odd. No employees onsite... It was Tuesday morning.

Moments later, another story. *Biotech's invisible hand. The story of illegal clinics.*

It was about HSU and Veronica. This one was from The Enquirer and dug deeper.

Little is known about the mysterious Health Services Unlimited, an underground clinic specializing in procedures ranging from banned brainSTEM transfers and untested neural implant interfaces to the more obscure and risky. And as for its leadership, or corporate structure, all records were wiped before this morning's raid.

It's reported to be the black market clinic of choice for world leaders, politicians, and CEOs, and yet, no records were found.

Somehow, they'd nuked their system, everything. These guys were good. Schmidt, Amir, and I were the only ones who knew the truth. And HSU got off clean, again, as did DDI.

How many shots would we get?

How many would we survive?

MIKE

Three more votes. Just three more votes. We might make it, but time was running out.

I'd tried Sanders, Goran, Isaacson and Peters... there were only so many not in the pocket of LE. What about Gabby Kealoha? Smart, ambitious, passionate... the second-term Hawaiian senator could be perfect. Plus she was into yoga, or taichi, one of those earthy soul movements, wasn't she? LE wasn't natural, in keeping with the spirits and all that. That's how I'd play it.

It turned out she was in DC working on a sister bill to the updated marijuana legalization, something to legalize all natural compounds. Although what was defined 'natural' was the subject of some debate. The big controversy was around cocaine and LSD.

In theory, it was a good move. The war on drugs had cost this country hundreds of billions, maybe trillions. Our jails were overrun with simple drug offenders, poor kids with little option but to sling dope. Atlanta had its fair share, and dealers more, on the streets.

Most of Europe had made the plunge, and things were going well, except the Balkans. But that was the Balkans...

It was a short hop to DC. How people ever flew commercial was beyond me. Reggie, Wallace and I landed at one of the seven designated landing zones throughout the capital. We'd filed our flight plan hours early to avoid anti-aircraft systems. Since the April Fools' Day attack on the White House a decade ago, security was insane. Following San Francisco and LA's lead, the city was devoid of homeless, carted by the truckload to shoddy suburbs, away from the wealthy and worried leaders of the nation. Warren would be proud.

And Rodriguez wanted to pull that shit in Atlanta? Not in my state. Not on my life. But now wasn't the time. Enemy of my enemy...

The door opened and we stepped into the brisk sunlight of Lincoln Park, the high-security site reserved for dignitaries, politicians, and President Nguyen's few mass donors.

It was a busy day, ships coming and going as the powerful played at government, pushing their agendas and pulling the country ever closer to collapse. Why was I so pessimistic today? Jamie... That had to be it. Still nothing. Why couldn't science hurry up?

We had an hour to kill before meeting the senate's first ever surf champion, and spent the time walking the Mall, stopping at the Shakespeare Library, and keeping our heads down.

The Supreme Court loomed tall in the background, the highest house of law and order, where distinguished old men made young by LE decided the fate of the many. The soaring Athenian columns never got old, even after I'd visited Athens in college. Talk about a trip.

We made our way to the Lower Senate Park and headed for the gushing fountain on the way to the Japanese-American Memorial, taking seats around the sun-kissed kaleidoscope of rainbow arcs. This was the perfect hour, the lighting unreal.

Kealoha arrived thirty minutes later, apologizing for being late. Her guards waited on the far side of the fountain, and Reggie and Wallace walked over to them. Better to keep things on even footing.

She was a small, short-haired woman, lithe and athletic, tanned body forged on the board and maintained by a rumored regiment of hot yoga, calisthenics, and weight training that put many an Olympian to shame. She raised an eyebrow, saying all she needed to.

"It's about the LE bill," I said, once we'd covered the pleasantries.

She said nothing. So, she was going to make me beg? "I need your help."

"You know LE's big with my constituents. Medical tourism drives a good deal of our economy. The beach is the best place to have a rejuv."

Not a good start. I *needed* this. "But it's wrong, Gabby, you know that," I shook my head. "It's not natural, not right."

She pursed her thick lips. "Is it any different than locking up a kid for dealing, or worse yet, for trying something once?"

And here we go, the real reason she'd agreed to meet. "Is that what you want?" I asked.

She nodded.

I could get behind that. Drugs hadn't played as big a role for me as most, but I'd had my share of shrooms in the day. "Done," I said without hesitation. "Thanks, by the way. I've been wanting to propose something similar but didn't have the pull. What'd you think?" I gestured to the sprawl of the city. "Is it everything you imagined?" She was young and innocent, it'd be interesting to hear her unsoiled perspective.

She laughed a cold irony. "If they'd have told me it was this bad, I'd have stuck to surfing. But now," she shrugged, "feels like my duty to fix it. You know?"

I did. "Tell me about it." The question, would it kill me? I'd dodged a few political shanks in my day.

We split not long after. She had a meeting with the DEA later, and needed to change out of her yoga pants, which were quite flattering. I on the other hand needed to make the rounds, drum up support. Two more to go… Let the begging and ass kissing begin.

We could change everything, but I was going to need more coffee.

Now, who owed me a favor?

* * *

"**A**re you sure that's the one?" I gave Jamie a skeptical look.

She twirled in the long Vermillion red dress, admiring herself in the simulated dressing room mirror, pinching her lips. She tilted her head like her mother, and said, "It's perfect. Can I get it, daddy?"

She only said daddy when she was trying to manipulate me. It worked. How could I say no? She'd been through so much these past few months. This could well be her *last* high school dance. I couldn't protect her and swallowed hard. "Sure, Jame. It looks beautiful, and so do you."

She beamed, twirling again, until another girl appeared across the dressing room, shooting her a catty look. Jamie blushed, grabbing my hand. "Let's go, Dad."

What was that about? I was about to ask when an urgent notification buzzed. "One second, Jame. You go ahead and pay." Stopping in the middle of the crowded Nordstrom—one of the few brands to survive the e-commerce boom—I checked my messages.

Top Secret: DDI intel

A furtive glance. No one was watching, not that it mattered. I opened the email. It didn't have a sender listed or an IP.

Senator Schmidt,

I work for DDI and want to help you. There are things you should know. It's much worse than it seems. We're talking serious bribes, extortion. We need to talk.

Worse than it seems? Jamie finished paying as I fired off a response. *Tell me when and where. What is it?*

We headed for the exit. "All good?" I asked, mind anywhere but clothes.

She nodded, and led the way out of the store. "Now if I can just find a date," she said with a frustrated voice.

Bribes, extortion? Was this—concentrate, Mike. She needs you. "Any boy would be lucky to—" Another notification. I froze, opening the message.

Tonight, 9pm. Piedmont Park, at the Peace Monument. Was it a trap? Or the break we were looking for? My head spun.

Jamie gave me a sideways look. How long had I been standing here? "Everything okay, Dad?"

Heck no! "Yeah, everything's fine, Jame."

A whistleblower... Holy shit.

ETHAN

"What do you mean we have a problem?" I snapped at Tracy. How many more freaking 'problems' did we need? What now?

My Head of IT held her ground, sitting taller as he dev's shoulders hunched over the keyboard. "I mean," she said, matching my cutting tone, "someone used a work computer to contact Senator Schmidt. Thought they were being tricky, used a VPN, encrypted browser, and decentralized email protocol. That didn't matter."

"Are you saying we have a traitor, a fucking whistleblower?" I asked.

She opened a holographic display, a message thread appearing. "Henrik Hauser, in R&D."

Henrik-effing-Hauser. I should have known. Shit. What had he seen? Project I wasn't on the up and up, like half our Lab Two moonshots. "Thanks, Tracy. Lockdown his computer and access. Don't let him download or export anything, period! Or leave the building. Call security." At the door, I said, "Tracy, *this* never happened. Wipe those messages. I don't want any record on our systems. Nothing."

She nodded. "On it, Ethan."

It was three p.m. There wasn't much time. How'd he know about the bribes? Things were spiraling fast.

Heading for a soundproof office, I activated jammers. Didn't need anyone listening in, NSA, SLI or otherwise.

'Vlad, I need a favor.'

'Anything, boss,' he said. 'That's what I'm here for.'

And that's why he alone made the big bucks.

I told him what happened. 'Can you take care of it?'

'When you say take care of it—'

'Take care of it,' I said. 'You know what I mean.'

'On it, boss.' He clicked off.

Damn. Did I just order a hit? I slumped back in my chair. What did Hauser just make me do? Everything was slipping out from under me.

Mom called.

Shit!

* * *

"Y ou're *sure* you want to do this?" I asked for at least the tenth time. She couldn't, she couldn't... After what happened to Bobby, after all we'd been through...

Mom nodded, a peaceful smile on her face. And the room was peaceful, the perfect place to die, if you were into something hideous like that. Made my skin crawl. The walls nearest us were transparent, sweeping Savannah coastlines. And behind us, the Italian masters: Monet, da Vinci, Botticelli... an impossible assortment of beauty and vibrance. For some, it was to die for, not for *my mom,* though.

I slid my chair closer to the inclined foam bed where she was hooked to a slow-drip dimethyltryptamine (DMT) solution to *"ease"* her into enlightenment. It was a load of horseshit. The entire industry was immoral, pursuing death... Who needed psychedelics or mystical experiences, there was more than enough to live for.

"Ethan, are you even listening to me?" she said.

Distracted, even on her deathbed... Maybe that was my way of coping. No, I didn't need to cope, I was fine. *Come on, Ethan, pull your-*

self together. Her eyes were glazed, the drugs sapping her system, more DMT than her pea-sized pineal gland could ever produce filling her brain with...—I was doing it again, drifting...

"I'm here, Mom. I always will be."

"You know why I'm doing this, right, Ethan?" she whispered, reminding me of better times and secrets amongst our tight-knit trio.

Of course not, but what was I supposed to say? 'Cause you're abandoning me like dad did?' One last shot. My fists tightened. "You're sure you want to do this? I can—"

Her eyes rolled back, going blank. "The universe is calling me," she said in a soft drag. "A flowing connectedness, a consciousness. All things... It's so, so... Oh, E, I wish you could see it."

A call, Vlad. Dammit, whatever it was, it could wait.

Closing my eyes, I squeezed her hand. Mom! This was it. This couldn't be it... Who else did I have? Why was she doing this, leaving me alone. I'd cured aging, cured death, dammit! But it was happening again, just like last time...

The sliding door opened and a cocky, spiky-haired nurse with a *COEXIST* multi-creed tattoo on his hand walked in, smiling as he pulled Mom's notes. "How are you doing, Ms. Anderson?"

Was this clown fucking kidding? My jaw twitched. It was new age idiots like this that convinced people—mainly women, like my fall-for-anything mom—there was nobility in death. There was *nothing* noble about dying. I'd seen hundreds, no, thousands of life donors... nothing *grand* about it. They needed the money, that was it. It was the circle of life, and I'd conquered it, dammit. And it didn't matter...

Mom hadn't said anything for a while, lying in a trance-like stupor. Screw this. "Unhook her!" I commanded in the toughest voice I could muster. My voice broke. "I can't let you do this." My face burned as memories flashed, making me angrier. My eyes even moistened. Would I cry? It'd been decades...

The deadbeat prick had the nerve to smile. "Sorry, sir, nothing we can do. Happens all the time, loved ones, second thoughts..." He shrugged. "She's going to a better place."

These damn Gaia hippies. Fucking Luddites. "I'm going to sue your ass for this. Bankrupt this whole shithole of a scam."

The infuriating nurse said nothing.

Another call from Vlad. I checked Mom's pulse, fifty beats per minute and dropping.

Forty-five. Forty... My body shook. I couldn't do this, couldn't be here, not now.

He called again. Shit, what? Couldn't this wait? At least I could escape for a second.

Gathering myself, I stepped into the hallway, deepening my voice before answering. Vlad couldn't see me like this. 'What?' I snapped. 'I'm kind of busy.'

'We missed him, boss. He got away, Hauser...'

I couldn't deal with this either. 'Goddammit. How? What happened?' How'd those idiots mess this up?

Vlad muttered something about misdirection and outside help. 'We've got his place cased, but...' He shrugged. A missing man in midtown Atlanta... that was worse than a needle in the projects.

Shit, shit, shit. 'Deal with it.' I clicked off. Did I have to do everything myself? Idiots... I slipped back into the miserable room.

The beeping was gone. The EKG had flatlined. I'd missed it. Too late.

Swallowing hard, I batted away the semblance of a tear and headed for the clinic's landing pad. Fuck this place.

Pain is weakness leaving the body.

Pain is weakness leaving the body.

Pain is weakness... Dammit! My knees sagged and I slumped outside the bathroom, slamming my fist into the wall. Mom... Jeez!

She was gone. I was alone.

Alone...

MIKE

"And you're sure this is credible?" I asked, stunned.

The German-looking little fellow in the button-up seated opposite me at the hole-in-the-wall Roasty Toasty cafe nodded, sipping his rum-spiked coffee, despite the hour. He shifted in his seat, green eyes scouring the busy street, hat low over his distinctive face. "I worked there, I saw things."

"And you're prepared to testify?" I asked. "To go on the record?" It was almost too good to be true, *almost*. Like a universe-level intervention.

"Yeah, but I need reassurances, need protection." He swallowed hard, hands fidgeting. He was a fidgetter all right, and it was driving me nuts.

"Of course, of course," I said. The man was overreacting, but that was normal for a whistleblower. "So, tell me again, what happened?"

The skinny guy sat bolt upright. "Did you disable GPS?"

I nodded. Did I look like I was born yesterday?

"Good, sorry. You can't be too careful. So, where to begin?"

By the end, I was on the edge. I hadn't read a thriller this good in years. "You're kidding?" I asked when he finished. "Bribery, blackmail? Do you have proof?" Busting Rodriguez would be icing on the cake, and boy did I love icing, as Jamie could attest.

He shook his head. "Why would I?"

Damn. Made sense. "What about names?" I asked. "Or projects involved?"

Hauser had only watercooler gossip, but it was enough to get started. He ordered another alcoholic pick-me-up and asked again about protection.

"Let me make a few calls. I'll be a minute." I rose and strode out the door, catching Wallace's eye as he nursed a latte. It was sunny and beautiful, Atlanta without the crushing heat. Reggie gave me a look from his table off to the left—better for countersurveillance, or something—but I shook my head, tapping my ear. He snapped back to attention, eyes on Ponce de Leon Avenue.

Who could I trust? If it was as bad as Henrik said, half of Atlanta was on the dole, and tons of politicians. He must be exaggerating... It couldn't be *that* bad.

But where to put the guy? They'd already tried to take me out. And it's not like he could stay at my place... Speaking of, Jamie. A quick check-in. *Hey, Jame, how's it going with you guys?*

I waited. No reply, so I called Jones. No one knew we were connected. 'I need a favor.' I told her everything, the message, the meeting... how we could skewer DDI.

'I'm in,' she said without hesitation as soon as I'd finished, sounding more charged than she had in weeks. 'What do you need?'

Soon it was settled. There was an abandoned house two blocks from hers, a perfect safehouse. Hurrying inside, I paid our bill and ordered a ride. "Time to go." Wallace and Reggie descended, covering both sides, and we jumped into the car the second it reached the curb. Not taking any chances.

"See anyone?" Hauser's eyes flittered between Reggie, Wallace and the windows.

"Nah." Reggie turned again. "Looks like we're clean. To be sure, take us for a spin," he added.

This spy shit was getting old—I'd had enough the last few months to last an enhanced lifetime. We drove past Sam's street and down a small cul-de-sac off Ashby. She stood next to rotten steps leading up to the dilapidated blue house, complete with boarded windows and a standalone green garage. As we hurried inside, she slipped her lock-picks into her pocket, and bolted the door behind us. It was low tech, as was the house: spider webs, plastic-wrapped furniture, and drop-ping-covered cheap laminate. The smell was atrocious.

Sam eyed Hauser. "This is him?"

Hauser's eyes narrowed to match, but he said nothing. Don't bite the hand that feeds you. "Anyone need a drink? Coffee, water?" She offered, as if it were her home and she was being generous.

"I'll take a beer," Hauser said.

Screw it. "I'll have one too." It had been a helluva morning, and it wasn't getting any easier.

"What's the plan?" Reggie asked once she returned, a pair of Millers and three coffees in tow, sipping pitch black with a look of relief. Maybe I should have taken an espresso.

I nodded. "The idea's to catch DDI, and folks they've bribed with their pants down. We're two votes short on the bill, and I'm not sure either will budge." It wasn't worth explaining the intricacies of the Senate, and no one said anything. "If we caught them though, between the leverage and the public outcry, it would be a walk in the park... If we had proof, that is."

"What?" Sam exclaimed, looking between Hauser and me.

We told her, which began a long-winded debate on how best to tie DDI to the wrongdoings.

"We could force a confession," Wallace said.

"Do you know who you're dealing with?" Hauser asked.

"And it wouldn't be admissible," I added. "As much as I'd like to."

Sam stood up, stretching. "How does HSU tie into all this? Shouldn't that be enough?"

Wow, they knew nothing about the law. I shook my head. "Same deal, no proof. We can't prove Anderson, or any of them, knew what the company was engaged in. It's the same reason we couldn't nail them with Toran, the hitman." My stomach seesawed again. I was living on borrowed time.

A notification, Jamie. *All good, Dad. Uncle Joe said not to worry about us.*

That helped. We'd been friends with Craig and Ivy for years, ever since Ava got that job eons ago. At least, if something happened to me, she'd be safe. They were reliable.

"I haven't heard anything on my end either," Sam said. "Couldn't we just—" She froze, eyes widening, looking at Hauser before staring me down.

A subtle shake of my head. *No, I didn't tell him you were a murderer.*

She relaxed, folding her tense body into a ratty chair. And I thought I had demons...

"There is one thing," Hauser said, after finishing his second can. He looked like someone who could handle a few... "I didn't save it, but..." He said some convoluted nonsense about cloning transfusion stem cells.

"English, please," Reggie said with a schoolboy's contempt.

"Oh, sorry," Hauser blushed. "The genomic profile—the DNA—I was working with, it was for third party client—not DDI, off the record. We were trying to make the Qin process work. If we trace the contract—"

The Qin process? Why have I heard of that?

"So, we've got our client," Wallace cut in.

"And proof," Sam added, eyes unsure.

Henrik nodded and tapped his interface, fingers flying through the air. "One second. Proxy tunnels and employee encryption." A pause. "Shit. It's gone, everything." His jaw dropped. "My research, all of it... Everything is gone. But that means..." He swallowed hard. "That means they know."

SAM

The senator ran his hands through his unwashed hair. "Wait, don't you have the files?"

"I do," the little man said. "I was checking the updated versions."

My spine tingled, a sixth sense tuned in Riyadh's winding streets and bazaars. I jumped up. "We need to get out of here!" The others didn't move, faces confused.

"Come on!" I snapped. "If they know about Hauser, DDI will have detected his sign-in location. They'll be suiting up as we speak."

Recognition dawned, and Schmidt's guards reached for their weapons.

"Don't bother," I said. We'd met Vlad's friends a couple of times at a bar north of here and their tats spoke volumes. The regiments they'd served in, the tours they'd done—made Vlad and Boris look like teddy bears.

"What are you saying?" Schmidt asked, hand on the door handle.

"The easiest solution to Ethan's problem—who'd delegate it to Vlad—would be to kill Hauser," I said, mind racing. "I can keep a lookout but—"

"K—Kill?" Henrik interrupted in a shrill voice, stopping dead. "What do you—"

Ignoring the pussy, I grabbed Schmidt's arm, which made Reggie stiffen. "You told him about the assassin? Actually, nevermind. We need to go." My hand went to my gun. Good, still there. I ordered a ride. "You guys coming?"

They plowed after me. Idiot checked his work drive... And he was the one who got paid the big bucks?

Once we'd escaped the neighborhood, we switched cars twice, and continued south to the outskirts, life expectancies dropping with each rundown block, much like the folks we passed.

It was a shitty place, South Atlanta. Dealers lined the corner, jostling with hoes for placement, each fighting to scrape a shell of a living, and escape the slums fate had forced upon them. Even a mile or two north made all the difference. I sighed, but the others—except the senator, who fidgeted in his seat, eyes pained and conflicted—didn't react.

Once we reached Tri-Cities, we were golden. Even Hauser, who'd been bitching the entire time, ran through his data dump. "No matches," he said as we pulled to a stop outside the abandoned roofless high school. "Nothing."

No one said anything. Our surroundings didn't look promising. Neither did our situation, and the scientist's face was crestfallen as the spraypainted rafters dangling from the busted barbed wire beside us.

"Look on the bright side, Henrik," Reggie said with a sarcastic optimism. "You're not dead yet."

"Might as well be," the whiny man replied, face sullen. "Why'd I have to grow a freaking conscience?"

Replaying the murders in my head, I understood. What had I done? Did *I* feel guilty? Was it wrong? Those were good questions I wasn't emotionally equipped to answer. Not now, at least.

A horn honked, and three junkers skidded to a dusty stop. Here comes trouble.

"Hands where I can see 'em!" someone yelled.

MIKE

F our kids stepped forward, each no more than fourteen or fifteen, holding dated guns. The pale lanky one with the pornstar stache pointed at me, leveling his pistol. "You there! Your cash, now."

A sunken-eyed Latino in a Falcons tank top hurried over, raising his weapon, hands trembling. "Do it!"

"Hold on a sec," Sam said. She stepped towards the kid, as did Wallace. This wasn't going to end well...

"Not another inch," the skinny black tomboy hissed. She didn't have a gun, but her pals had the firepower to convey the message. Her bloodshot eyes raked Reggie. "Don't even think about going fer that gun of yours. You either, big guy." She eyed Wallace.

"You don't want to do this," I found myself saying. "There are always other options. Don't do something you'll regret." She was barely older than Jamie. And living on the street...

"Easy for you to say," the emaciated one with pockmarked arms covering Sam retorted. "We ain't born with no silver spoon."

The girl shot me a withering look. "Need food fer a spoon to matter. Transfer what you got, the full cash balance, and we'll let you live."

"Ok." It's not like my mobile account had much.

To my right, Wallace moved. Shit. No… The Latino spun, shaking. *BANG.*

Wallace dropped, shots echoed. Chaos everywhere as guns rattled. What was going on?

Sam's weapon was out in the blink. She aimed, fired.

Bodies flew as I stood there, frozen. Childish screams as both boys collapsed.

My ears rang. The girl turned to run. No!

A shriek. She crashed to the pavement, clutching her chest, face smashing into the concrete with a bone crunching *crack.*

There was blood everywhere. My heart was racing. No one moved…

It was all over.

What the fuck just happened?

The sidewalk was a regular inner-city crimson canvas.

I thought we were the 'good guys'…

ETHAN

"What do you mean we lost him?" I flung the dumbbell at the wall and the fifty-pounder crashed to the padded floor in a cloud of drywall, a gaping dent next to the climbing wall. This wasn't how it was supposed to go. Everything had been shit since the clinic.

Five hours. Hauser had been loose for five freaking hours. Who knew what kind of damage he'd already caused. "And we know he's with Schmidt?" I asked to distract myself from Mom's lifeless eyes. Nothing was going my way, and my own employees were turning against me.

Vlad nodded, grimacing as he avoided looking at the wall or asking about Mom. "Probably. Our guys arrived fifteen minutes after he accessed our servers. There was no one, just a foreclosed shit hole north of West End."

Grabbing the pair of weights, I started my next set. I was fine dammit. Why was he looking at me like that? "And?"

He shrugged, looking down. "No idea. We're running down possible leads with transit, but you know how Tesla is... so much data. And that's not including scooters or Waymo."

He was right. It was borderline impossible. Pushing out the last few reps with that prick doctor's face in my head, I said, "Why hasn't he made demands?" I should have canned his ass years ago. Was I losing my edge?

My forearms strained as I imagined choking the life out of that backstabbing bastard.

I'm fine, dammit.

* * *

Bee dee dee dee.

Dammit. Freaking alarm. Blinking, I opened my eyes. It was so comfortable. Not today...

I turned over in my king-sized sleeping pod, thinking of Mom, grabbing the pillow. Ashes, ashes, we all fall down. My five a.m. alarm buzzed again, but I closed my eyes.

Not today, not today. It was all pointless anyway. Let someone else deal with it.

* * *

What a trainwreck of a night. I stood straighter, eyeing my annoying Board, holos assembled around La Chance, my ever-evolving bean bag laden creativity room which could go from Borneo to Burma without warning. It was Christ the Redeemer at the moment, ironic to say the least. At least mom hadn't gone Catholic. No one had so much as asked about her. Cowards.

'Where are we at on the SLI deal?' Collins asked. The ancient shark smelled blood, and a safe exit for her fund. Given the current political landscape, I couldn't blame her. But I did. She didn't trust me, none of them did. But this was my ship, dammit.

"I had a call yesterday with Lee," I said evenly. They were testing me, but I had supervoting shares. Question was, should I use them?

'You know what we'd recommend, Ethan.' Ha Eun eyed my scruffy face, not a fan of my new look. 'We should cut our losses and merge.'

'Damn, Ethan!' Nancy Collins snapped. 'Don't let your ego get in the way. There's a future with SLI, look how the winds are blowing.

There's serious push behind this senate bill.' Several Board members nodded agreement. They were all quite vested in the company, none more so than Nancy. But it was my company, not Lee's. And they were all turning on me.

I cleared my throat to buy time. It was a lot of money and it means I could be done with the whole bullshit industry. But it wouldn't bring back mom or Bobby. Why did people choose to die? And it was Sun Lee, dammit. "The writing's not on the—" A loud knock on the door. Now what? "Come in."

It was Jones, her face beet red like she'd run a 10k. "Vlad says they found him."

Well, hot damn. Thank you, Jones. "This meeting is adjourned." I cut the Board's connection before they could protest. "Tell me."

MIKE

I couldn't believe it. All those kids, dead, and Wallace... We'd dropped him at Amazon Med, and checked him into Urgent Care. His wife, Emily, was frantic when I called. She'd left the kids with their aunt, breaking all speed records to get there.

It was a long night, but doctors said he'd make it.

Sam had been the one to suggest the Motel 6. It's not like I could go home... And she had to work.

The three of us sat in the slinky motel room around the uneven table, sipping much-needed shit coffee. We had a plan, of sorts, if you called using Hauser as bait, a plan.

"So, tell me again why it needs to be me?" Henrik asked for at least the fifth time, staring into his mug. The murky reflection didn't seem to be helping him.

Reggie didn't bother answering, and neither did I.

Acid guilt poisoned my gut. Those kids had been right—privilege. I'd been lucky, they hadn't. It was as stupid and simple as that. They didn't even have a dive of a joint like this to live in. Who wouldn't try drugs? And Big Pharma sure made them addictive enough.

I sighed. We'd need more than luck to pull this off. Even Reggie—

the consummate, if sarcastic, optimist—had serious doubts. It would come down to Sam, the insider

A buzz. It was a message from Sam.

They leaned closer.

Anderson's thinking of paying off Henrik. Call him to get the ball rolling.

I told the others and Hauser winced but said nothing. He was out of options.

A quick call to check on Jamie. No answer. My stomach lurched. Was she fine?... *Busy, dad,* she replied. Seconds later, *At the Braves game.*

Dammit, Craig. I'd told him to stay home, but he had a soft spot for his hometown team, and they were playing the Mets. It wasn't safe. Both Craig and Ivy spoiled their almost-daughter. I'd talk to Ivy later. At least I could reason with her.

For Craig, life was a game, competitive, the occasional elbow, nothing worse than a scrape or missed shot entering his innocent mind. I missed those simple days on the courts under the noon sun as we clashed and posted up. We'd been a good team.

Reggie tapped my shoulder. "Mike, what do you think?"

Had I been daydreaming?

"They're willing to meet," Reggie said. "Tomorrow morning, seven a.m. Stone Mountain. He wants Henrik to sign a few things to have leverage on him."

Tomorrow? Already? Was this really happening? "We need to talk to Sam."

"Yeah, Sam," Henrik said, as if any delay would do. Reminded me of a jittery squirrel.

She was on until eight tonight. "She should get back here to go over things." I stood, pacing the dinky joint. "Reg, know anyone who could help?" If Anderson tried anything, we'd need backup. And please don't ask me to use a gun.

"Give me a couple hours." The big man headed out to make some calls, tapping his ear as he went.

Shit was about to get real.

SAM

'Okay, we'll do it. Seven am, northern entrance to Stone Mountain. No funny business.' Ethan clicked off a moment later and turned to Vlad who'd been plugged in from his rotating command pod. "It's done."

Did they know I'd turned? They couldn't, could they?

"Jones," Ethan said, "coordinate with Gonzalez. We need to land at six forty."

I nodded. Don't say something stupid... "Anything else, sir?"

Ethan looked at Vlad, and back at me. He shook his head, but said nothing, brow furrowed in a complicated expression I couldn't read. Crap. Why was he such a mask? "On it." Were they onto me? Was it coincidence they sent me out?

My mind spun as I hurried from the comms center toward the elevator. The lift opened and Boris and Gonzalez stepped out, expressions dark. I took a step back. Shit.

Footsteps down the hall.

It was always going to end like this.

I went for my gun.

MIKE

Where the heck was Sam? I checked the time again. Eight thirty p.m. She was clockwork normally.

A call came in, a username I didn't recognize. The others jumped, the room dead silent as I tapped my ear. A hurried conversation. Not good.

I fought to keep my eyes from floating to Hauser.

So much for well-laid plans...

* * *

It was a misty, eerie morning of hoots and animal sounds as we huddled in the dark forest of oak, elm, and little else, feet scrunching pine needles as we paced. Reggie's guys arrived an hour before the meet—two guys and a chick he'd known in the Rangers. All three—including Reg—wore patterned camo, AKs at their sides, and paint under their eyes. Graphenite vests and hunting knives at the hip completed the Rambo getup. Even I had a Glock, but the safety was on. How he'd talked me into it was beyond me.

"You'll rendezvous with Anderson at the old railroad station," Reggie was saying. We'd been over this before. Reggie's crew would have us surrounded, and in theory, protected. The chasm in my stomach wasn't so sure, and it was winning.

If I was worried, Henrik was a wreck. Reg had given him a joint on the ride over to "take the edge off." It was working, but barely. Hauser shivered beneath a concealed graphenite vest, rubbing his exposed neck like he'd nicked himself shaving. "How do we know they won't shoot—"

"They won't," Reggie said without much conviction. "Besides, we're filming the whole thing."

Wouldn't be much saving grace for the researcher, but it would serve its purpose. I shuddered. Was I that callous? No... "I'll go with you," I volunteered, surprising myself.

Reggie pulled me aside. "Mike, after all we been through—"

I cut him off. "No chance." He shrugged, and his guys got into position, ghosting into the trees with little more than a crackle.

Thirty minutes.

Were Ethan's men already here? And what happened to Sam?

Henrik looked at me, eyes beyond wide. Was I *that* pale?

What had I signed up for? I touched the Glock shoved into my waistband.

Oh my god, Jamie.

Was this thing loaded?

* * *

A black VTOL streaked in from the darkening north as rain clouds threatened, touching down in a small field overlooking the murky pond at three minutes to seven. Two heavies hopped out, weapons leveled, clearing the area. One wrong move...

A second later, DDI's towering owner emerged, stretching and looking around. He leaned towards one of the men and said something. The man nodded, pointing towards the old railroad and the trio set off, heading towards us.

The forest was quiet and ominous, a stark contrast to my hammering heart.

"Senator?" Ethan said in surprise as we came into view on the elevated wooden platform, quaint yellow station building covering our backs. "Fancy seeing you here."

"Anderson," I hissed. A tingle shot down my spine. One way or another, it ended now.

"Traitor." Ethan glared at Hauser with a lion's disdain, rippling forearms ready to maul him. "I always knew it'd be you, Hauser. What do you want? Money, power, immortality...? How about fifty million?"

Henrik's eyes ballooned. *Hold on there, cowboy.* We hadn't expected near as much. He could ruin everything.

I clapped my hand hard on his shoulder and Hauser jumped. Twin rifles spun towards. "No sudden movements," a thick voice rasped.

"It's over, Ethan," I said.

The billionaire laughed, sounding nothing like a Bond villain. "Because we're surrounded? Your men going to close in?"

Something in his voice terrified me and I hesitated. Did he know? No... he couldn't.

A man stepped forward, raising his visored assault helmet, weapon at his side. Hair cascaded down, and she smiled.

My jaw dropped. Hauser did a double-take.

Fuck. It was Sam.

She'd betrayed us... "You bring the shovels, Boris?"

ETHAN

I smirked at the pair, puffy clothes making it obvious they wore graphenite. As if that would help. "Bring them out, Vlad." My hand floated to the gun at my belt. Vlad had been giving me lessons since Cape Town, not that I'd need it today.

One by one, a series of shrubs waded towards us, Schmidt's B-level guards walking before them, hands in the air, weaponless. The flowing green strands of Vlad's near-invisible Ghillie suits waved in the wind with an unsettling *whoosh*.

One of the bushes raised its arms, removing the alien hood. "We detected five cameras as well. Looks like those detectors came in handy after all, Jones."

Veins twitched in Schmidt's neck, mouth agape. He clenched fists as I stepped forward, patting him on the shoulder. I laughed. "Better luck next time." I wanted no part of what happened next, and turned for the ship. "I'll see you back at the compound." Next time, bring your A-game.

Vlad nodded, double-checking the silencer on his pistol.

Two birds, one stone. Today was going to be a good day. I'd break out the Dom Perignon. Some occasions demanded a bit of bubbly.

"Freeze, Ethan. Don't move." It was Jones, her gun was leveled at my head.

What the fuck? Was this a joke?

Everyone froze, Jones' finger on the trigger. A raw hate glinted in her eyes. Was this it?

The clearing had gone dead silent, even the birds.

SAM

Ethan's face soured. "What the hell are you—"

"Shut up. Vlad, order your men to stand down." My heart hammered. Six-to-one... These were terrible odds. Why the hell didn't Reggie bring more guys? "Don't make me fucking do it."

"Jones, what are you doing?" Vlad's gun twitched as he yelled in more than a whiff of Russian.

"Jones," Ethan said. "I can make you rich beyond your—"

Money, like money could bring back my family... I stepped closer, lifting the barrel to Ethan's chin. "Tell me about HSU!" Vlad's men had lowered their weapons, but remained rigid and ready. One slip-up, and I was a dead. "Tell me everything."

No one moved or said a word.

No one so much as breathed.

Ethan broke the cutting silence. "What does that have to do—"

"You killed my daughter," I whispered. "My husband too."

Ethan did a double-take. "Your daughter?"

"You despicable fuck."

"Ohhh." Recognition flashed in his wide eyes. He bit his lip. "HSU?" He didn't wait for my reply. "Shit!"

Movement to my right. I pulled a second weapon and leveled it at

Boris. "Don't!" He froze. "I'll put a bullet in both your heads if I have to. Toss it to Reggie."

A moment's hesitation. It all came down to this.

Time died in the staredown. A gun clattered to the ground and shattered the stillness. Another, another. Reggie's speechless men looked dumbstruck. "Hurry up!" I snapped. They leapt to life and rounded up the weapons. "Check for spares." My eyes hadn't left Ethan for a second and he glared back, sizing up his options.

I took a step back towards safety and stumbled. Ethan sprang, tackling me to the ground. Powerful hands crushed my throat as my elbow pummeled his temple, stunning him. A palm strike demolished his nose as Boris surged. Reggie fired a warning shot, and everyone stiffened. He wrenched a bloodied Ethan off me as his crew shoved the unarmed prisoners into a small circle.

"It's over," I said at last. "So, HSU?"

Ethan clenched his pouring nose and walked me through the ins and outs. "Not that you can prove anything," he added with a confident snarl. "We weren't involved, not in the day to day at least. We'd send special cases their way, stuff like that. But what's it matter, what's the point?"

"Wouldn't that make you complicit in her daughter's murder?" the senator—who'd been quiet for some time—asked.

"What's done is done!" Ethan snapped. "I can't change the past. And besides, you have nothing, no proof."

I smiled. "If you taught me one thing, Ethan, it's to *always* have a backup plan." I tapped my ear. "We scanned *them* for mics and cameras, but this confession should do."

His mouth opened, closed, and opened again. "Shit!"

MIKE

"So, here's what you're looking at in terms of options," the blond district attorney with the people's chin and prosecutor's poise said. Ethan was seated across from the DA and I in his orange jumpsuit, hands chained to the heavy wooden table in the center of the bone-bare interrogation cell with the one-way mirror behind us. I fought the urge to smile, if not laugh. Karma's a bitch, *bitch*.

"You can work with us; cut a deal and skip prison time in exchange for testifying," the DA continued, outlining the spiel we'd perfected earlier. "You'll get off on house arrest, or a few months in a low-security facility. That, or you're looking at at least twenty-to-thirty. Two counts of espionage and attempted murder, five of illegal cloning, sanctioned genetic material licensing, and a litany of other charges."

If Hauser's list was even half true, we were looking at the biggest case of corporate bribery in history, some forty-odd senators and congressmen on the dole. It'd be a landmark case. Ramsey knew what it'd do for his career. So did I...

"Can you at least get these off me." Ethan shook the cuffs for emphasis with the scorn of someone used to getting their way.

"One thing at a time," Ramsey replied with a smirk. He was enjoying this too. "Do we have a deal?"

"I want zero jail time and the ability to sell my shares before the news hits," Ethan demanded.

Ramsey gave me a sideways look. Was he getting off *that* easy? It was a big case though, a lot at stake. I nodded.

It was a deal I could live with. We'd break it to Sam later. "You've got a deal."

* * *

Reggie and I slumped out of the lift to my door, exhausted. It was only ten p.m., but it had been a hell of a few weeks. The door opened.

"Hey, Dad, hey, Reg." Jamie was curled in her favorite chair, but quit whatever she'd been doing. "How'd it go today?"

Like hell. What had we been thinking? If I never saw the inside of another courtroom, I'd be a happy man. "We'll get convictions. But it will take time."

"It's all over the news. So is your bill. When's the vote?" Teenagers... they never paid attention. It's all we'd been talking about for at least two weeks.

"Next Tuesday," I said. Dang, I needed another coffee. That'd make seven today.

Jamie went back to whatever she was doing, and Reggie blended something gross. I grabbed a seat alongside Jamie and checked my messages. It had been a constant stream since teaming up with the DA. Ramsey's people were thorough. A good thing too, I was never a details person.

A message from Sam. *WTF! He's getting off clean? We need to meet ASAP.*

I sighed. Knew that was coming. Why the media couldn't keep things under wraps was beyond me. Good for nothing vultures.

* * *

W hat the— My eyes blinked open. Where was I? Sam's daughter, I had to help her... She was... What was going on?

Jamie grabbed my arm. "Come on, Dad, let's get you to bed."

Was I dreaming? It had felt so—Jamie dragged me down the hall. When did the apartment get so big? Where was I?

I collapsed into bed.

ETHAN

I closed my eyes. This wasn't happening.

The Board was meeting in-person for the first time in ages. And Lee was here, polluting DDI's executive suite with his mere presence, an army of advisors at his heel. We were all seated around the Old Hickory, the massive oval table that served as our nerve center. The gleaming views of Atlanta's towering skyline did little to brighten my mood, as, on all sides, thirty-some-odd men and women gambled the future of my empire.

"All in favor of the sale?" Collins asked. She'd assumed the Chair after I'd been arrested, citing provision 27.1. Her first order of business, recapping the company and eliminating my super-voting shares. I was an employee now, nothing more. A bloody employee! After all I'd done for this company, for this industry... Sure, I owned twenty percent, but I was at the mercy of shareholders, and the Board. And the acquisition...

One by one, they raised their hands. It was a horrible deal, a fraction of what DDI was worth. Lee had decreased his offer twice since the initial proposal. It was pennies on the dollar, at best. But Collins and the rest didn't care, not after news of bribery broke. The stock had tanked. Who could blame the markets? I'd sold too, the fifty percent

Ramsey and I had agreed on. Ten billion was a decent-enough retirement sum, I guess.

The motion passed and Lee gave me a smirk, the same off-the-boat ugly he'd given me all those years ago in Chem. But he was my boss now. Only thing left was the paperwork. Fucking paperwork...

How had things gone so wrong?

Fuck Jones too. I'd deal with that bitch later, somehow.

SAM

Tuesday morning was an early one with little sleep, despite the king-sized Marriott comfort. It all came down to today's vote, and while Schmidt assured me things would work out, I'd be happier once it was over.

Over? A strange thought... Could something like this ever be over? Was this how the Germans felt after the Holocaust; Truman after Nagasaki? How do you live with something like that?

In reality, it's not like it mattered, everything we'd fought for. If the US banned LE, elites would go overseas. It was better than nothing though. My mind raced, bouncing off cookie-cutter perfect Executive Plus white walls. I had to get out of this upscale IKEA prison. A run?

Slipping on shorts and my trainers, I headed for the sparkling lobby complete with chandeliers, emerging into the chaos of Capitol Hill. Fancy suits bustled and news VTOLs hovered over the center of American law and order. The energy was electric, the air humid. It was odd there were no drones, but this was DC. Airspace regs.

A shirtless whacko on the corner of Independence and 4th held a crumpled sign, resting his tired lungs as he eyeballed me. *The reckoning is upon us. God will judge ye sinners.* Pushing past Agers, Catholics, and various screaming protesters for and against LE, I stepped over a pile of dogshit. Or was that human? Two guys begging for coke wrestled another with a *Schmidt for President* sign. Just another day in America.

After arriving three days ago, I'd spent two exploring. It'd been a while since I'd been to DC—a Senate hearing on embryo enhancement where clueless farts had tried to grill Ethan. A lot had changed. Schmidt had taken me a few places, but in general, been busy, a celebrity amongst gold diggers. Everyone wanted a piece.

After the third *Schmidt for Pres* sign, I stopped. Was *that* possible? He hadn't said anything. I'd have to ask. A lot was riding on this vote.

Schmidt had tried to get me access to the Capitol Building, but I'd been turned down thanks to my history with DDI. Oh well.

I headed into a small cafe beloved by staffers, The Grind, known for counterculture coffee, avocado omelets, and Microdosed Mondays, a blend of Arabic, Lion's Mane, and half-a-gram of inspired psilocybin. Settling into a Burning-Man booth in the corner, I grabbed a tall black, and opened the news, waiting. Proceedings were set to start at noon. But what else was I going to do?

A Times story about the EU caught my eye. *German-English Alliance to Follow Schmidt's Lead Banning LE.* I skimmed the article.

Was this serious? According to the BBC, approval ratings for LE had plummeted the past six months throughout the remaining EU. Even serious talk about banning it in France and Italy as well, despite their separatism and tourist industries. Malea always wanted to visit Paris... I missed her. My stomach scar tingled.

What would I do when this was all over? I'd been asking myself since Ethan's arrest. Who was I? Did I have a purpose? Me, a fucking midlife crisis...

My mind flashed to Veronica. I hadn't found much. Her address in New York was a front, and even Ethan hadn't known much about her, at least according to the DA. And Ethan, damn... No jail time! Total bullshit.

A notification: it was starting. The ugly-carpeted semi-circular chamber came into view, a hundred of the most powerful elites in America seated around a podium where the Senate chaplain and presiding officer posed alongside the flag like actors in some play.

A bell rang three times, announcing the quorum. The chaplain stepped forward to lead the congregation in prayer. Really? The Pledge of Allegiance too? A little quaint, don't you think? But government was anything but innovative.

Stay positive. This is what you've been waiting for.

Should have got the spiked coffee.

Schmidt said this would work. It had to.

MIKE

At last, it was time.

Months of hard work and grinding, of shaken hands and sordid offers, of blackmailing and blue balling until the cows came out to pasture.

Standing amidst my fellow senators, I went to the rostrum to make the formal announcement. This was it, my big moment, the start of something new... Everything was riding on this vote. Would we pull through?

I made my opening arguments, sweat dripping down my spine before I opened the floor.

Time flew, and before I knew it, both sides had spoken. It was time, and each representative voiced their vote.

Then, it was over, approved, 56-44.

I couldn't believe it. And onto the next order of business, a bill addressing rising housing costs and the need for government intervention.

It was surreal. But there wasn't a moment to celebrate, wheels of democracy hurrying on. History waited for no man.

When we broke session, reporters cluttered the exits, lining the Capitol's sweeping staircase in a gauntlet of gotchas, a piece of meat dangled before rabid hounds. And some of these jokers were vicious... But we owed the public a photo op, an image to commemorate the occasion. "Senator Schmidt, Senator Schmidt! How does it feel to be—"

"Are you running for President?" another pushy reporter cut in. More voices yelled.

From amidst the masses, someone said, "Are you the next Lincoln?"

It all woozed over me as another voice yelled: "What'll happen to—"

"Are you worried about—"

Everything melded together, the noise overwhelming. If I could just turn back, become a nobody once more.

Reggie and an army of cops marched through the reporters and milling crowds. Signs everywhere praised and condemned our efforts, some more colorful than others. Some bearded religious group in tunics cheered our pro-life stance while a firebrand preacher with the devil's tongue shrieked about the evils of ending LE, proclaiming my eternal damnation.

A path cleared, and we slipped into the waiting car, my heart thundering, sweating despite the weather. Reggie slammed the door, and wheels screeched as we pulled away.

"Damn," Reggie murmured.

I nodded. Damn, indeed. We'd done it. I was lost for words.

And so, the world changed. At least our world, at least a little. But the law wouldn't go into effect until the following year. Moving a fat-ass bureaucracy like the US government took time, but that didn't stop markets slashing the leading LE companies. Beyond Human folded within the month, and DDI completed its shitty merger with Shanghai-based rival SLI not long after. I'd pay to see the look on Anderson's face.

The economy was in turmoil, but also booming with a strange optimism I hadn't expected. Economists said it helped the EU put a similar proposal on the ballot. Plus according to Phil, my investment guy, there were no more "safe bets" to park your money, "outside of

Asia." And while China was booming, I, like most capitalists, had a healthy skepticism of centralized economies. Then again, look how well we did running things...

* * *

We zipped along North Ave back to the office, a full slate of meetings for the afternoon. Atlanta was healing. Only a few hundred homeless on the ride over and half as many tents. Without the prospect of donoring, folks were forced to choose between life and death. And while there'd been a string of suicides, on net, things were improving.

If only I could say the same about Jamie... I had to get my mind off her, which got harder every day. How could so many specialists fail so spectacularly? At least there hadn't been any symptoms, not yet. She was as vibrant and active as ever.

The car pulled into the underground lot. Let's see, Chang. I flipped through the slides Reggie had prepared on the young interim mayor. Tech grad, former city councilman, engineer by trade. He even volunteered at the local shelter. Patrick Chang had all the makings of a promising mayor, and with the rushed pseudo-national elections to fill the many vacancies our convictions—which the media had taken to calling the "Purge"—had created, the typical heavy hitters hadn't had the time and resources to make their campaigning count. We should do this more often.

Chang had potential.

* * *

"Thanks for taking the time," Chang said. The tall, dark-haired Asian man stood, extending a hand and welcoming me into my own waiting area. "I was a little early."

We'd met twice before, Chang and I. He wore his signature slacks and polo, but it was obvious from how he carried himself and his lack of a finessed swagger, he was anything but a golfer. "I know you have been busy, Senator. I won't take much of your time, your upcoming campaign and all..."

I was tempted to roll my eyes. The press had been saying for weeks I'd throw my hat in, but I had no interest in the presidency or the shenanigans that came with it. "What can I do for you?" I asked.

He pulled out a list—*a handwritten list*—and ticked off items. By the end, we'd covered affordable housing, inner-city schools, Mayor Rodriguez's shady Russian dealings and the slew of blackmarket clinics popping up. I thought of HSU and Sam's crusade, but said nothing. Nobody could know about that, nobody.

It was a productive meeting, but my alarm buzzed. "Sorry, Pat, I've got an eleven o'clock."

Chang rose, thanked me with a two-handed shake and headed for the door. Two minutes later, Sims—one of Reggie's guys from the meeting with Ethan, and Wallace's replacement while he was on the mend—opened the door. "Should I let them all in, sir?"

Sir... I'd have to break that habit. Wait, "all" of them? "What happened to Senator Kealoha?" This was supposed to be about her drug reform bill. We were a dozen votes short.

"She's here," the ex-forward from UGA who'd been a jump shot from getting drafted said, adjusting his unfamiliar cuffs. He was new and didn't realize I could give a damn about dress code.

"Oh, open up!" snapped an unfamiliar voice. "We won't bite, Michael."

Michael? Only a handful of people—The door opened and six suited heavy-hitters entered.

Shit. "I'm not interested."

"Michael, it's been too long." The DNC Chairman hustled over.

* * *

"Y̲ou can't be serious. Me?" My voice was off as I struggled to breathe and avoid hyperventilating. Gabby had set me up, ambushing me with half the Democrat brass and a marching band in tow. "You want me to run?"

Finnegan nodded, vibrant Irish fervor of his forebearers alive and well in his sparkling green eyes, the perfect fit to his light gray Hugo Boss and sharp features. "You're a shoo-in. The president's been a lame duck for three years and she knows it. She's on board," he said with a dealmaker's flourish, little hands anything but small. "Your convictions have driven her approval ratings through the roof, and three-quarters of the bastards you nailed were Republican or Independents. We can do some real good if we control the House and Senate."

I didn't say anything, buckling under their collective gaze. It was quite the assault team they'd put together, senior statesmen and youngblood alike.

They *really* wanted this.

"Think of the housing and work initiatives you were telling me about," Senator Kealoha cut in.

What was her role in all this? She was off to the back a ways, so it couldn't be prominent. Could it? No yoga pants this time. Too bad. "Can I get you folks some coffee?" I asked, to buy time.

"Are you hearing what we're saying?" the chairman asked, putting his arm around me. "Chance of a lifetime. We need you, Michael. The country needs you."

I said the first thing that came to mind, "I have to talk to my daughter."

"Of course, of course," Finnegan said with a patronizing smile.

Whispers and handshakes all around. They thought I was kidding. I didn't care.

They left not long after, after discussing logistics, gossip, and all manner of political underpinnings. When they closed the door behind them, I sank onto the floor, ignoring my cluttered desk and busier mind. Was there no rest of the weary?

Was I *seriously* considering? I'd seen the before and after pictures. But Mr. President had a nice ring to it.

President Schmidt...

What about Jamie?

ETHAN

House arrest I could tolerate, but watching Sun Lee and SLI dismantle everything I'd worked for... I crushed another set of bench presses, Boris sweating above me as I blasted a fifteen rep personal best, fuming. They'd abandoned me, everyone. At least Jones had the decency to confront me. The rest were vultures, swooping in for the kill.

In the end, we sold for ten percent of our cap, a measly sixty billion. The sharks in Shanghai must be licking their lips, buying assets at a frenetic pace. Four-month timeline didn't help.

Worst of all, Schmidt was running for president. Bastard was a lock. Polls had him at seventy-five percent, other candidates toying with the remaining twenty-five. No one thought there'd be any contest, and they weren't wrong. An effing victory lap.

"Where do we stand on tracking down Jones?" While Schmidt would get away with it, there wasn't a chance in hell Jones would. Sure, she had some diplomatic cover, but the public were oblivious. And I was marked man.

Ratting on forty-nine elected officials, that was a record. Each had a score to settle after wrist-slap sentences. I'd doubled security in the past two months, and doubled it again to be safe. But they were politicians anyways, their bark much worse than their bite.

Boris' eyes flashed. "Nothing so far, sir!" It was personal for him too, he'd been bested, and knew it. "We'll find that bitch," he said through gritted teeth.

We freaking better. "Check with our contacts in Chinese Intelligence. And ask Sun's people." Maybe that two-bit bastard could be good for something after all.

Two more months of this shit. Two months, and I was out of here.

What then?

I had nothing left... Maybe that was a good thing.

SAM

It'd been harder and harder to get ahold of Schmidt after the bill passed. Between 60 Minutes, CNN, FOX... he'd been everywhere. I couldn't blame him. But despite everything, I was empty inside. The void hadn't filled or dulled, not an ounce. Malea was still gone, Daron too. No amount of legislation could change that.

I slipped into a toity restaurant with lacy tables and azaleas as the door opened. My quarry, Felipe Mendoza checked his shoulder before hurrying on. Felipe was ex-DDI—in their R&D department, and had come into a great deal of money after the merger, at least according to colleagues. He arrived at work the last day in a personal VTOL and cleaned out his desk, leaving with the haughty air of someone who'd cheated the system, and won.

If it wasn't for the melancholy depression that had driven me to their corporate headquarters that fateful day, I wouldn't have found him.

We'd slayed the beast, but my enemy had sprouted another head and disappeared into the shadows. Rumors of HSU and others like it cropped up daily. Hence why I was here, following the stumpy researcher as he snuck through spraypainted, trash-laden alleys of Atkin Parks' old industrial area. He rounded the corner, and I reversed my dual-sided jacket, popping a Braves cap on my head. Shoving hands into my pockets, I hurried after him.

In the middle of the alley, Mendoza swiped a scanner, slipping into a recessed doorway eerily similar to HSU's last location. I waited, having learned my lesson. If there weren't armed guards and security systems lacing this place—maybe the entire street—I'd be stunned.

But interrogating Mendoza was my best bet at unearthing HSU's inner workings. He'd had an old brick townhouse in posh Ansley Park, but upgraded a month ago to a beautiful Midtown penthouse not too dissimilar to Schmidt's: armed guards, secure parking, and not a chance in hell of me getting access. Something was up.

I backtracked to a small cafe with a view of the entrance to wait. It was two p.m. How long would he stay?

* * *

It took five hours, but three espressos and a cheap sandwich later, he appeared, walking fast. I tapped my bill, and rose. I'd ditched the hat and changed earlier in Le Paris's cramped bathroom. The wannabe-French owner with the twang of a Scot had given me a funny look, but said nothing. He waved as I left, but I didn't break stride. A good thing too, because a car rolled to the curb.

I grabbed an e-scooter, paying with a swipe, and hopped on. Should be fine. Only a few miles. Gripping the handlebar, I zipped off, one of many fleeing the corporate rat race that defined our world.

Catching up on tenth, I tailed him for blocks. No luck. He didn't stop, and proceeded to his underground parking lot. Reinforced gates closed in a flash as I sized up the lofty highrise, a burly pair watching me from behind bulletproof glass in the sparkling lobby. No chance. Secondary guards lined reception. But I was getting closer...

Tomorrow, I told myself, if he didn't re-emerge tonight. No more waiting.

I *had* to do something.

* * *

I   t was a long night, and a short one, little more than a wink.
            Coffee fixed that.
            Back at Mendoza's at seven. I didn't have to wait long.
Another coffee and some cheap artificial eggs later, he appeared. Interesting. Early riser for a Saturday.

Dressed in denims and an AiDC shirt, he crossed the street,
headed toward me. Was my cover blown? My pulse quickened.

At the last second, he passed my stool, and grabbed one by the
pastry shelf. He grabbed the sugar-free OJ pitcher with the Save the
Dolphins sticker and poured himself a glass. Adjusting my seat, I had
the perfect vantage of the India-inspired cafe, pictures of Krishna,
Hindu gods, and yogis lining the tan walls.

"The usual?" a young aproned girl at the counter with enough
flour on her face to be the owner asked.

He nodded. "Thanks, Izzy."

She reached for silverware on the hooks above her. "Nearly ready,
saw you coming. How's the new job?" The blonde flipped the green
naancake, and broke three real brown eggs on top, yolks sizzling
approval. Weird.

The researcher looked at his hands. "All good. You know how it is."

Izzy rolled busy eyes. "You never tell me anything. How long you
been coming here?"

I leaned forward, feigning interest in my near-empty plate. Neither
noticed.

"It's different," Mendoza said at last, "more experimental."

She slid the strange dish over as the espresso machine activated
with a nutty kick.

"Not sure about the boss yet," he added. "Meeting her Monday.
I've heard... things."

My shoulders stiffened. It couldn't be.

"Show her that Latin smile of yours," Izzy said. "I'm sure the
ladies love it."

Mendoza shrugged, looking at the girl when she turned away,
longing in his dark eyes. So that's why he came here. Poor kid.

Another patron entered, and soon Mendoza and I were forgotten, the unnatural redhead cooking up a storm until help arrived.

Felipe finished his meal and left soon after, no longer of interest to his crush. I waited thirty seconds, and followed. Choices... Confront him, or wait for a possible meeting with Veronica? But they'd meet at the office...

He headed for Piedmont Park, hands in his pockets, whistling a doleful tune. Not quite happy go lucky... A man walking his Rottweiler by the entrance to the park made Mendoza jump. We locked eyes at twenty yards. Shit.

"Do I know you?" he asked.

I strode forward. Decision time. I was getting sloppy.

His eyes narrowed. "Hey, you're the same—"

"Shhh." A finger to my lips. "They're watching us, watching you."

He took a step back, eyes wide. "What? Who?"

"HSU," I said in a hushed voice. "Follow me." I led him past the one pristine public bathroom in Midtown, along the farmer's market path where hippies were setting up stands. One love, and organic and all that. At least they provided some cover. Here goes nothing.

"Who are you?"

"Agent Smith," I lied. "Department of National Security."

He turned white, freezing in the middle of the jogging path, almost knocking a pair of bikers over. They yelled a few choice words. "Wh— what do you want with me?"

"It's about your new employer." Where was I going with this? "If you cooperate, I might be able to get you off without prison time."

He quivered, raising his shaking hands. "Prison, who said anything about—"

This might work... "I need you to tell me everything you know about Health Services Unlimited. You help me, and I'll put in a good word with my boss."

"I, I just started there." Sounded like he might pee himself. "Check with your people. I—"

I put a reassuring hand on his shoulder, and tears came pouring.

He told me everything. "I'll give back the bonus, get you a client list, anything…"

Some people were such suckers. Especially men. "That's a good start. Here's what we're going to do."

* * *

Over the next two days, Mendoza fed me what little he had on HSU: his nondescript work contract, contacts within the company, even a few names he'd on next week's schedule: two congressmen and some ambassador whose name escaped him. HSU was alive and well, as was the demand from its influential patrons.

But I was interested in Veronica, the mastermind behind it. He was meeting her Monday, a brief midmorning before jetting off who knows where. This was my last chance. The hackers I'd hired couldn't make heads or tails about her. And according to Felipe, the lab was locked down tight: "as Fort Knox."

I pushed my half-eaten plate to the end of our chromed booth. The Shack did a decent burger—even for lab-grown—but I wasn't in the mood. We'd picked the 80's diner for its solidarity, near-empty until at least five p.m. Once Mendoza finished off his grain-free BLT, I asked, "Could you get her to meet out of the office? Maybe lunch, or something?"

He shook his head, wiping salty crumbs from his mouth. "I don't have any way to contact her. And I doubt she'd change her plans." His eyes flicked to the neon door every time it opened.

A pair of punk teens in all black walked in, and he relaxed, slumping in relief.

So, Veronica? It came down to how to confront her. The more personal, the harder it would be. But I wanted to see her eyes, let her know I'd bested her, make her feel what so many of her victims had… I wanted that bitch to suffer.

But how bad did I want that? Enough to risk success?

"Okay, here's what we're going to do." I outlined a plan.

MIKE

If someone told me a year ago I'd be at Stanford University debating Henrietta Marks, the staunch conservative, pro-life advocate who'd passed bills in her home state of Utah banning in-vitro fertilization and leading Republican primaries, I'd have called bullshit. Me? Yeah right.

The hard-nose righty moderator, some political anchor from CNN, turned the question to me. Here we go... The auditorium was packed, and everything would be broadcast globally. Hundreds of millions tuning in or catching newscaster breakdowns... *no pressure.*

I braced myself on the all-too-small black podium, conscious of copious makeup and bright lights blanketing my sweaty face as the sharp-eyed African-American senator—and world, at large—stared me down.

"So, Senator Schmidt, same question. How would you deal with—"

Someone screamed.

BANG.

Was that a gun?

The crowd exploded in a flurry of action.

Reggie tackled me to the floor and Secret Service materialized, surrounding Marks and I, bulging chests and bulky shoulders guiding us to the blinking exits with inhuman precision as time froze and chaos erupted.

* * *

"We caught him, sir," Agent Kelt—one of the younger and brighter eyed servicemen with a fighter's build and face for podcasting—said. We were stuffed in the bunker under the auditorium, a dozen Secret Service agents lining the doors and every nook and cranny, political posters tagging all the walls. "His wife was scheduled for a LE treatment last month which never happened... She didn't make it," he added without a touch of empathy. Maybe we had perfected robotics...

The news—especially Google and FOX—had been highlighting the few unfortunate consequences of the bill and ignoring the thousands of lives already saved by our efforts. If it bleeds, it leads... I'd never felt so under the microscope, and every day made it worse. They'd dug up old girlfriends, test scores, even a drunken party pic back in high school.

I hadn't asked for any of this, had I?

Senator Marks' daggers bore into me from across the gala-esque hors d'oeuvres bar. She'd let me know *exactly* how she felt. It wasn't pretty. Her party blamed me for everything from inflation and the recent economic blip to the deteriorating environment—ironic to say the least, falling education standards and increased crime—which if we were honest, was due to economic inequality and India's growth.

Sitting in the corner, I prepared to go back on stage.

Finnegan called, breaking my concentration. 'How's it going, Michael? I saw what happened.'

'What do you want?' I didn't have time for his *top o' the mornin' to ya* cheer.

'We found some dirt on Marks,' he said. 'I'm sending it through. Thought you could use some firepower.'

What'd I care who she was sleeping with? 'I'll look into it,' I said. 'I've got to go.' Sighing, I clicked off before he could say more, popping a crab puff and opening the message.

Speaking of sex... Henrietta couldn't have kids. She'd undergone IVF four times. Explained the in vitro bans; jealousy. 'If I can't have kids, neither can you...' What a hypocritical bitch. If that came out, it'd be the end of her.

How had I not heard before?

* * *

"So, Senator Marks," the brainy blonde from CNN asked after I'd answered my question, as if nothing had happened. "There are rumors out of Shanghai and Seoul of successful 'designer' babies: increased intelligence, immunity, and aesthetics... How would you have America proceed? Your state banned in vitro..."

Marks swallowed hard, looking away before leaning on her podium and regaining composure. "We have to ask ourselves what is natural, what is right?" She launched into a scripted tirade on the dangers of gene editing and unforeseen consequences, never once mentioning IVF.

"So, you're willing to let China lead?" the moderator asked pointedly. Whatever happened to America first?

Marks mumbled something about God's will. She couldn't have set herself up better if she'd tried. No one realized how clouded her judgment was. And while I was against LE, safe genetic engineering was the only future we had as global temperatures rose.

"And, Mr. Senator?"

Moment of truth. Could I out her on national television? Fertility was something so personal. But she'd ripped open my relationship with Ava... even brought Jamie into the picture.

"Contrary to popular belief," I began, outlining all the reasons I supported a robust biotech industry in America. "And when it comes to IVF—" I stopped myself. No, I couldn't do it. Marks and I locked eyes, and hers widened, her hand going to her mouth. Her shoulders tensed.

"Actually, I have nothing further to add," I finished.

"And Senator Marks, how would you respond?"

ETHAN

Two more days and I was a free man. What was I going to do with my time?

DDI had been my life for the past twenty years, and it was gone. The SEC had barred me from working in biotech for at least ten years, let alone starting something. And I couldn't leave the country. Good luck enforcing that. What they didn't know, couldn't hurt.

This is what it felt like to be a free agent again. I hated it. Pacing the kitchen, I sipped Yerba mate but nothing came to mind. My life's work and purpose were gone... Decimated. And China was going to win. They'd all betrayed me.

The phone rang. I tapped in. 'Hello? Ethan Anderson.'

It was Veronica. She was in town and wanted to meet. 'Really? What time Monday?' My schedule was freer than free, and I couldn't wait to get out of here.

Eight. Whole. Weeks.

We made plans to meet at her newest office and clicked off. What'd she want? Probably to gloat, the bitch. I'd hear her out. Those angel investments would pay off a hundred-fold. And the shell companies would offset the capital gains.

It was good to be king.
Now, what to do with my life?
Shit, good question.

SAM

Monday took forever coming around, and the day passed slower still. By the time we were supposed to meet Veronica, I'd hit the gym, ran, meditated for all of two minutes, and taken three showers. Waiting, I sat on Malea's bed in her half-princess and volley-baller room, flicking through old pictures, tears seconds from crushing me. I couldn't bring myself to clean it out. Too many memories, too much pain.

I'd failed her as a mom, as a protector... my little girl. Guilt gripped me.

At two forty-five, I rose from bed, and got things ready, double-checking my bag. The newest wig and spare outfit were there. Same with the untraceable gun from the "Taxman" killings. It'd been buried in a safe north of Stone Mountain since I wiped it clean months ago. Should give the blue bloods a ride.

Attaching the fake nose, I put in green color contacts, and checked myself in the holographic mirror. Perfect. Plenty of time.

I'd meet Mendoza at the French coffee shop and wait until Veronica was about to leave.

Popping the cartridge, I inspected the rounds one last time. The gun was in order, and I slid it into my holster, heading for the door. One way or another, I was ending this. *Today.*

* * *

A**n encrypted message from Felipe woke me from my trance in the wrought iron chair outside Le Paris, twirling the unnecessary sugar spoon in a clockwise whirl as passersby with plenty to live for hustled here and there. *The golden goose has landed.* Damn, Mendoza. He'd seen too many spy films.

Affirmative, I shot back. Another sip. Stretching, I snatched a glimpse of the entrance. How had she slipped past me? I hadn't seen a thing. This might be harder than I thought.

Waving at the owner, McCrae, I said, "Be right back. Save me seat." Couldn't help imitating his highland rattle. After paying my tab, I slipped out the picket fence and beelined for the alley parallel to HSU's entrance. Shuffling along, hands in my pocket, I did my best drunken stupor, limping. The cramped passage had more than enough bums to provide me cover.

Halfway down was a door, an industrial lift defaced with street art. I'd missed it last time. Stumbling further, I tripped. There were cameras around, had to be. I roared a drunkard's frustration, wobbling to my feet, and continuing down the side street before collapsing in a ball.

This would work.

The alley stank of feces and cheap beer, something scientists hadn't fixed, try though they might. I closed my eyes. It'd be great if I'd slept last night... The trash heap was too comfy.

ETHAN

W hat to wear? What to wear? I surveyed my two-story walk-in closet. Was I vain? No. It'd been a week since I wore real pants, and I deserved some closet time.

I settled on some minimalist blue jeans and a red micromodal button-up. Didn't need much to look good. Two of the new guys were waiting on the roof, Gonzalez too. Let's get the fuck out of here.

We hopped in and took off, the repressive prison shrinking as we accelerated. Guess who's back...

HSU didn't have a landing pad for obvious reasons, so Gonzalez put us down in Springdale Park. One side of the landing pad was fenced off, leaving us exposed. "How do you want to handle this, boss?" Boris asked. He'd become a lot more deferential after the Jones incident, humbled by the whole ordeal. He damn well better be.

"We'll pick her up at the address I gave you," I said. "I don't care about the details."

Boris nodded while the others cleared the area, scaring an older black lady and sending a homeless kid running for the hills. Bernie's ice-cold eyes and facial scarring would do that.

A big black Tesla sped to the edge of the park and skidded to a stop, war-ready doors popping open. Boris scuttled me forward, past staring onlookers, and into the waiting armored cage.

Atkins Park was a slum, no mistake about it. Boards on the windows, junkies on the sidewalks, hoes on the curb. Half the businesses were empty or closed, and it was only seven p.m. Talk about lazy.

The GPS took us through the rotting city to HSU's coordinates, but the dark alley was too narrow for the hulking vehicle to navigate. Bernie stayed with the idling car as the four of us exited, heading for the door. Veronica was nowhere in sight. There were more than enough gutter dwellers to see why. Two lights glowed, another flickering with creepy regularity.

Why'd she pick this dump, of all places?

A call came in. 'Veronica? We're here.'

'Two minutes. Problem client, LNS...'

Grimacing, I hung up. Wouldn't want to be *that* guy. "Two minutes."

A bum sandwiched between trash bags stirred. Gonzalez leveled his gun. "Stay down," he warned.

The hobo looked familiar but my mind flicked back to Veronica. What could she want?

SAM

E than? I reached for my gun, freezing as Gonzalez stared me down. Shit. Did he recognize me? Closing my eyes, I pretended to sleep, pulling my face deeper into the filth. This wasn't the plan.

A *whirr*. The loading dock began to open. She was coming. She was meeting Ethan? Why? Now what?

I opened a map of the scooters and Teslas in the area. Might need a fast getaway, or to tail them. But four against one... not good odds.

"Ethan, there you are. How's it feel to be out?" an acid female voice asked. Veronica stepped into the dim night, wearing a tailored pantsuit, a pair of black guards flanking either side. Shit, six.

"Veronica," Ethan countered in a force voice. "To what do I owe the pleasure?"

There was an awkwardness between them. At least it kept them distracted. What was going on?

"We should get out of here," Boris said.

The group headed for the waiting ride. This was my chance.

"I wanted to talk to you about..." She leaned closer and whispered something in his ear. Ethan stood straighter.

"I see. Can I invite you to dinner? The Lif?"

"You read my mind," she said.

The doors slammed shut, and the car disappeared around the corner before I had a chance to do anything.

I jumped up, forgetting my act and hurried for the nearest scooter. No car would let me ride like this, but scooters were hobo-friendly.

Mhm, Ethan and Veronica... Maybe I could kill two birds with one stone.

* * *

The Lourde and Lif was located in the northern part of Midtown, the most exclusive area, at least for bars and nightlife. Hopping off at the west edge of Piedmont, I snuck into the park to find a good bush. A piss and change of clothes later, I was almost ready. The smell was the problem. I reeked.

Walking along Peachtree, I found a luxury shop and stepped inside, heading for the fragrances. A manicured salesman with a perm came over, eyeing me, confused. "Can I help you with—"

"I'm good thanks." I kept walking.

He gave me a sideways gay look but disappeared into the augmented dressing rooms with a *humpfh*.

The place was fancy, not a price tag anywhere. Skirting the real leather jackets, I found the perfumes and applied more than enough Chanel. After running a display comb through my disheveled blond wig, I scrutinized myself. Good enough? It would have to do.

I left without paying.

Back on the street, I made it to the Lif in less than five. No one so much as stared, which was a good sign. This could work. Visualizing the layout in my head, I tried to play things out.

We'd eaten here often enough, at least Ethan had. It was his favorite place to woo potential clients and bigwigs. After trying the food, it was easy to see why. While broad-backed tuxes and slim celebs strode towards the looming Medieval Scot-esque entrance some ex-Nike designers had perfected, calling in historians, archeologists and the like, I waited in the shadowy alley across the way. A plan would be great about now.

At least I knew the security setup. Looks were deceiving. Don't frighten the guests. That'd been head chef, Louis' motto. As such, the front of the house staff, the doormen, even the guys and gals manning the palatial restrooms, were all ex-military or law enforcement. This was Fort Knox with a fork, hence the ease with which rich and powerful streamed in, not a care in the world—personal bodyguards waiting nearby. There'd never been an incident at the Lif, ever.

That was about to change.

Success had softened them. Just this year, Louis had banned weapons in the place. So, while five heavies manned the door for intimidation, if I could make it in...

I checked my wig one last time. Emerging from the alleyway, I strode towards the entrance with the arrogance of a trust fund kid, flashing a bimbo smile at the uglies on duty and pretending to tap a call. One of them stepped towards me. "Name, ma'am?"

I raised an eyebrow and waited. The man paled. Holding up a finger, I said, 'One second, daddy. I'm having trouble with these buffoons.' My eyes narrowed. "Is my table ready?"

The ex-Slav with the hook nose opened his mouth. "Sorry, ma'am, right this way."

Nodding, I continued my faux conversation while the soldier with a sweet spot for pullups led me forward. We passed cavernous, chandelier-lit rooms into the great room, bedecked in twelve-pointers, Scottish and Gaelic masterpieces, and a fair few pikes and maces. Eyes followed my ass as rumors buzzed.

My whiskey barrel table was by the roaring fire, warm glow and easy atmosphere making it easy to blend in. Where were Ethan and Veronica? "Will anyone be joining you, ma'am?" the man asked.

I shook my head.

"Virtual or physical?" he asked.

"Oh, what the heck, let's be crazy. I'll take a real menu."

The waiter—Nikita was his name, odd for a man—ran off, reappearing moments later with handbound leather. "Take your time." He left, and I pretended to peruse the options, searching the room. It's not like I could afford anything. A basic meat pie was forty-five bucks.

Standing, I headed for the bathroom, and slipped into the adjoining Throne Room—Ethan's inner ego on full display. Sure enough, he sat at the place of honor, a six-seater covered in three courses for their covert discussion. Lackeys enjoyed a decent meal several tables over.

Ethan leaned closer, whispering something I couldn't make out.

Veronica laughed with ironic mirth. "Things are booming. Added four new cities in the past month, seven since the ruling. Without the up-and-up, we're the best option."

Ethan raised an eyebrow, skewering his quail. "Why am I here?"

"Sometimes, roles reverse. I need your help."

"I'm listening."

And so was I, but how to avoid being noticed? Continuing to the echoey stone bathroom, I sat in the heated stall for a moment's privacy. There was no way I could pull this off, and escape.

I was washing my hands when the thin attendant stepped forward. "Anything I can help you with, miss?" Her eyes pleaded for a tip. The salaries were abysmal, what with the excess labor. My eyes settled on the fire alarm. Could that work? Would it trigger sprinklers? Not without fire...

Tapping her palm, I transferred her a few bucks. "Good luck."

MIKE

J amie had chosen this place, of all places...

To be fair, the Lourde & Lif had an excellent reputation, the best in the city. And it was Jamie's first time. I closed the menu display on our table, enjoying my kilt-themed wrap-around armchair. "Know what you're going to have?" I asked, cognizant of the Secret Secret agents two tables over, and the ones by the door. They'd barely glanced at their menus, hawkish eyes never leaving me.

She bit her lip, nose turning in a mirror image of Ava, same as it always had when making a tough decision. "I'm deciding between..." She said something but I wasn't listening. Was that Sam? A figure slipped by, heading for the restroom. Nevermind, look at the nose on her. Doppelganger maybe. When you'd get so jumpy? Relax, Mike.

"What were you saying, Jame?"

She couldn't stop staring at the shielded crests behind me lining the masoned wall. "Pretty cool, don't you—" *Phew.*

Water exploded from the ceiling, heavens opening as an alarm blared. *EEOOEEEOEE.*

People jumped to their feet. Someone screamed as plates and tables clattered.

"Fire!" another yelled.

Pandemonium ensued in a mad dash for the door, glasses shattering. I grabbed Jamie's dripping hand as servicemen rushed towards us, knocking bystanders to the ground. It was chaos as sprinklers rained down on and elbows jostled.

The guards pulled us forward and a shadow figure appeared, our eyes met. It *was* Sam after all. Green eyes... What was she doing here? Her face was calm and cool, focused. Had she caused this?

Ethan's voice broke the din. "What the hell's going on?"

It clicked. Ethan, Sam...Shit!

The crowd dragged us towards the streaming exit, flashing lights illuminating the way. Jamie's nails dug into my palms, her hands shaking. Only I knew Sam's true identity. Was she here for me? Tying loose ends...

Shit, where'd she go? The crowd swallowed her whole, wrenching us from the Secret Service as we spilled onto the busy street. Horns sounded, people clamored, and others cried. Jamie threw her arms around me, eyes like headlights. Someone bumped me towards the road. Sam? No.

What was going on? Where was she?

We wouldn't wait to find out. Seizing Jamie's hand, we hurried away, checking our shoulder every few yards.

Better safe than sorry.

ETHAN

A fire, in my restaurant? What idiot—let's get this over with. Things had been getting interesting too. Taking over North and South American operations was right up my alley. Veronica hadn't *officially* made the offer, but... Wait, where was she?

I pushed through shell shocked crowds towards the door. "Get out of the way." It's just a fire, people, jeez.

Hundreds of people spilled onto the sidewalk, some moron elbowing me in the ribs. "Relax, people, everything's going to be—" There she was, by the curb. "Veronica!"

She didn't hear me, face panicked, as she moved with the mob. And she was with another—wait, she looked familiar. Why? Was she ditching me?

They turned towards me, and I got a good look. No way.... It couldn't be. Jones? The hair and eyes were wrong, but... it had to be. She moved with the same controlled prowl. That fucker.

"Move, idiot." I shouldered a fat man out of my way and was halfway there when a car pulled from traffic and skidded to a stop. Veronica got in and Jones followed, something in Jones's hand. Had they been in this together all along? It clicked. It made so much sense.

I'd been played, twice. She'd been working with Veronica? And she was probably in league with Lee.

Damn.

Didn't see that coming...

She'd get what was coming to her as well.

SAM

"Get in the car." I shoved Veronica, gun pressed into the small of her rigid back. She could handle herself, but did as she was told. We zipped away before her guards or the Lif's staff caught sight of her. I activated my jammer.

"Don't even think about it." I pointed at the door with my gun and her eyes fell.

"What do you want?" she asked. "What did I ever do to you? Is it money?" Her voice was calculating, shoulders defiant.

A shrill laugh erupted, bordering on insanity. Her face turned pale and her body shook.

"You have no idea," I whispered. "My daughter, my husband... you've taken everything from me." The words poured out, pent rage and frustration. *Everything...*

When I finished, she stammered, "It, it wasn't personal. It was only business."

Why was it business people always said that? As if I give a damn whether it was personal. This was it. I had *nothing* left, nothing. And *that's* all you have to say?

I raised the gun to her head, and signaled the car to open the door.

"Well, this is fucking personal." Firing, I shoved her out the speeding car.

Thump, dump.

We sped away, the hole inside me dark as ever.

A deep breath. I opened my mouth and shoved the silencer in.

Poetic justice.

ETHAN

I t was all over the news. Between the fire which hadn't been and the unidentified woman's body on the steps of DDI's headquarters, it'd been a great effing night. The vultures descended again, smelling blood. Not that I'd give them any.

After talking with officers—three different sets of incompetent blue bloods due to some blowhard jurisdictional dispute—I'd been allowed to go. "Allowed," as if they could *allow* me to do anything. At least I was home.

Of course, the body had been Veronica's. No one knew. No one needed to know. She'd had few enough friends, and plenty of enemies. The question: what would happen to HSU? Could I grab the whole thing?

So, Jones had gotten her revenge after all... Despite everything, I felt a strange admiration. Veronica always was a bitch.

Now what? Was she after me too, or just Veronica? That was the question. If she'd managed to get her at the Lif, well, that wasn't promising. I'd have to be more careful and stay at home, or leave the country. What about Asia, or South America? Maybe even South Africa.

Screw it, who else did I know at HSU?

It was time to push the envelope.

It was time to be back in business.

Those fuckers were going to pay for what they did to my company.

Let the games begin.

MIKE

"Are you ready, Mr. President?" Stepping forward, I thumbed the lucky coin Jamie had given me the day she'd returned from Rome to "watch your back, Dad." There was a whole film crew, directors, lighting, the whole nine yards. The demolition team gestured towards the red, white, and blue cartoony detonator as cameramen squared their shots and drones hovered overhead.

"We're live in sixty seconds!" someone yelled.

It was a pleasant day outside DDI's long-abandoned headquarters, rigged to blow, fireworks and everything. A decent crowd gathered. We'd debated for a while but decided people needed a change, a visual image to signify the end of LE and start of my presidency. "What better way than with a bang?" Those had been Jamie's exact words, and ever since, my chief of Staff, Vickie, along with teams of assistants, had seen to the details. I couldn't piss without planning a calendar event. And even those were scheduled, hurried, and had to help the people, saving water for the dolphins in the process.

What had I gotten myself into? This suit was ridiculous. I looked like a clown.

"Ten, nine, eight..." Mayor Chang counted down as I readied

myself, eyeing the foreboding building one last time—Ethan Anderson's legacy. The billionaire had vanished off the face of the earth. Whether he'd died or gone rogue, no one knew, and frankly, no one cared—the IRS, the one exception. He owed hundreds of millions in back taxes. "Now, Mr. President!" someone yelled.

I slammed the unnecessary T-shaped handle home with a satisfying umph.

BWOOM. Bwoom. Bwoom. A series of timed explosions ripped through the tower, scattering debris around the roped off demolition site as level upon level of the colossal structure collapsed inward, floating, as if suspended in midair before smashing to the ground in an ode to equality. *Okay, that was cool.*

A cheer as the last of the building thudded to the earth. It'd take weeks to clean up, but symbolically at least, LE was no more. The truth was, blackmarket clinics like HSU were more popular than ever. But that would come, one of the early goals of my administration. 'My administration'… what a weird thought.

After, Vickie got her photo op—Chang and I shaking hands in the wake of the billowing destruction—we hurried towards the next engagement, a meeting with EU Council President Juergen Wolf on unified negotiations with India and China and the economic ramifications of including Africa in the proposed free-trade zone. It was all too much for a simple boy from Syracuse… Thank god for advisors.

ETHAN

Thailand was growing on me. Between the craziness of Bangkok, the laidback Chiang Mai and the interest in medical tourism for all types of rejuvenation, stem cell treatments, and LE, business was booming. SLI was furious, which was a big plus. And with lax drug laws, almost no tax, and the world's best beaches in under an hour, I could get used to this.

I'd bought five of the largest monasteries and medical resorts in the country, dozens of politicians and numerous impenetrable estates throughout the beautiful land. Thai women saw to my every need, always there to keep me company. The daily fucks and massages were a nice add-on.

Things were moving, hence the need for this meeting on the top of my inaccessible villa, headquarters for our illicit juggernaut of a startup. The five of us sat around a small bamboo table, views of the jungle and gleaming shoreline below blacked out to avoid the distraction.

"Where are we at with HSU's European assets?" I asked Lin Na, my old—and now new—CFO. We'd poached DDI's best people, got rid of legal, and after a few hiccups, hit our stride. We were two orders of magnitude off old revenues and treatment numbers, but within two years we'd pass that, and within five, we'd best the combined SLI-DDI merger for the largest health tech conglomerate, at least by revenue—and it was tax-free. Lee had about shit himself when he'd heard the news. Wished I'd gotten that on video. Bastard deserved it.

"Pretty well, Ethan. The EU will roll out bans in Q1, but most legal clinics have folded. We can't keep up with demand, and SLI's weak in Europe, regulations and such." For once, Europe's prudishness was plus.

We rushed through status updates on South America and Africa before I had to duck out. King Ramata was joining me to talk big picture. The Thai government was hurting for cash, and we were happy to help if our operations were left alone. The question, how little could we offer? I cut the best deal, always did.

Hurrying across the concrete patio overlooking the jungle, I skirted the infinity pool where ladies lounged, barely noticing the palm and papaya trees edging towards the towers of my thirty-two-thousand square foot Phuket villa. It had stunned me the first few days: mangoes and midget bananas with out of this world sweetness, glittering beach a mile away.

But today, I had other things on my mind.

* * *

The meeting went well, all things considered. Thirty million a year was a small price to pay. Ramata had offered to provide military protection, but I wasn't falling for that. Pablo Escobar had kept his own personal army, and for good reason. And even he ate it at a certain point. But I'd studied history and wasn't worried.

"How are things?" I asked Vlad. He sat in the command center of the palatial compound surrounded by impassable forest, the occasional Bengal tiger or obnoxious macaque, and little else. His war room was a mirror of the one in Home Base One, albeit with an ironic

blue-bellied Buddha in the corner—Russian humor. Vlad hadn't meditated a day in his life.

"We're up to twenty, sir." Vlad said. "A few of our old FSB friends
are flying in next week to round out the squad."

Good. I wasn't taking any chances. "Any update on Jones?" She'd
disappeared after the fire and the traitorous skank was keeping her
head down. Vlad's old intelligence and mafia contacts hadn't even
been able to locate her. Bitch was a ghost.

Vlad's jaw twitched. "Not yet, sir, but we're looking. I upped the
contract, should bring the players out in storm."

It better. Half a mill was serious cash, at least for offing a washed
up bodyguard. "Good. Have you asked Sun's people for help?" Maybe
Chopsticks could be good for something after all. Plus, it'd lure him
into a false sense of security. If Lee thought we were on good terms,
he'd be easier to access.

"No, sir," Vlad said through gritted teeth. "Should I?"

The pride of these guys... "Do it. I want that hoe in a bodybag by
the end of the week. Speaking of, we're headed to Chiang Mai on
Tuesday." Maybe Jones had other family we could lean on.

Vlad ran off, and later, walked me through the transition plan
while Boris tried to find weaknesses. When we were done, I was
impressed. They'd taken it up a notch since Veronica, true profession-
als. I'd increased their salaries after the incident, with a few contin-
gencies. No reason to leave loyalties in question. More performance
bonuses and perks too, plus an extra $100,000 once Jones bit it.

And Jones... how had I missed that? Her daughter, her husband...
She was a simple, weak nothing who was bound to crack. Why hadn't
she seen my vision, where we could take humanity? Instead, she'd
ruined everything over petty bullshit. Women...

I hoped they didn't kill her. A quick death was too easy and Boris
had said something about a Russian needle method that put CIA
waterboarding to shame. She'd pay, all right. She'd pay.

And unlike Veronica, I was untouchable here. Let Jones or anyone
take their best shot. This was a fortress. Short of an aerial SAS assault

or a Stinger missile strike—which Vlad assured me we'd shoot down —you'd be hard-pressed to reach our five-meter towering walls, let alone get inside.

A smile touched my lips.

Ramata may have just left, but it felt good to be king.

SAM

He thought he was so clever, a villa in the mountains. The compound loomed, shattering the wild jungle with impossible human fortitude. I could see why he'd chosen it. Even the king—who'd met with him earlier this morning, flying in by royal VTOL—couldn't touch the place. Walls five meters high and featureless, covered with an assortment of pale, battle-tested soldiers and anti-drone missile systems the Israelis could have made use of.

Since arriving two days earlier, armament had accelerated. Shifting in my thermal-isolating ghillie suit, I turned the zoom on my high-end lenses up, careful not to turn my head too fast. They were changing shifts, and I marked the time. It seemed to be random, which didn't help.

If only I could get a shot off from here. But those damn walls meant I didn't have a chance of penetrating the facility. Short of scaling the walls—which would be a clusterfuck—I was SOL. I buckled down, waiting. Maybe the bugs would pay off.

That was the one nice thing about the jungle, made countersurveillance impossible. Good luck sweeping for non-electric listening devices from a quarter-mile.

But in a week, it wouldn't matter anyway. He was headed to Chiang Mai.

* * *

'**D**iving one last time before we leave,' Ethan's voice said. What was that? Had I been sleeping? My eyes opened. It'd been a long and stuffy night. Everything itched.

Holding a finger to my ear, I tried to playback the scene.

'I don't know if we have—' Boris began.

'We'll be fine,' Ethan replied with his usual arrogance. 'I own the entire cove, and we can make up the time in the air. When's the next time I'll have a chance?'

'But we haven't set a proper perimeter.'

To Ethan, such things were mere details, and in the end, Boris was overruled. No surprise. Falling back, I melted into the thick underbrush, hurrying toward the sex tourism fueled town packed with ex-Soviet thugs. There wasn't much time.

ETHAN

Boris radioed ahead, alerting teams on the beach to lock down the water.

We landed fifteen minutes later, and Boris pointed out the concealed army amongst the palm trees and snaking banyans, invisible given the unspoiled aquamarine waves lapping the postcard perfect shore no ultra-res could ever do justice. The stranded coral took my breath away, rich lapis lazuli and pink carnations fit for a queen. No wonder I chose this, of all places.

"Have fun, you two." Boris faded into the background. He wasn't much of a swimmer but I'd never found out why. Didn't Spetsnaz have amphibious training? Whatever. His loss.

Vlad and I suited up as Boris updated Gonzalez. Vlad was a certified Dive Master, and in his black neoprene, swinging the buoyancy compensator (BCD) on backpack style, before I'd finished checking my tank pressure. He'd run me through hardcore certification when we got here, dusting off FSB training and plenty of submerged raid stories with the practiced air of a pro, moving with frogman ease through crystalline waters.

Slipping his black fins on, he looked back at me from behind his blood-red mask and checked my tank and gauges, helping me to tighten them.

"Can you hear me?" he asked in a voice beamed into my earpods.

I nodded. "One second."

The gear weighed a ton and we waddled toward the water two minutes later, Vlad flying as I limped through sand and shells in what could have been a baby's pathetic first steps. Even Achilles had his heels. *Come on, Ethan.*

At last, I hit the water and dove in.

It was warm and clear, a perfect Thai day. Phuket's beaches were renowned, nothing compared to Koh Phi Phi—where they'd filmed Alex Garland's novel, *The Beach*—or Krabi, a natural wonderland accessible only by boat, but outstanding nonetheless. And there were plenty of Russians, Phuket being popular for the hearty folks from the North.

Kicking my flippers, I dumped air from my BCD, vest deflating, and sank like a slow-motion rock. Vlad waited at five meters, floating near a glimmering school of Red Fire Goby that hugged a pink polyp formation, and turned on a dime as I approached. The blue and gold coral formations froze me, a whole new world. I tried to soak it all up but there was too much.

Dull rays coasted over crannies, mixing with burnt red seagrass, mushrooming colonies of growth, and a life force I'd never experienced on the mainland. Sometimes, I wished I could spend all day down here. It was the one place I escaped my head.

Vlad waved me on and we headed towards the unexplored depths further out. How had it taken thirty years to find diving?

"How we looking timewise?" Vlad asked.

He quizzed me from time to time. It was weird having the shoe on the other foot, but as he liked to say, "Anything could happen down there." To be safe, my dive computer was state of the art, Shearwater, all key readings displayed in my mask and on a backup wristband.

We had two hours of air and I was in no hurry. "We could—"

"Ah!" Vlad's shrill voice erupted in my ear.

What was that? Where was he? "Vlad? You okay?" Spinning, I tried to reorient myself.

Everything gyroscoped and something kicked up a cloud of dirt on the ocean floor. I swam towards it, the water darkening.

"Everything okay?" Boris asked from ashore.

Vlad didn't respond. Was this some bullshit Russian humor? We'd have a talk after this.

The dust cloud cleared in a muddy fog.

A floating body. Holy shit! It was Vlad.

What was going on? "Boris, we have a problem!" I yelled.

CIA?

SAM

There he was. A murky figure floated towards Vlad, hand flying to his earpiece. I screwed the second needle onto the rod and kicked, diving towards him, tranquilizer leveled. A sixth sense made Ethan look up. His eyes met mine as our bodies closed above the bristling ocean floor.

Jabbing the tip through his suit, it thudded into his thigh. He screamed a stream of bubbles, body contorting before going slack. I grabbed his hand, reaching behind me and unhooked the handheld, torpedo-shaped sea scooter as a speedboat roared towards us.

Hurry. Strapping his weight belt to mine with a basic carabiner, I turned the SEAL-grade propulsion system on, angling for deeper waters, it's fifty pounds of thrust gliding us forward at a *whopping* 1.7 miles per hour.

Searchlights illuminated the crystal water as we dove deeper, now ten meters, following the busy ocean floor. I dodged corals and rays with what little control I had. The system had one-to-two hours of runtime. At best, two miles. Make them count.

At least they hadn't found us yet. I could always slit his air tube and be done with it, if it came to that.

A boat raced our way. This was it. I reached for my knife.

At the last second, it veered toward shore.

Would we make it?

* * *

We reached the inaccessible edge of rocky Laem Krating and I unhooked the snap, letting Ethan float in the shallow rhythmic tide as I uncovered the pontoon boat I'd hidden earlier, clumping the camouflaged cover into the storage box. Within two minutes, Ethan was in the boat covered with gear, and we were off, shooting up the western coast of the skinny island.

A VTOL whizzed overhead, another. Out of time.

We swerved towards a sandy banana tree-lined cove as a third bore down on our position. This one hovered before descending. Shit. I reached for the waterproof gun taped under the instrument dash. Where was it?

The craft landing gear thudded, bouncing on the white sand as doors flew open.

It was Boris and Gonzalez, flanked by three other men, all rocking Oakleys and packing serious heat, weapons drawn.

* * *

"It's all over, Jones!" Boris yelled. A red dot appeared on my chest as the group advanced.

My hand came up empty as I slid desperate fingers. Dammit. "Don't!" Boris snapped. "Last chance." They spread around the small nook, making a shootout unwinnable for me. Plus, they all wore vests.

Malea, Daron... I couldn't quit, not now.

Ethan groaned, and fidgeted under the pile of gear. He was waking up. Great... His bloody fucking health regiment was paying off. Should have been out another hour.

Why hadn't I slit his throat?

Boris and Gonzalez reached the inflatable raft, the others waiting, guns trained on me. "It was nice knowing you, Jones," Boris said. "I get why you did it, your daughter and all. But I need the money."

"Me too." Gonzalez looked away. "Wife and I want to have a second."

My fists clenched. "You're cowards, both of you."

One of the lackeys, a bear of a man with scars and a beard to match stepped forward, pressing his AK to my head. "You talk a big game. It's too bad I'll have to—"

"Shut up, Bernie!" Boris snapped. "Any last words, Jones? I'd take care of your family, but..."

A stabbing emptiness. I shook my head, and Boris sighed. A soldier's nod as he raising his weapon. "I better get a fucking raise—"

Pht. Pht.

Blood erupted from Boris' head, splattering me as a series of silenced rifle blasts dropped the remaining guards.

Motionless, covered in death, I closed my eyes, waiting for the inevitable.

It never came. I opened my eyes.

Figures emerged from the jungle. What the hell?

* * *

The black-clad masked figures hurried towards me, stopping a safe distance away, silenced weapons at the ready. Lifting my hands in the air, I searched for some hint of my fate. Thai? American? The Brits? What was going on?

A short man with a gymnast's body stepped forward, surveying the situation before removing his mask. Chinese. "Hello there, Ms. Jones."

My jaw dropped. Sun Lee.

* * *

"W hy?" I asked, once shock wore off.

"Business," the chinaman said, his eyes flashing in a more-than-personal way. "And he threatened my family. Where is Ethan Anderson?"

I managed to avoid looking at the debris littering the skiff, and faked a smile. "Dumped the body. You won't have to worry about him or HSU anymore." What was I doing?

Lee nodded an almost imperceptible twitch. "I see." He held templed hands to his stoic brow. "Very well. You're free to go."

It took me a second. "I, I am?" Was this some cruel joke?

His devilish eyes flashed. "I'd offer you a job, but you betrayed your last employer. Ethan never was the brightest. Good luck. Make sure we don't meet again." With that, the hit squad left, slipping into the undergrowth without a sound. I didn't move. I didn't believe him.

The bullet was coming.

Any. Second. Now.

* * *

E than awoke an hour later, flailing under heavy equipment before pulling himself to his feet. "Jones?" he said with a relaxed nonchalance.

"Ethan," I spat.

He nodded, smiling to himself. "Well played. How about this, I'll give you—"

Jerking my hand up, I fired. *Pht.* The pistol kicked as Ethan collapsed to his knees, eyes frozen in shock. No more speeches, no more games—it was over.

Shuddering as I stepped ashore, it hit me how close I'd come to killing myself after murdering Veronica. I hadn't been ready, and still wasn't.

But now what? Ocean waves lapped my feet, sandy pebbles grounding me to this impossible moment. It was over, all over. A beach lay before me, bird calls and the occasional motorbike breaking peaceful silence. Peace, it'd be great to find peace.

I looked down at the gun in my hand, which had dominated my days. No longer a mother, no longer a wife... My days as a killer were over too. Flinging the pistol into the ocean, I sat on dunes, staring off into infinity, left to ponder my life...

Screw it, this was Thailand.

Maybe I'd join a monastery. Maybe I'd find peace.

MIKE

G abby Kealoha was right, drug usage was way down. Even as the economy struggled and industries sought to replace high paying LE jobs with more humane forms of healthcare, crime was falling. We'd taken six-hundred thousand off the streets in the two months following legalization, and now, a big push to forgive past possession charges and free the half-million-plus imprisoned on minor drug charges.

The system was working, somewhat, and hope was on the rise. There were still slums of impromptu housing and a wealth gap to rival the Grand Canyon, but we were off to a good start. Would it be enough?

What kicked off that thought train? Oh, the trippy dream last night... maybe it was the wine. General Secretary Huang could pound Sake bombs and aged Bacardi with the best of them.

I rolled out of bed at six am, first of many coffees ready and waiting on Jackie Kennedy's tea table. It was too much, the embroidered four-poster bed, the two-tiered chandelier, the hideous beige carpeting Nguyen had insisted on during the last administration. When I was sworn in, the staff had told me every president updated the big house in their own way. "Anything, say the word." But taxpayer dollars made all this possible and in the grand scheme of things, my comfort wasn't *that* important.

A double black Americano with the Presidential Daily—to clue me into the most important news—before reviewing my schedule. Busy, as always.

Breakfast with the Joint Chiefs, a nine o'clock with the African Alliance Commissioner, a slew of speeches and fundraisers for the Equal Housing Initiative—at least that mattered. A quick physical at three in time for my three-thirty with Chairman Finnegan, who was already talking re-election and stacking the House. It was hard not to think about legacy. There was so much I wanted to accomplish, and yet Washington, bureaucracy…

Time flew by, always did. The doc drew some blood, Finnegan was fired up about fundraising and the evening boasted five galas, two of which I showed my face at before retiring to my quarters for a relaxing movie night with my girl.

I missed Jamie. Between my schedule and her schooling—now the nation's best private tutors—plus her recent interest in ancient Roman architecture since her trip, we'd had little time to ourselves.

Curling up in my king-sized bed, watching the latest Pixar block-buster, it hit me. This was the most important thing I'd done all day. I pulled my baby closer, and to my surprise, she didn't push away. Things couldn't have been better.

A high priority call ruined the moment. So much for personal time.

Couldn't it wait until my hectic morning?

"One sec, Jame, I gotta take this." She gave me a pained but familiar look that tore into me. I'd make it quick. 'Hello, this is Michael Schmidt.'

The voice on the other line shocked me, rattled me to my core. There was no way…

It couldn't be.

* * *

"Wait, what are you saying?" I squeezed Jamie's shoulders tighter, holding her close on the stiff 20's era tan couch. The quiet doctor with more degrees than even Mom would have liked fidgeted with her charts across from us in the center of the West Sitting Hall. It was comfier than most, and homier too: beige walls, simple upholstery, no-frills. We'd almost put in a foosball table, almost.

This was Dr. Mendelson's first time in the big house, and the two Servicemen behind her—Qin and Varner—knew it, hands a whip's twitch from their holstered Sig Sauers as the little brunette felt presidential heat. "Remember you asked me to run those tests?" she asked.

I put my arm around Jamie's bare shoulders, unable to believe it was true.

"Well," she said, "the results came back negative." I stood, and she added, "That's good news. Great actually. She doesn't have early-onset ALS, or any form of the CCNF, BNIP1 or KIF5A mutations."

Oh, negative, duh… My knees collapsed as I fell back onto the couch. "H—how? How is that—" Could it be? Please god, or allah, or whatever…

"What's she talking about, Dad?" Jamie's voice cracked, eyes widening. "ALS? What do you mean?"

Mendelson looked between us. "You didn't tell her?"

How could I? "No," I said at last. "Are you sure?" I added, terrified of the answer.

She smiled, nodding. "One hundred percent. We had four different labs run the bloodwork. Your daughter's fine, Mr. President. Just your average sixteen-year-old."

Clutching my chest, I laughed and cried all at once, tears streaming down my face. If I believed in miracles… "Jamie, you have no idea…"

"Dad." She wrapped confused arms around me, tears falling as her makeup blurred. "Dad?"

I told her what happened, about the blackmail, false blood tests, everything.

"Wait, you knew?" she demanded when I finished. Her body stiffened. "And you didn't tell me?"

Uh-oh! Ava's fire flared, filling me with regret. "I wanted to protect you." How could I explain?

Jamie stood, half-snarling, running into the echoey Center Hall, feet pounding towards the East Wing as wails intensified.

SLAM. The Queens' Bedroom.

Teenagers.

But she was going to be okay. Nothing else mattered.

"So, explain it to me again," I said. I wasn't taking any chances.

* * *

Everything was set. I walked the East Room one last time, checking the ballroom-esque tablecloths and bouquets, name tags, and old-fashioned menus, ensuring things were ready. It all had to be perfect. This was her big day.

Wow, four whole years. We'd made it. She'd made it! Twenty...

Ethan Anderson was a bastard, a good-for-nothing son of a bitch. He'd let me believe Jamie was horribly sick, a rare, near untreatable condition. Rot in hell, or whatever dumpster he'd decided to disappear to. The intelligence agencies were looking, but no one held out much hope. Consensus was, someone had caught up to him, one of his many enemies.

Served him right. Karma's a bitch.

Come on, Mike. Tonight's about Jamie. One last check. Regardless what happened in the upcoming election, this was her night. My little girl.

Vickie roused me, high-heels machine-gunning toward me as the steel-eyed brunette with an impossible knack for names thumbed docs a mile a minute. "Mike, you have the Brazilian ambassador here at two. We've blown him off twice."

Darn coffee harvests. "I know, Vick. Give me a minute."

The wiry woman did, or as close to fifteen seconds as she ever let up before leading me to the famed Oval Office, which wasn't all that special.

I talked trade terms with the charismatic Brazilian, promising a good word with the Minister of Commerce and sampling the repurposed Rainforest blend. Thank god for climate-combatting capitalism. We were teetering on two degrees as it was, but my mind was wandering.

Jamie. The big two-oh. Four hours until the surprise. We'd kept everything under wraps, and thanks to Vickie, it'd be a party for the ages. Boy bands, a Triple Chocolate Rocky Road cake, and all her friends from DC and Atlanta. A night to remember.

You only turn twenty once.

* * *

"Hey Jame, come here. I want you to see something." She was the image of beauty as we navigated the marble-columned maze that was the Cross Hall, her silky red dress swishing the red carpet as I took her hand, passing distinguished portraits of my predecessors. *That's why I smiled for pictures, Mr. Jefferson.* Could you look whinier?

She pulled away. "Dad, I'm twenty. I know it's my birthday, but I don't need you to hold my hand or—"

The towering East Room door opened with a cheer, and a piano kicked in, crowd bursting into a passable "Happy Birthday" as Jamie's hands flew to her mouth. "All this? For me..."

I gave her a hug, which couldn't come close to how I felt, as her friends and White House staff surged forward to congratulate her. We stepped into the low-lit hall as music started, rock and pop, even a bit of soul, not a sharp-elbowed politician in sight.

Things couldn't have been better.

Reggie and I were sitting at a table by the glowing dance floor, reminiscing about all we'd been through the past four years—his Secret Service appointment, the birth of his son, Wallace's retirement

—when "My Girl" came on. A spotlight blared on us as everyone turned to watch us.

Ah, the father-daughter dance. I was a klutz, never much of a dancer. Being elected hadn't helped.

Jamie appeared in the middle of the dance floor, and Reggie pushed me forward. "Go for it, *Mr. President.* Let's see what you got." Even ramrod Varner offered a whistle as I made my way to the empty dance floor. Jamie walked towards me, looking beautiful. She'd grown up, and was a woman now. "Jame," I said when I reached her, taking her trembling hands. "May I have this dance?" Ava would have loved this...

She smiled, soft tears padding her cheeks and mine.

And so, we danced, "talking 'bout my girl" in the background as I held *my* little girl tight. It was all so—

Crack. Her heel snapped. Jamie twisted, falling backward as time slowed.

WHAM. Her head slammed the floor.

Screaming. Blood everywhere.

I fell to my knees. No! "Jaammiiieeeee!"

Bodies raced towards us. What just happened?

"Jamie?" I yelled.

Someone ripped me away. *"JAMIE!"*

* * *

"What do you mean her brain's been damaged?" I demanded of Dr. Kapoor, the tall Indian doctor before me who was supposedly the best.

We were sitting in Georgetown University's Urgent Care facility, in their world-renowned brain trauma and neuro ward, Jamie hooked to more tubes and sensors than it took to run a Tesla. The room was white and heartless, lifeless with its twice per hour cleanings, anti-bacterial floors, and quiet demeanor that terrified loved ones.

"How bad is it?" I asked, dreading the answer.

How could he look so damn calm, hands in his pockets while my daughter was dying? Do something, dammit!

"It's not good, Mr. President. The newest scans came in. Over a third of her brainstem and corticospinal tract have serious lesions and trauma, and she's been unresponsive for six hours."

Jeez, had it been *that* long? Six hours... And corticospinal, that sounded bad.

Reggie put his hand on my shoulder, and I lost it. "What does that mean?" Reggie asked as my voice failed me.

"Basically, the brainstem is the part of her brain connecting the other regions." Kapoor winced. "Like an intersection at a four-way stop. If we don't do something soon, she's going to go into a coma."

A coma? Jesus, a coma. Everything spun. Hold it together, Mike. I ran my hands through my receding hairline, sinking into the chair again. "What are our options?" I was the president, dammit. Someone could do something, someone, anyone...

Kapoor shook his head, considering. "She needs donor brain stem cells for a chance at repair. That, or embryonic ones, which were outlawed decades ago. Otherwise, her body won't be able to repair itself, not with so much damage. There's not much I can do. It's all illegal thanks to *your* LE bill."

This wasn't happening. This was some sick dream. "There has to be something, anything. As your president, I'm ordering—"

"I'm sorry, Mr. President," Kapoor said, holding up helpless hands. "There's nothing *I* can do. You'd need a donor, and to change the laws. I'd lose my license. Clinics here can't..."

A long silence.

"What are you saying?" I asked at last. Don't be what I think it is...

"I'm not saying anything, sir. Only explaining your options. We'll give you a moment with your daughter." He gestured for Reggie and the two Servicemen to join him in the hall, leaving me alone to ponder everything in this sickening white emergency room.

Dammit. What had I done? Banning the very thing that could save her.

Here I was, the most powerful man in the world, and there wasn't a damn thing I could do. The universe had a cruel humor.

What if I took her overseas, or reversed the ruling? Maybe the ban wasn't such a good idea... If I could just—No! I shook my head, disgusted with myself. What was I thinking? Me, of all people... Talk about hypocritical.

But Jamie...

The window called me, and I rose, trudging towards it, staring at Reservoir Road with a mix of trepidation and guilt. Were my morals worth my daughter's life? We couldn't roll back the bill, it had accomplished so much good.

Couples strolled the blustery park lined with vibrant cherry and oak trees, med students and aspiring leaders, enjoying a beautiful fall day in the nation's capital that was sunnier than my mood. One, in particular, caught my eye. Their daughter looked at me from two hundred feet, her eyes piercing my soul. She looked like my little girl, like my Jamie, years earlier.

What was I going to do? What could I do?

Trembling, I reached into my pocket and pulled out Jamie's lucky coin. I never went anywhere without it. Aurelius's resolute face stared back at me, and I sighed. "What do I do?" He said nothing.

I flung the coin into the air. "I love you, Jame..."

Was I *really* leaving this to chance? Time stood still.

The catch, the flip... It came back negative.

Something imploded inside me, memories flashing in a painful happiness. This couldn't be happening, not after all we'd been through...

Not her too, I couldn't lose Jamie. Being truly alone terrified me.

No, fuck that, I was the president.

I made the call.

'Hey Vickie, tell them to fire up Air Force One. We're headed to Shanghai...'

AUTHOR'S NOTE: PLEASE READ!

GET FREE ADVANCE COPIES OF MY UPCOMING BOOKS

Building a relationship with my readers is the best part about writing. I hope you enjoyed Death Donor and continue to read my books. The whirlwind adventures will continue, I promise.

I occasionally send newsletters with details on new releases, exclusive offers and discounts, and free copies of my books for early beta readers.

And if you sign up to the mailing list, I'll send you:

1. Free copies of my upcoming books to review.
2. Dozens of hours of interviews with leading biotech researchers like the director of the Human Genome Project, the lead science advisor to the Jurassic Park series, the world's foremost expert on longevity and anti-aging science... plus tons more.
3. Polls on future book titles, cover designs, character names, and more...

You can access everything, be the first to read and review my future books **for free,** and get tons of BONUS hours of content by signing up at **mattwardwrites.com/freebonuses**.

Enjoy this book? You can make a big difference!

Reviews are the most powerful tool in my arsenal when it comes to getting attention for my books. Much as I'd like to, I don't have the finances of a New York publisher. I can't take out expensive newspaper ads or plaster subway stations, *yet*.

But I have something even more powerful and effective, something publishers would kill for.

You guys! A committed, loyal bunch of readers.

If you enjoyed this book, a positive review would be greatly appreciated as it affords me the opportunity to focus more of my energy on my writing and helps persuade others to read my work. Just visit the link below and click: *Write a customer review* at

mattwardwrites.com/donor

Reviews are enormously helpful when it comes to Amazon's rankings and allowing more readers to find my books. And I personally read each and every one!

And don't forget to join my newsletter and FREE advance beta reader team to get exclusive early copies of my upcoming books and more at: mattwardwrites.com/beta

Thank you for taking the time. I hope it's been more than worth your while.

Cheers,

Matt Ward

mattwardwrites.com

ABOUT THE AUTHOR

 Matt Ward is an author, entrepreneur, host of the Disruptors.FM tech podcast, and the #24 ranked futurist worldwide. His work focuses on the intersection of exponential technologies and the ethical issues confronting humanity in the 21st century, as do his novels, which are inspired by the cutting-edge scientists he interviews on his show. Today, Matt writes fast-paced science fiction, fantasy, and speculative fiction technothrillers with a dystopian bent on the question: what does it mean to be human?

You can find Matt online at mattwardwrites.com. Or, you can connect with Matt on Twitter: @mattwardwrites, on Facebook: facebook.com/MattWardBooks, or Instagram: @mattwardwrites, or email him at matt@mattwardwrites.com if you'd like to say hey.

ALSO BY MATT WARD

COPYRIGHT

Peachtree City, GA 30269
mattwardwrites.com

CPSIA information can be obtained
at www.ICGtesting.com
Printed in the USA
LVHW082012270520
656683LV00008B/206